D0055277

Edgar Pangborn
was born February 25, 1909, in New York City. He studied at
Harvard University and the New England Conservatory of
Music, leaving to farm in Maine from 1939 to 1942. He served
in the U.S. Army Medical Corps and, in 1947, became a free-
lance writer. His first science fiction story, "Angel's Egg" (1951),
has become one of sf's best-loved classics. Mr. Pangborn died
February 1, 1978.

**"His work addressed itself to the great problems of life and
death, the mystery of existence, and personal worth. . . . Above
everything else, Pangborn brought an overpowering sense of
beauty to science fiction."**
—George Zebrowski

**"[Pangborn's work reflects] the regretful, ironic, sorrowful,
deeply joyous—and purblind—love of the world and all in it."**
—Damon Knight

A Mirror
for Observers

o o o o o o o o

Edgar Pangborn

Bluejay Books Inc.

Manufactured in the United States of America

First Bluejay printing: December 1983

Library of Congress Cataloging in Publication Data

Pangborn, Edgar
  A mirror for observers.
  Reprint. Originally published: New York, N.Y. :
Equinox Books, 1975 printing, ©1954.
  I. Title.
PS3566.A56M5 1983 813'.54 83-15869
ISBN 0-312-94305-9

to John V. Padovano

. . . But I observed that even the good artisans fell into the same error as the poets;—because they were good workmen they thought that they also knew all sorts of high matters, and this defect in them over-shadowed their wisdom; and therefore I asked myself on behalf of the oracle, whether I would like to be as I was, neither having their knowledge nor their ignorance, or like them in both; and I made answer to myself and to the oracle that I was better off as I was.

—PLATO, *Apology*

note: *all characters in this novel are fictitious except possibly the Martians.*

prelude

The office of the Director of North American Missions is a blue-lit room in Northern City, 246 feet below the tundra of the Canadian Northwest Territory. There is still a land entrance, as there has been for several thousand years, but it may have to be abandoned this century if the climate continues to warm up. Behind a confusion of random boulders, the entrance looks and smells like a decent bear den. Unless you are Salvayan—or Martian, to use the accepted human word—you will not find, inside that den, the pivoted rock that conceals an elevator. Nowadays the lock is electronic, responding only to the correct Salvayan words, and we change the formula from time to time.

The Abdicator Namir had not been aware of that innovation. He was obliged to wait shivering a few days in that replica of a bear den, his temper deteriorating, until a legitimate resident, returning from a mission, met him and escorted him with the usual courtesies to the office of the Director, who asked: "Why are *you* here?"

"Safe-conduct, by the law of 27,140," said Namir the Abdicator.

"Yes," said Director Drozma, and rang for refreshments. A century ago Drozma would have fetched the fermented mushroom drink himself, but he was painfully old now, painfully fat with age, entitled to certain services. He had lived more than six hundred years, as few Martians do. His birth date was the year 1327 by the Western human calendar, the same year that saw the death of Edward II of England, who went up against Robert Bruce at Bannockburn in 1314 and didn't come off too bloody well. In Drozma's web of

11

wrinkles were scars from the surgery which, about five hundred years ago, had made his face presentably human. His first mission into human society had been in 1471 (30,471), when he achieved the status of qualified Observer during the wars of York and Lancaster; later he made a study of three South American tribes even now unknown to human anthropology; in 30,854 he completed the history of the Tasmanians, which is still the recognized Martian text. His missions were far behind him. He would never again leave this office until it was time to die. He was not only Director of Missions, but also Counselor of Northern City, answerable to its few hundred citizens and, after them, to the Upper Council in Old City in Africa. He carried the honor lightly, yet in all the world there were only three other such Counselors—those of Asian Center, Olympus, and Old City itself. A strangely short while ago there were five Cities. We remember City of Oceans, but it is better to let the mind turn to the present or the deeper past. Soon enough a successor would take over Drozma's burden. Meanwhile, his thought was crystalline-calm as the canals that wind among the Lower Halls of Earth. The Abdicator Namir watched him pet the little ork curled at his feet, the only breed except our own that survived the journey from slow-dying Mars more than thirty thousand years ago. It purred, licked ruddy fur, washed itself, and went back to sleep. "We had word of you recently, Namir."

"I know." Namir sat down with his drink, gracefully in spite of his own advanced age. He waited for the girl who had brought the drinks to pat Drozma's cushion, smile and hover, and go away. "One of your Observers identified me. So I came, partly, to warn you not to interfere with me."

"Are you serious? We can't be intimidated by you Abdicators. I value Kajna's reports—she's a keen Observer."

Namir yawned. "So? Did she mention Angelo Pontevecchio?"

"Of course."

"I hope you don't imagine you can do anything with that boy."

"What we hear of him interests us."

"Tchah! A human child, therefore potentially corrupt." Namir

12

pulled a man-made cigarette from his man-made clothes and rubbed his large human face in the smoke. "He shares that existence which another human animal has accurately described as 'nasty, brutish, and short.' "

"I think you came merely to complain of humanity."

Namir laughed. "On the contrary, I get sorry for the creatures, but the pity itself is a boredom." He shifted casually into American English. "No, Drozma, I just stopped by to say hello."

"After 134 years! I hardly——"

"Is it that long? That's right, I resigned in 30,829."

"I notice you've picked up human habits of conversation."

"I did interrupt—beg your pardon. Please go on, sir."

Not in rebuke but from a private need, Drozma meditated fifteen minutes, hands folded on his belly, which eventually bounced in a chuckle. "You are bored with the society of other Abdicators?"

"No. They're few. I rarely see them."

"As one Salvayan to another, how do you put in the time?"

"Going up and down in the world. I've become quite a wizard at disguise. If I hadn't long ago used up my scent-destroyer your Kajna could never have eavesdropped on my talk with the Pontevecchio boy."

"The law of 27,140 provides that no assistance can be given to Abdicators by Salvayans of the Cities."

"Why, Drozma, I wasn't hinting that I wanted scent-destroyer. I don't find it hard to avoid horses, they're so scarce nowadays. Odd how no other animal seems to mind the Martian scent—Salvayan: you prefer the antique word even in talking English? Must have been tough in the ancient days before the destroyer was invented. But since human animals can't catch the scent, I don't need the stuff, except to help me avoid your sniffier Observers. . . . The smart thing, five or six thousand years ago, would have been to develop an equine epidemic, get rid of the damned beasts."

Drozma winced in disgust. "I begin to see why you resigned. In all your life I think you never learned that patience is the wellspring."

13

"Patience is a narcotic for the weak. I have enough for my needs."

"If you had enough you'd cure yourself of resentments. Let's not argue it: our minds don't meet. Again, why have you come here?"

Namir flicked ash on the mosaic of the floor. "I wanted to find out if you still imagine human beings can ever amount to anything."

"We do."

"I see. Even after losing City of Oceans—or so I heard."

"Namir, we do not talk about City of Oceans. Call it a taboo, or just a courtesy to me. . . . What did you ever hope to achieve by resigning?"

"Achieve? Oh, Drozma! Well, perhaps a spectator's pleasure. The interest of watching the poor things weave a rope for their own hanging."

"No, I don't think that was it. That wouldn't have turned you against us."

"I'm not against you particularly," said Namir, and pursued his original thought: "I thought they had that rope in 30,945, but there they are, still unhanged."

"Tired of waiting?"

"Ye-es. But if I don't live to see their finish, my son will."

"A son. . . . Who is your Salvayan wife, may I know?"

"Was, Drozma. She died forty-two years ago, giving birth. She was Ajona, who resigned in 30,790 but continued to suffer from idealism until I effected a partial cure. The boy's forty-two now, almost full grown. So you see I even have a father's interest in hoping to witness the end of *Homo quasi-sapiens*. . . . Might I ask your current population figures?"

"About two thousand, Namir."

"In all the—er—four Cities?"

"Yes."

"H'm. Bigger, of course, than our few dozen of the enlightened. But that's deceptive, since you are all dreamers."

"Men vanish, and you repopulate from a few dozen?"

"I don't suppose they'll vanish completely. Too damn many of 'em."

"You have plans for the survivors?"

"Well, I don't feel free to give you blueprints, old man."

"The law of 27,140——"

"Is a routine expression of Salvayan piety. You couldn't use it against us. After all, we have a weapon. Suppose men, with a little help, were to locate the—remaining cities?"

"You couldn't betray your own kind!" Namir did not answer. . . . "You consider the Abdicators peculiarly enlightened?"

"Through suffering, boredom, observation, disappointment, realistic contact—yes. What could be more educational than loss and loneliness and hope deferred? Why, ask even Angelo Pontevecchio at twelve. He adored his dead father, there's no one he can talk with, childhood keeps him in a cage with life outside—result, he begins to be quite educated. Of course he's a directionless kitten still, a kitten in a jungle of wolves. And the wolves will give his education another lift."

"Love, if you'll excuse the expression, is more educational."

"Now I could never make that mistake. I've watched human beings fool around with love. Love of self mostly, but also love of place, work, ideas; love of friends, of male and female, parent and child. I can't think of any human illusions more comic than those of love."

"May I know more about what you do, outside?"

Namir looked away. "Still an Observer, in my fashion."

"How can you observe through a sickness of hatred?"

"I observe sharply, Drozma."

"You confuse sharpness with accuracy. As if a microscopist forgot to allow for relative size and saw an amoeba as big as an elephant. . . . As I remember, after your resignation you were first seen by us in 30,896, in the Philippines."

"Was I?" Namir chuckled. "Didn't know that. You get around."

"They say you made a convincing Spaniard. In Manila, a day or

15

so after the official murder of José Rizal. You had some part in that?"

"Modesty forbids—no, really, his human killers could have managed perfectly well without me. Rizal was an idealist. That made his slaughter almost automatic, a human reflex action."

"Other idealists have—oh, I think eternity would be too short to argue with you. Not a single kind word for humanity then?" Namir smiled. "Not even for Angelo Pontevecchio?"

"You're truly concerned over that child? Ridiculous! As I said, he's a kitten now, but I'll make a tiger of him. You'll hear the lambs bleat with blood in the throat even up here among your pretty dreams."

"Perhaps not."

"Would you dare to bet on it?"

The Director reached for a primitive telephone. "If you like. It won't affect the outcome. Nor would any Observer I send, maybe. However . . ." He spun the crank. "Regardless of whom I send, Namir, your real antagonist is not the Observer, not I, but Angelo himself."

"Of course. Telephones! Getting modern as next week."

Drozma said pedantically: "It happens we invented the telephone in 30,834. Naturally when Bell reinvented the wretched thing independently in '876 he made some improvements. We're not gadget-minded. And his successors—oh dear! Fortunately we don't need all those refinements. Anyway we had to wait till men brought their lines north of Winnipeg before it was convenient to talk City-to-City. Now I suppose you might call us—ah—unofficial subscribers. We have a full-time Communicator in Toronto, sorry I'm not free to give you his name. Hello . . . ? Hello . . . ?" Namir chortled. Drozma said plaintively: "I suppose the operator is in contemplation. Does it matter? I can always call again. You know, Namir, I had this—ah—gimmick installed simply because I can't easily walk around any more. I don't actually like the things. I—oh, hello . . . ? Why, thank you, my dear, and on you the peace of the laws. When you have time, will you send word that I

16

want to see Elmis? . . . Yes, the historian. He's probably in the Library, or else the Music Room, if this is his practice time—I can't remember. Thank you, dear." He put away the receiver with a twiddle of pudgy fingers. "A gimmick."

"Can't wait till you grow up to radio."

"Radio? We've had excellent receiving sets ever since human beings invented it. Obviously we mustn't broadcast, but we hear it. Have you forgotten your history? Radio was known on Salvay, one of the little techniques our ancestors abandoned—from lack of important need, I suppose—during the first miserable centuries in this wilderness. Don't you ever think of ancient times, Namir? The shock, loneliness, no hope of return even if Salvay had not been a dying planet—except to the Amurai, I suppose. They could wall themselves in, accept the underground life that we rejected. And then we had to accept it here after all! Think of the ordeal of adaptation too. History says it was two hundred years before the first successful births, and even then the mothers usually died. What an age of trial!"

"History is a dead language."

"Can't agree. Well, our mathematicians study the human broadcasts. Over my head, the mathematics, but I'm sure radio's immensely useful."

"Immensely emetic. While we wait for your big-time operator, would you care for a word of advice?"

"Certainly. Television too—damn it, I love television. You were about to say?"

"On my way here, I passed six settlements in northern Manitoba and Keewatin District, all new since the last time I was near there, in 30,920. The icecap goes faster all the time. You're losing the Arctic shield. No concern of mine but I thought I'd mention it."

"Thanks. Our Observers watch it. The waterlock will be finished before we need to close the land entrance. And did *you* know that the human plastics industry is almost ready with greenhouse dwellings, size limited only by convenience? In a few decades there'll be garden villages all through the Arctic, independent of climate, and

17

in a century the population of Canada will probably match that of the States—if they're still technically separate countries by that time. Personally I'm pleased about it. Come in, Elmis."

Elmis was long-legged, slim, powerful, his complexion close to that colorful pallor human beings call white. From his agony of surgery long ago, his face and hands were properly human. The brown-haired scalp and artificial fifth fingers had been almost-normal parts of him for over two hundred years. If he had to show himself barefoot, the four-toed feet would pass for a human anomaly. Drozma explained: "I'm sorry to call you from the work you prefer, Elmis. I know you'd hoped never to go out as an Observer again. But you're much better qualified than anyone else available, so I can't help myself. This is Namir the Abdicator."

Elmis' manlike voice said in English: "I think I remember you." Namir nodded inattentively. "You've returned to us?"

"What an idea! No, just passing by, and I must be on my way. A pleasure. By the way, Drozma—care to put up some little consideration to make that bet interesting? Say, a human soul?"

"Why, assuming anyone could dispose of a human soul——"

"Sorry. For a minute there I thought you wanted to play God." He squirmed into his arctic gear. "So long, children. Keep your noses clean."

"?" said Elmis, and entered contemplation, head on his knees.

Presently Drozma sighed. "A time factor, Elmis, or I wouldn't interrupt your thought. Would the name 'Benedict Miles' suit you?"

" 'Miles'—yes, a nice anagram. Urgent, sir?"

"Maybe. A human child becomes a man more swiftly than one can write a poem. Is your work in such state that you can leave it?"

"Someone else can always go on with it, Drozma."

"Tell me more about it."

"Still tracing ethical concepts as lines of growth. Trying to see through the froth of conflicts, wars, migrations, social cleavages, ideologies. I was restudying Confucius when you called me."

"Tentative conclusions?"

"A few, confirming your own intuition of a hundred years ago:

18

that a genuine ethical revolution—comparable to the discovery
of fire, of agriculture, of social awareness—might be in progress
about 31,000, and might develop for the necessary centuries. The
germs are present. Hard to see, but certainly present, just as the
germ of society was latent in pre-language family groups. Of course
one can make no allowance for such unpredictables as atomic war,
pestilence, a too sudden rise in the water level. Fortunately the
dream of security is a human weakness we needn't share. As a very
rash prediction, Drozma, I think Union with them might be possible
late in my son's lifetime."

"Truly . . . ? Seems very soon, but it's a refreshing thought.
Well, here's your mission. Observer Kajna came home yesterday.
She was overdue, and with the worst of the journey ahead of her,
when she had to wait on a train connection in Latimer—that's a
small city in Massachusetts. She spent the time in a park. A nice old
gentleman was feeding the pigeons and talking to a boy about
twelve years old. Kajna caught the Martian scent. She renewed her
scent-destroyer, listened in on the conversation from another bench.
The old man was Namir. She'd seen him once using a similar disguise in Hamburg, years ago. You know we try to keep track of the
Abdicators so long as it doesn't interfere with more important work.
Kajna happens to feel rather strongly about them. She wanted to
follow Namir, she had to get home to us soon, and as she listened
a third necessity developed. In the end, when the old man and the
boy went different ways, Kajna followed the boy, not Namir. Followed him to a lodging house where he lives. She inquired about a
room, enough to start a conversation, pick up a few facts. The boy
is the landlady's only child—Angelo Pontevecchio. The landlady,
Rosa Pontevecchio, is—Kajna used the term 'sweet-minded.' Not
much education, and on a very different psychophysical level; a fat
woman in poor health. Kajna saw and empathized enough to suggest valvular heart disease, but wasn't sure. Well, then Kajna came
home. Used her own judgment. As you will have to do."

"And Namir?"

"Oh, he identified her after all. Mentioned it when he was here."

19

"Whatever brought him? More than a century since he resigned."
"I think, Elmis, he has some rather dirty little plans for Angelo, and wanted to find out what plans we had, if any. We have none, except as they will develop in your good Observer's mind. The boy may or may not be as potentially important as Kajna felt he was. I hope he is—you know I wouldn't send you out for a trivial cause. You're to go there to Latimer, live in or near that lodging house as Benedict Miles. On your own. I must have your independent judgment. That's why I won't tell you any more about the child, and I'd rather you didn't talk with Kajna about the mission before you go. As for Namir, you know the law of 27,140. The Abdicators aren't to be acted against, so long as they do no positive harm." Drozma stroked the ork as it rose to stretch squabby legs. His voice shook. "I can imagine situations in which you might have to review the definitions of that cloudy word 'harm.' You know also that an Observer must not risk violating human law, unless he is prepared to —to prevent betrayal of Salvayan physiology."

"Sir, we don't need euphemism, you and I. I'll ask Supply to give me a suicide-grenade recheck. And, I think, a spare grenade, unless you object."

Drozma bit his lip. "I don't object. I've already told Supply to have everything ready for you. . . . Elmis, the bitterness I saw just now in Namir—I'd almost forgotten such feelings could exist. Be careful. I suppose he's always in pain. His own thought turns on him and eats him like a cancer. Salvayan pain, remember. No matter how human he acts, don't ever forget he has our lower threshold of suffering along with our greater endurance. I'm sure he still meditates, though he might deny it. And if his angry heart is set on a thing, he'll turn aside for nothing except superior force." Drozma shifted fretfully on his cushion. "It's an extended mission, Elmis. If you feel you should stay for the whole of that boy's lifetime, you have my leave. Spare no expense—be sure you draw all the human money you'll need, and I'll authorize the Toronto Communicator to honor any emergency requests. But even if you return quite soon I may not be here, so I think I'll give you this."

From under his cushion he took a wrapped package, heavy but small. "A mirror, Elmis. Unwrap it and look at it later if you like, not now. An Observer—his name is lost—brought this in 23,965 from the island now called Crete. Bronze—we've kept the patina away from the best reflecting side. I don't suppose it's the first mirror made by human beings, but surely one of the first. You might want the boy Angelo to look at his face in it. You see, we think it possible that he's one of those who can learn how to look in a mirror."

"Ah . . . ! Am I good enough for such a mission?"

"Try to be. Do your best. The peace of the laws be with you."

part one

The problem of darkness does not exist for a man
gazing at the stars. No doubt the darkness is there,
fundamental, pervasive and unconquerable except
at the pin-points where the stars twinkle; but the
problem is not why there is such darkness, but
what is the light that breaks through it so remarkably;
and granting this light, why we have eyes to see it
and hearts to be gladdened by it.
—GEORGE SANTAYANA, *Obiter Scripta*

Accept, Drozma, assurance of my continuing devotion. For reasons of safety I write in Salvayan instead of the English you prefer. This report was begun in greater leisure than I now have, and it follows a humanly fashionable narrative form: I had your entertainment in mind, knowing how you relish the work of human storytellers, and I only wish I had their skill. I have blundered, as you will see. The future is clouded, my judgment also. If you cannot approve what I have done and what I still must do, I beg you will make allowance for one who admires human creatures a little too much.

1 The bars are genial in Latimer in 30,963. A warmer life fills the evening streets than on my last visit to the States seventeen years ago. People stroll about more, spend less time rocketing in cars. It was a June Saturday when I reached Latimer, and found the city enjoying its week end snugly. There was peace. A pine-elm-and-maple, baked-beans-and-ancestors, Massachusetts sort of peace, to which I am partial. Getting born in the Commonwealth would help, if one had to be a human being.

Latimer is too far from Boston to be much under the influence of what Artemus Ward called the "Atkins of the West." Latimer can make its own atmosphere: five large factories, a population over ten thousand, a fairly wealthy hill district, a wrong side of the tracks, two or three parks. The town was more populous a few years ago. As factories become cybernetic they move away from the large centers; the growth is in the suburbs and the countryside. Latimer in this decade is comfortably static—yet not quite comfortably, for there is a desolation in boarded-up houses, a kind of latent grief that few care to examine. In Latimer the twentieth century (human term) rubs elbows with the eighteenth and nineteenth in the New England manner. There is a statue of Governor Bradford half a block from the best movie theater. A restored-colonial mansion peers across Main Street at a rail-bus-and-copter station as modern as tomorrow.

I bought a science-fiction magazine in that station. They still multiply. This one happened to be dominantly grim, so I read it for laughs. Galaxies are too small for humanity. And yet, sometime . . . ? Was our own ancestors' terrible journey thirty thousand years ago only a hint of things to come? I understand men will

25

have their first satellite station in a very short while, four or five years. They call it "a device to prevent war." Sleep in space, Salvay —sleep in peace . . . !

No. 21 Calumet Street is an old brick house on a corner, two stories and basement, not far from the inevitable Main Street, which travels from right to wrong side of the tracks. No. 21 is on the wrong side, but its neighborhood is not bad, a residential backwater for factory workers, low-pay white-collars, transients. Five blocks south of No. 21, Calumet Street enters a slum where dregs settle to a small Skid Row, no less pitiable than the massive human swamps in New York, London, Moscow, Chicago, Calcutta.

I found a "vacancy" card in the basement window. I was admitted by the one whose life I was to meddle with. I knew him at once, this golden-skinned boy with eyes so profoundly dark that iris and pupil blended in one sparkle. Perhaps I knew him then as well as I ever shall, in that mild moment of appraisal before he had even spoken or given me more than a casual friendly glance. When we admit that the simplest mind is a continuing mystery, what height of arrogance it would be to say that I know Angelo!

He was carrying a book, his finger holding a place, and I saw he was lame, with a brace on the left ankle. He led me into a basement living room to talk with his mother, whose body, like a disguise, billowed over a rocking chair. She had been mending the collar of a shirt that sprawled as if alive on the mountain of her lap. I noticed in Rosa Pontevecchio her son's disturbing eyes, broad forehead, sensuous mouth. "Two rooms free," she told me. "First-floor back, running water, bath one flight up. There's a second-floor back, but it's smaller, maybe not so quiet—well, it's that awful copter noise, I swear they try 'n' see how close they can skim the roof."

"First floor sounds all right." I indicated a portable typewriter I had bought on impulse in Toronto. "I'm writing a book, and I do like it quiet." She was not inquisitive nor obsequiously impressed. The boy spread his book face down. It was a paperback, selections from Plato, opened near the front to the *Apology* or *Crito*. "My name is Benedict Miles." I kept my phony autobiography simple, to lessen the nuisance of remembering details. I had been a schoolteacher, I said, in an (unspecified) Canadian town. Thanks to a legacy, I had a year of leisure for the (undescribed) book, and wanted to live simply. I tried to establish an academic manner to go with my appearance of scrawny middle age. A shabby, pedantic, decent man.

She was a widow, I learned, managing the house alone. Its income would clearly be inadequate to pay for hired help. She was about forty, half her tiny lifetime gone. The latter half would be burdened by hard work, the gross discomfort of her flesh, many sorts of loneliness; yet she was cheerful in her chatter, outward-looking and kind. "I don't get around too good." Her lively hands spoke of her bulk in humorous apology. "Doing the place mornings is my limit. Angelo, you show Mr. Miles the room."

He limped ahead of me up a narrow, closed-in stairway. This house was built before Americans fell in love with sunlight. The first-floor back was a large room and would be relatively quiet. Two windows overlooked a yard, where a pudgy Boston bulldog snoozed in the last of June daylight. When I opened a window Angelo whistled. The dog stood on her hind legs to waggle clumsy paws at him. "Bella's a show-off," Angelo said with unconcealed affection for the pup. "She doesn't bark much, Mr. Miles."

One never knows how a dog will react to the Martian scent. At least they never object to the overriding scent-destroyer. Namir had no destroyer. . . . "Like dogs, Angelo?"

"They're honest." Commonplace, but not a twelve-year-old remark.

I tested the one armchair and found the springs firm. The impress of other bodies was appealing, and gave me a sense of sharing human qualities. I tried to consider Angelo as another human being might. Two things seemed plain: he lacked shyness, and he lacked excess energy.

His father was dead, his mother not strong nor well. Premature responsibility could account for his poise. As for his quiet—I watched him as he moved about softly, drawing away a curtain in

27

a corner to show me the hand basin and two-ring gas stove, and I changed part of my opinion. There was surplus energy, probably intense, but it was a steady burning, not dissipating itself in random muscular commotion or loud talk. "Like the room, Mr. Miles? It's twelve a week. We rent it as a double sometimes."

"Yes, I like it." It resembled all furnished rooms. But in place of the customary tooth-and-bosom calendars and prints there was only one picture, an oil in a plain frame, a summer landscape of sunlit fantasy. You would as soon expect a finished emerald in the five-and-dime. "I'll take it for a week, but tell your mother I hope to be here longer than that." He took the money, promised to bring keys and a receipt. I tried a wild shot: "Have you done many paintings like that, Angelo?" A flush spread on his cheek and throat. "Isn't it yours?"

"It's mine. A year ago. Don't know why I bother."

"Why shouldn't you?"

"Waste of time."

"I can't agree." He was startled, as if he had been braced to hear something else. "I admit it wouldn't please the modern cults, but so what?"

"Oh, them." He recovered, and grinned. "Sissy though. Kid stuff."

I said: "Nuts." And watched him.

He fidgeted, more like a twelve-year-old now. "Anyway I don't think it's very good. I don't hear that birch tree."

"I do. And the grass under it. Field mice in the grass."

"Do you?" Neither flattered nor quite believing it. "I'll get your receipt." He hurried, as if afraid of saying or hearing more.

I was unpacking when he returned. I let him see my clutter of commonplace stuff. The hair dye to keep me gray passed for an ink bottle. The scent-destroyer was labeled after-shaving lotion and would smell like it, I understand, to a human nose. The mirror was wrapped. The flat grenades were next to my skin of course. Angelo lingered, curious, willing to get acquainted, possibly hurt because I volunteered nothing more about his painting: bright as he was, he

28

wouldn't have outgrown vanity at twelve. He asked innocently: "That typewriter case big enough for your manuscript?"

Too smart. When I decided that Mr. Miles was puttering at a book I neglected to pick up anything but the typewriter and packages of paper still unopened. "Yes, it is for the present. My book is mostly here." I tapped my head. I knew I should dream up some mess of words, and soon. I didn't think he or his mother would poke among my things, but one tries to avoid even minor risks. Fiction? Philosophy? I sought the armchair and lit a cigarette (again I recommend them to Observers deprived of our thirty-hour periods of rest: smoke is no substitute for contemplation but I believe it softens the need). "School finished for the year, Angelo?"

"Yeah. Last week."

"What year are you? Shut my mouth if it's none of my business." A smile flashed and faded. "Sophomore."

The average age in that class would be around sixteen. He would be holding himself back, I knew, in self-defense. "You like the *Crito?*"

Alarm was obvious in the studied blankness of his face. "Ye-es."

Certainly it would be difficult to convince him that I was not talking down, not making secret fun of his precocity. I tried to be idly conversational: "Poor Crito! He really tried. But I think Socrates wanted to die. In the reasoning to prove he should remain, don't you think he was talking to himself more than to Crito?"

No relaxation. Strained youthful courtesy: "Maybe."

"He could have argued he owed Athens nothing; that an unjust law may be violated to serve a greater. But he didn't. He was tired."

"Why?" said Angelo. "Why would anyone want to die?"

"Oh, tired. Past seventy." (What should I have said?) It was enough for the moment, I thought, or too much. At least it was an attempt to let him know I honored his intelligence, and it might help me later. It would have been easier if I had been required to hold a soap bubble in my clumsy hands, since a soap bubble is only a pearl of illusion and if it bursts that's no great matter. More like

29

snuffy Mr. Miles, I said: "Wonder if my typing will bother the other tenants? It's a noisy old machine."

"Nope." Angelo was plainly relieved at the prosaic turn. "Mr. Feuermann's bath and closet are between the rooms. Room over you is vacant, and the folks upstairs—the old ladies and Jack McGuire—they won't hear it. We won't downstairs. This is above the kitchen. Don't give it a thought."

"Not even if I split an infinitive?"

He stuck a finger in his mouth and snapped it to make a pop like a cork out of a bottle. "Not even if you treat a spondee as an iambus."

"Ouch! Wait till *I* get educated, can't you?" He grinned sweetly and fled. And that, I thought, is the child whom Namir wants to corrupt. This was the moment, Drozma, when the enigma of Namir himself truly began to torment me, as it still does. I must accept fact: it is possible for a being, human or Martian, to see something beautiful, recognize it as beautiful, and immediately desire to destroy it. I know it's so, but I don't, I never shall, understand it. One would think the mere shortness of life would be a reminder that to destroy beauty is to destroy one's own self too.

I fussed about, as a human creature should in a new nest. I reviewed Observers' Rules. The risk that has always worried me worst is that some trifling injury might reveal the orange tint of our blood. I am prone to bark shins and bruise hands. Our one-to-the-minute heartbeat is not only a risk but a source of regret. It annoys me that I must be cautious in all physical contact, and it's too bad having to avoid doctors—they could be interesting. Observers' work must have been more entertaining as well as safer (except for the horse problem) in the old days when magic and superstition were cruder and more crudely accepted. And I turned the package of the bronze mirror over and over in my hands, wondering at some of your meanings, Drozma. I did not unwrap it. I wish that I had, or that I had examined it in Northern City. Doubtless you supposed I would, but there were many last-minute errands, and I have studied so many human antiquities that my curiosity was dulled. I

30

did not learn its nature until a time when it caught me unprepared. That evening I put the package in the bureau under some clothes, and wandered out to explore the city.

And I met Sharon Brand.

My immediate objective was butter, bread, and sliced ham, though I had it in mind to do any Observer's work that might turn up as a by-product of my mission. A delicatessen on Saturday evening can be a listening post. People lounge, linger, cuss the weather, and talk politics. I found one at once, by drifting toward the grimier end of Calumet Street. It was a tiny corner shop three blocks from No. 21, and the sign said EL CAT SEN.

No one was in it but a girl about ten years old, sitting almost hidden behind the counter with a comic book. Her left foot was on another chair. Her right leg was wrapped around her left in a sort of boneless abandon that might have been experimental or just comfortable. I examined the cases, waiting for signs of life, but she was far away. The wooden shaft of a lollipop protruded from her mouth with a sophistication that went well with a pug nose and dark shoulder-length hair. "All by yourself?"

Without looking up she nodded and said: "Uh. Oo i owioffsh oo?"

"Yes, I do rather." It wasn't baby talk. She just didn't find an immediate need to take out the all-day sucker, but wanted to know if I liked lollipops too.

But then she glanced at me—startling ocean-blue eyes, inescapably appraising—and waved at a box, and gradually got her wide mouth unstuck, and said: "Well, pick one. Heck, they're only a penny, heck." She reversed legs, wrapping the left around the right. "You couldn't do that."

"Who says I can't?" There was a third chair behind the counter, so I got into it and showed her. With our more elastic bones, I had an unfair advantage, but I was careful not to exceed human possibility. Even so she looked slightly sandbagged.

"You're pretty good," she admitted. "Inja-rubber man. You forgot your lollipop." She tossed me one from the box, lemon variety. I got busy on it and we have been friends ever since. "Look," she

31

said. "Heck, could this autothentically happen, I mean for true?" She showed me the comic book. There was a spaceman with a beautiful but unfortunate dame. The dame had been strapped to a meteor—by the Forces of Evil, I shouldn't wonder—and the spaceman was saving her from demolition by other meteors. He did it by blasting them with a ray-gun. It looked like a lot of work.

"I wouldn't want to be quoted."

"Oh, you. I'm Sharon Brand. Who are you?"

"Benedict Miles. Just rented a room up the street. With the Pontevecchios, maybe you know 'em?"

"Heck." She took on a solemn glow. She threw away the comic, and unwound and readjusted her skinny smallness. Now she was sitting on both her feet, and had her elbows hung over the back of the chair, and watched me for a time with eyes ten thousand years old. "Angelo happens to be my best boy friend, but you better not mention it. It would be most unadvisable. I would be furious."

"I never would."

"I'd probably cut your leg off and beat you over the head with it. If you detonated."

"Detonated?"

"Aren't you educated? It means shoot off. Your mouth. Some people call him stuck-up on account he's always reading books. You don't think he's stuck-up, do you?" Her face said urgently: Better not detonate.

"No, I don't think he is at all. He's just very bright."

"I'd probably turn a ray-gun on you. Tatatata-taah. He happens to've been my boy friend for years and years, but don't forget you promised. Heck, I hate a rat. . . . You know what?"

"No, what?"

"I started piano lessons yesterday. Mrs. Wilks showed me the scale. She's blind. Right away she showed me the scale. They've fixed up to let me practice on the school piano for the summer."

"Scale already, huh? That's terrific."

"Everything is terrific," said Sharon Brand. "Only some things are terrificker than others."

32

2   Later (I hoped my friend Sharon was asleep, but somehow I had an image of both those children turning on furtive night lights, Sharon with her spacemen, Angelo wandering critically through the intricacy of Plato's dreams) I went out to taste the city's middle evening again, going through the railroad underpass to the "right" side of the tracks, drifting with other masks past shopwindows, poolrooms, dance halls. I played the watching game with myself: "One I'd like to know, a gleam of intelligence. . . . Ah, the Face that Foreclosed the Mortgage! . . . A face of bitterness, member of the weasel totem. . . . A genuine dish. . . . Gracious with age. . . . Savage with age. . . . A schoolmarm (?)—a pickpocket—a plainclothes cop—a salesman—a possible bank teller . . ." In that game you have their voices too, never finished: "So he gets his gun on this other guy, see, only the Ranger's behind the bush——" "I told her, I said, if I don't know my own size in girdles by this time——" "I wouldn't believe him if he had brass knucks——"

I followed a street uphill. Separate houses with lawns, somber men being walked by small dogs. At the crest one looked down at city lights fantastically calm. My night vision, better than human, allowed me to see beyond them to distant fields and woods, delicately secret even in daylight with lovable small life in the grass and bushes. The moon was rising. I strolled in that placid region, admiring some of the houses, reflecting that the owners used the same type of aspirin as their neighbors downtown. I returned to the business district by another route, wondering if it could be true that someone was following me.

A sly footstep never quite heard, a shadow never quite seen

33

against hedge or doorway. Oh, I had been fretting more than I realized, about Namir. That was all, I thought—that and fatigue. The movie theaters were closed. The crowd had thinned and changed: fewer of the cheerful, more of the predatory. I bought a late newspaper and shoved it in my pocket after a glance at the headlines. The present seems to be an interlude of relative calm, but now human beings are too shrewd to suppose that the volcanoes under the surface are dead. They were fooled that way, I recall, in the '880s and '890s. They have learned a few things since then. The United States of Europe is functioning rather well if creakily, though everyone is afraid of the logical next step of Atlantic Federation, and the One World Government boys and girls are clouding the issue as usual with well-meant enthusiasm. There are three Iron Curtains now: Russia's, China's, and the curious new one, growing higher each year ever since the death of Stalin, between Russia and China themselves. But the seven or eight major civilizations of the world are cohering; except for those two eclipsed by ancient despotism, the civilizations may be feeling their way to an enduring compromise. One doesn't look for the small promises of an ethical revolution in the headlines: the ocean's currents do not derive from the ocean's tempests. . . . Eisenhower's successor appears to be a reasonable man: I gather that few seriously dislike him, though it's hard to fill such a pair of shoes. The trend is likely to be against him in '964, with the customary jump a little too far left. That doesn't worry me.

Back on the wrong side of the tracks, I entered a park up a side street near Calumet. It was mere leftover space created by an angling cross street. Brick walks too bumpy for roller skates, patches of stubborn grass. Two old men were playing checkers under a park lamp. I rested on a bench in the moon-shadow of a maple, wondering if this might be the park where Observer Kajna had overheard a certain conversation.

A hundred yards away were two clusters of benches, deserted except for a gaunt fellow, head bowed in his hands. Drunk, sick, or derelict, I thought. Two soldiers and their girls sat down near him and he got up and lurched away, on a path that would bring him past me. He did not pass me, and I looked again. He was stumbling off in the other direction, crossing grass as if to avoid the checker players' lamp.

My bench was deeply shadowed. He could hardly have made me out with drunken human eyes. I caught no Martian scent, but the breeze was wrong. My own scent-destroyer was fresh, but I had made no change in my face since Namir saw me in Northern City.

Dismissing uneasiness, returning to the now indolent night life of Main Street, I entered a bar (not my first that evening) and listened to the long gush of words, variations on the silly, wise, obscene. That was restful. It spoke well for my manner and appearance that nobody gave the skinny rye drinker a second glance until I invited it, rambling into an argument with a plumber over the future of the world's fuel supply. It has become fashionable to fret about that. We bought three rounds. I said solar energy, wind, water power, and alcohol, but in the end I let him have his atoms, what the hell.

"Thing is," he said, "you got to hitch to a star. When I think of the things my kids'll see! You figure there's life on Mars?"

"No atmosphere," said a fat man the plumber called Joe.

"Now it stands to reason," said the plumber, and pounded a puddle on the bar and apologized for splashing me. "They see green in the telescopes, don't they? How about that?"

"Lichens," said Joe. "Meant to say not *enough* atmosphere, see?"

"You can take your lichens," said the plumber, "and—well, it stands to reason, and anyway why couldn't they live underground, seal in the atmosphere, what the hell?"

"Not me," said Joe. "I'd get this now clusterphobia."

"All the same you can take your lichens——"

I was back at the lodging house before midnight, happy about moonlight on square quiet houses, happy about someone plinking a mandolin late and gently behind drawn curtains, happy about our Salvayan capacity for alcohol. My plumber had gone home under

35

convoy of Joe and another, the three of them operating rather like a minesweeper with a one-eyed pilot.

There was a night light in the hall, and more light from the open door of the first-floor front. That would be Mr. Feuermann, I remembered, and I saw him, a white-haired old gentleman in an armchair, his feet up on a stool. He was cherishing a horse-head meerschaum. Purposely I tripped. He cleared his throat and came stumping out. "All right?"

"Yes, thanks—turned my ankle a bit."

We examined each other with the furtive measuring of human strangers. He was obviously lonely. "Too bad," he said, and studied the carpet with some hostility, plainly worried about trouble for Mrs. Pontevecchio. "It looks all right."

"It wasn't the carpet. Fact is I had one too many."

"Oh." A solid old man, though tall and not stout. "Sometimes," he said, "if you make the hair on a long-haired dog a mite longer . . . ?"

So I went into his room and he broke out a pint of bourbon and we discussed it for an hour. He claimed he'd left the door open to clear away stale smoke, but then admitted he was always hoping someone would drop in. He had been a railroad engineer until twelve years ago, when he retired, because of age, because Diesels were hooting the end of steam and he was too old for new techniques. He had been a widower for six years; his only child, a daughter, was married and living in Colorado. Once his work had taken him all over the States. He spoke warmly and poetically of that wandering on steel pathways, but Latimer was home and he would not leave it again.

I did not try to steer the talk to the landlady's son: the old man did so himself. Jacob Feuermann had lived in that house since his wife died. I understood, without words, that the Pontevecchios had become an adopted family for him. Their troubles were his, and perhaps he knew that there was on him a reflected glow of Angelo's strangeness.

He remembered Angelo as a huge-eyed six-year-old, not talkative but intensely observant, given to fierce fits of temper—caused, Feuermann believed, by frustrations that would not have badly troubled ordinary children. In retrospect, Feuermann took a sort of proprietary pride in those tantrums. Angelo had never been a naughty child, he said. Angelo took punishments with good grace and rarely repeated an offense; but a toy out of reach, a tumbling block house, a missing jigsaw fragment could turn him blue in the face. "Even now, when he's got over that, you couldn't call him a happy kid, and I don't think," Feuermann said, "the bad leg has much to do with it. . . ." When Feuermann first came to the house, Rosa had been bearing a private crucifixion of despair over those temper fits, her mind approaching and skittering away from the word "insanity" (that fog-word, Drozma, still terrorizes any human being who has learned no discipline of definition). She had confided much in Feuermann. He also remembered her husband in the flesh.

Silvio Pontevecchio seems to have been a baffled alcoholic marshmallow. Intelligent, Feuermann considered him, but unable to profit by it. Silvio had tried a dozen or more ventures, taking his dozen or more failures with the same meek surprise and a few quick ones. Even before Angelo's birth, Feuermann deduced, it was Rosa's work with the lodging house that supported them. Silvio did manage the furnace, but carrying ashes bothered his back. And so on. In the end (just as humbly and mildly, maybe) Silvio fell on the ice in front of a skidding truck, after drinking up money intended for a life insurance premium. "Poor bastard," said Feuermann with genuine pity—"couldn't even die right." That happened when Angelo was seven. Angelo had loved his father, who told good stories and was kind in small matters. A year after Silvio's death Rosa told her friend Feuermann how Angelo had said to her: "I will not, repeat not, lose my temper again." And kept his word. She quit worrying about his mind and worried instead about his small size and his impatience with the tedium of school. ("Enforced play"—but that was a term Angelo himself used, to me, and much later.)

"He skipped three grades in secondary school," Feuermann told me. "They didn't like it. The kid drove 'em, Miles—talked 'em into a position where they had to let him take the examinations, which were nothing to him. Made 'em look silly, so they went to fussing about his 'manner' and 'attitude' and—what's the word?—social adjustment, some damn thing. Brrah! Boy's bright, that's all, but wasn't bright enough then to hide how bright he was."

"Genius?"

"You tell *me* what that is—I dunno."

"Supernormal ability generalized, let's say."

"That he has."

"I sometimes wonder what the schools aim at nowadays."

He made a business of refilling the meerschaum, sensing that I honestly wanted his opinion. "My Clara—it's almost twenty years since she was in high school. I remember beating my brains about *her* schooling. They never seemed to want to teach her anything except how to be like everybody else. When she finished—bright, you know, nothing stupid about Clara—she could add a column of figures after a fashion, read a little if she had to. Hated books, still does. Always been a heavy reader myself, be lost nowadays if I wasn't. Damned if I know what she did learn. Self-expression before she could have anything to express. Social consciousness, whatever that is, when even now she hasn't enough command of language to tell you what she thinks society is. Scraps of this and that, no logic to hold 'em together. Everything made easy—and how are you going to make education easy? You might as well try to build an athlete by keeping him in a hammock with cream puffs and beer. Why, Miles, I've put in seventy years trying to get an education, and only done a half-baked job of it. I guess Angelo's school is about the same. Only, bless your heart, he's learned by now to treat it as a joke, and damn well keep the joke to himself."

"Maybe the schools have come to regard education as a sort of by-product, something it would be nice to have if it isn't too much trouble."

"Oh," said the gentle old man, "I wouldn't say that, Miles. I be-

38

lieve they try." He added, with I think no trace of humorous intent: "Maybe if they started by educating teachers it would help. And there still are a few with high standards—I found that out when it was too late to do Clara any good. . . . Anyway Angelo's a good boy, Miles—nice"—he was fumbling for words himself—"clean, goodhearted. Mean to say he's no damn freak. If it wasn't for his peewee size and that poor little game leg . . ."

"Polio?"

"Yes, at four. Happened before I came here. Gets better as he grows. Doctor told Rosa he might be able to drop the brace after his teens. It shuts him out of a lot. But he never seems to mind that much."

"Might've helped him develop his brains."

"Might." We left it there, for my friend was suppressing yawns. I sought my own room, went to bed lethargically like a tired human being.

I woke in a fog to a sound of snoring; my wrist watch said four-thirty. It was never my way, nor the way of any Salvayan, I should think, to wake with a thick head. The snoring was on the first floor, had to be Feuermann, but was unreasonably loud. I was aware of a nasty sweetish stench and my forehead was a block of dull pain. Something tumbled from my pillow to the floor, and another smell fetched me furiously wide awake: the Martian scent, individualized as it always is and certainly not my own.

I snapped the light on. The thing fallen from my pillow was a wad of cotton, still foul with common chloroform.

I thought at first that nothing was missing. Then I snatched up my bottle of scent-destroyer. Two thirds gone.

My door was ajar. Out in the hall, I learned the snoring was loud because Feuermann's door was open too. A street lamp showed me his bed. No chloroform here. I made sure the old man was un-harmed, his sleep natural though noisy. Back in my room, I saw that my clothing, hung on a chair, was disarranged. The bronze mirror in the bureau was safe. My wallet was too, the money intact, but a note had been shoved in among the bills. A note in our tiny

39

Salvayan script, which looks to human eyes like random dots. It was unsigned and casual:

Please observe that I play fair. Your S-D bottle is not quite empty.

Nothing so artless as a human-style burglary had occurred to me. But Namir was only following the oldest Observers' Rule: *Act human.* I stopped laughing when I considered one non-human element: I could not drive Namir into the grip of the police without betraying our people. He would exploit that fact and never lose sight of it. It was like yielding a handicap of two rooks to a chess player no weaker than myself.

One window was more widely open than I had left it. Namir had come in there from the back yard. A ladder rested against the wall short of my window sill, an easy climb. I had noticed it on its side yesterday by the fence, likely left over from a recent paint job on the window casings. And what about that bulldog? Sunrise was not far away. The wooden back-yard fence had a blank door to the side street—Martin Street. A pile of rags near it troubled me because I couldn't recall seeing it before.

I returned sniffing to the hall, a bathrobe over my pajamas. I heard a fuzzy murmur of another snore upstairs. No scent. Namir would surely be gone. He would not waste the scent-destroyer, but would wait till he could strip and dab it on the scent-gland areas. I tried the second floor. The bathroom was empty, and the vacant room over mine. The two tenants' doors were open a crack. From the room in the middle came that cozy snoring and a whiff of sachet. No chloroform. Angelo had mentioned old ladies. They were probably safe. I looked in the front room.

Here I did smell chloroform. I flipped on the light, snatched the pad away from the young man's pillow, and shook him. He struggled up and grabbed his head. "Who in hell are you?" Jack McGuire was built to ask such questions, a fine mountain of man, mostly shoulders. Redheaded, blue-eyed, and sudden.

"Moved in yesterday, first floor. Prowler broke in, but no-

40

body——" Mac was into his pants and barking about the old ladies before I finished, and then out in the hall shouting: "Hey, Mrs. Mapp! Mrs. Keith!" Nice boy. Plain-spoken. He'd have the house steaming in three minutes. Meanwhile I gave his room a photographic glance. Decent poverty, self-respecting. A work shirt with oil stains—mechanic? Glamor photograph on the bureau, a cute wench with a heart-shaped face; another beside it of a muscular lady unquestionably Mom. Razor, toothbrush, comb, and towel laid out as if for Saturday inspection by a second lieutenant. I shoved the toothbrush into a comfortable diagonal to please myself, and withdrew to a sound of screaming.

They were nice old ladies in a hugely cluttered nest. A double window overlooked Martin Street. That would be their headquarters in normal times, but now the thin one was standing up in bed and screaming while the fat one asked her if everything was all right. Mac said it was. Having touched off the eruption, he was shoving the lava back, barehanded. I liked Mac.

Agnes Mapp was stout, Doris Keith lean. I learned later that they were from New London, and had a low opinion of Massachusetts, where they had been living on widows' pensions for twenty-six years; this burglary was the first occasion when the Commonwealth had snapped back at them. Mrs. Keith subsided to the horizontal, and Mrs. Mapp took over the screaming, waving at the bureau. "It's all upsettled!" In that mass of furniture, corsets, workbaskets, china ornaments, and, yes, antimacassars, I wondered how she knew. "We never let the red vahz set next the pink hairbrushes, never! Oh, Dorrie!" she wept. "Look! He's stolen our album!"

I mumbled I'd call the cops. Mrs. Keith was recovering, and demanding in a severe baritone that Mac explain. He and I contemplated each other in a sympathy bridging the Salvayan-human gap. I went downstairs.

I met Angelo limping up from the basement in yellow pajamas. Feuermann, roused by the screaming, padded after me. I asked him to call police and he ducked back to the hall telephone without fuss. Angelo was muttering.

"Save Mama climbing the stairs."

"Sure. She needn't. Come back down with me. Just a prowler, maybe got away with a few dollars. Ladder under my window. Chloroform."

"Oops!" said Angelo, catching some normal pleasure of excitement. "But Bella——" He forgot Bella, hurrying to his mother as we entered the basement living room. She was in her rocker, grayfaced, clutching a blue wrapper. I wasn't sure she could get up. I tried to be stuffily humorous and soothing in the account I gave her.

"Never had *nothing* like this happen, Mr. Miles—never——"

"Mama," Angelo urged, "don't fret. It isn't anything."

She pulled his head against her. He drew free gently, and rubbed her aimless-wandering hands. Her color improved. Her breathing was almost right by the time Feuermann joined us. Reassuringly important, he said the police would be along shortly, meanwhile we'd better see what was missing. His common sense was golden, his Jovian fussing over Rosa more useful than my efforts. Angelo mumbled about Bella and slipped out. I spoke of the old ladies' missing album.

"Funny," said Feuermann. "If they say it's missing it is—couldn't misplace a pin in that room. They won't even let Rosa dust. Got a notion my own is missing. Remember, Miles, I showed you a snap of old 509 when she was new out of the yards, and one of me and Susan and Clara when she was twelve. Where'd I put that album when we were done with it?"

"Top of your bookcase."

"Right. Always do. Seems to me it was gone when I put on the light. Now what would a burglar want of pictures? Huh?"

I wondered if I knew. . . .

The others missed the small cry outside. My Martian hyperacusis is sometimes a burden: I hear too much I'd rather not. But it can be useful. I don't recall running. I was just there, in the back yard, in light from the kitchen window, with Angelo. He was kneeling by that pile of rags. It partly covered Bella, whose neck was broken. "Why?" said Angelo. "Why?"

I helped him to stand, frail in his rumpled pajamas. "Come on back in the house. Your mother might need you again."

He didn't cry or curse. I wished he would. He squinted at the ladder and the ground between it and the fence. Earth and paving stones were dry, unmarked. Angelo said: "I'm going to kill whoever did that."

"No."

He wasn't listening. "Billy Kell might know. If it was the Diggers——"

"Angelo——"

"I'm going to find him. I'm going to break his own neck for him."

3   "Angelo," I said, "stop that." And I searched my fair memory of the *Crito*. " 'And will life be worth having, if that higher part of man be destroyed, which is improved by justice and depraved by injustice?' "

He recognized it, and remembered. His stare turned up to me, foggy and sorrowful but at least becoming young. He tried to curse them, and it changed to crying, which was better. "The damn—oh, the damn——"

"All right," I said. "Sure." I held his forehead while he tried to vomit and couldn't. I steered him back into the kitchen, made him splash cold water on his face and comb his wild hair with his fingers.

There was a new bumbling voice in the living room, a broad-beamed cop getting the story from Feuermann and being nice to Rosa. His prowl-car partner was upstairs conferring with Mac. I took him outside to look at the ladder, and showed him Bella. "Why, the damn dirty——"

The difference was that Angelo had spoken from inner flame.

43

Patrolman Dunn merely resented violence and disorder. He didn't talk about breaking necks. Nor read the *Crito*. I learned from his comments that the job had the trademarks of someone named Teashop Willie—the back-yard approach, carefully non-lethal use of chloroform. Teashop would have an alibi, Dunn said, and it would be a pleasure to bust it over his think-box.

"Does he specialize in lodging houses?"

"Nup," said Dunn, not liking me much. "And this ain't a money neighborhood, Lord knows. But it's got the marks. You missing anything?"

"Haven't really looked," I lied. "My wallet was under my pillow."

Dunn went back in the house, murmuring: "Known the missus here ten years. People're mighty fond of Mrs. Pontevecchio, mister." There was warning in it, but only because I was what New England calls a foreigner.

They used up an hour or so, and sent for a fingerprint team. Teashop Willie rated that, as a favorite old offender; I suppose Dunn would have been startled if they'd found anything. I could have told him the burglar was wearing gloves. We were not grafting finger tips when Namir resigned in 30,829. The stolen photograph albums tormented Dunn. I think he decided Willie had gone whacky under the stress of a demanding profession. Feuermann and Mac had both lost a little money. The old ladies kept their cash in what Mrs. Keith referred to as a safe place, and she invited no deeper inquiry, implying indirectly that all policemen were grafters, Cossacks, and enemies of the poor. I thought: "Hoy!" Dunn and his pal left us at six-thirty with kind wishes. My only recollection of Dunn's partner is that he was a modest man with a modest wart, who told me personally that no stone would be left unturned. We never heard any more from them about it, so I picture him as still somewhere in the broad uncertainties of the world, turning stones. With all deference to Mrs. Keith, I think policemen are a very decent lot, and I only wish human beings wouldn't make things so tough for 'em.

The evening before, after an enjoyable half hour of space travel,

Sharon Brand had keyed herself up to selling me such items as coffee and bread. Her mother had been in the back room with a Headache, Sharon said, and Pop had gone to a lodge meeting. Sharon enjoyed minding the store. She had dealt competently with the two or three other customers who had interrupted our interstellar activities. Now opening my packages for breakfast reminded me of her, if I had needed any reminder.

I called it a justifiable preoccupation. If she was Angelo's (self-appointed?) Girl Friend, she ought to be studied for the sake of my mission. Then I stopped fooling myself. I admitted she had made me lonely for my own daughter in Northern City. I suppose Elmaja and my son will be living four or five hundred years from now, when nobody at all remembers little Sharon Brand. The one year's flower and the oak—it isn't fair of course.

Still the seed lives, and the flowering of individual selves can be glorious even in the niggardly threescore and ten.

I admitted more. Sharon as a person had reached me somehow, touched me in almost the way that Angelo had done. She lacks his precocity, she may lack his blazing intellectual curiosity. But you put me on my own, Drozma. Observer Kajna did not learn of Sharon. If she had . . . ?

From my window I saw Angelo and his mother go down Martin Street before nine o'clock, nicely dressed, to Mass. Rosa was walking with weariness, Angelo too spindling-small to help her much. I went out too, and strolled down Calumet Street the other way. The morning was muggy, sun pressing through windless haze, a tropical day, a day for the lazy, a day to make me remember the palms of Rio or a warm ocean dreaming against the beaches of Luzon, where I lived once—but that was a long time ago.

I heard trouble before I reached EL CAT SEN: Sharon's voice, cold, tight, and terrified, from the recessed entrance of a boarded-up house next door to the shop. "Don't, Billy! I'll never say it—*don't!*"

I hurried, but my steps must have made noise. Nothing seemed to be happening when I arrived. Sharon was leaning stiffly against the nailed-up door, almost hidden from me by a big-shouldered boy

45

who drew away from her as I appeared. Her right hand was behind her. I had an impression the boy had just released it, and he turned a blond head to stare at me. Much taller than Sharon, thirteen or fourteen and blocky, handsome but blankly so as if he were already expert at wearing a mask. Well, human beings are sometimes good at that. Sharon grinned feebly at me. "Hello, Mr. Miles!" The boy shrugged and moved away.

I said: "Come back here!" He only turned to stare again, hands in his pockets. "Were you bothering this girl?"

"Nope." He was unalarmed, unashamed. His voice was adult, no adolescent croak. He might have been older than he seemed.

"Was he, Sharon?"

Barely audible, Sharon said: "Nuh-nuh-no." She had a red rubber ball on an elastic string, and bounced it thoughtfully. I noticed she used her left hand for that. "Sharon, may I see your other hand?"

Reluctantly she held it out. I saw nothing wrong with it. When I looked up the boy was gone, around the corner. Sharon poked at a wet eyelid with annoyance. She said in a manner too ornate for the Court of St. James's: "Mr. Miles, how can I ever abdiquately thank you?"

"Think nothing of it. Who's the yellow-haired phenomenon?"

That helped. She nodded in acknowledgment of a valuable word. "Just Billy Kell. He is, heck, indeed a phenomenon."

" 'Fraid I don't like him. What did he want?"

Her mouth went tight. "Nothing." She bounced the ball with desperate concentration. "He's a mere phenomenon, think nothing of it." In need of small talk, she added politely: "I hear you had a burglary."

"Yeah. News does get around."

"Heck, I stopped by your house this morning before Angelo had to dress up for church. He says Dogberry will never abdiquately get to the bottom of it, and so phoo on Dogberry, don't you think so? By the way, do you swear never to tell if I happen to show you something?"

46

I said swearing was a serious matter; but she knew that. She studied me a nerve-twisting while, and made up her mind. She peered up and down the street, and darted down to the basement areaway. The lower entrance was half hidden under the front steps, only one board nailed to its wooden door. "You have to swear, Mr. Miles."

I examined conscience. "I swear never to tell."

"You have to cross your heart if it's going to be legal."

I did that, and she lifted away the loose board with slight effort, using her left hand. But she was not left-handed: I notice such things. I followed, closing the door behind us as she ordered, and we were in a hot dingy gloom, musty and vague, with a smell of rats and old damp plaster. I assured her I could see my way, but she gripped my thumb to guide me through a wilderness of empty crates and nameless litter, to a back room that had been a kitchen before the house was abandoned. There are too many such houses in Latimer, and the drift of population to the countryside may not be quite enough to explain it. I wonder sometimes if human beings have begun, a little, to hate the cities to which they have given such effort.

A large flimsy structure loomed in this kitchen, something knocked together from old crates, a house within a house. Sharon said: "Wait." She ducked into the contraption and struck a match. Two candles glowed. "You can come in now." As I squeezed in, she was hushed and solemn, the sea-blue of her eyes lost in enormous black. "Nobody ever did before, except me. . . . This is Amagoya." With obvious second thoughts and fear that I might not deserve the trust, she said: "Of course it's unequibblical make-believe."

It was and it wasn't. There was an altar here, the upturned bottom of a box. On a makeshift shelf above it was what some might have taken for a rag doll. "Amag," Sharon said, nodding to him. "Just merely a representation, used to be a doll. Dolls are so childish, don't you think so?"

"Maybe, but make-believe is real. The inside of your head is

47

real. Things outside are a different kind of real, that's all." The objects on the box-altar were flanked by the candles. A boy's cap, frayed at the brim, a penknife, a silver dollar. "Am I really the only one to see this, Sharon? Not even Angelo?"

"Oh no!" She was shocked. "Amagoya is me when I'm alone. And now you, is why I had to make you swear. Well, because you don't laugh only at the right times." A pity, Drozma, that I had to live 346 years before receiving a compliment of such magnitude. "The dollar, He got that for a school prize and gave it to me for a luck piece. The penknife because I wanted one and He said keep it." You could hear her capitalize the pronoun. "The cap He just threw away." There was no room for polite comment even from a Martian, and Sharon wanted no comment. I looked respectful and that was sufficient. She changed the subject with relief, saying apropos of nothing and with a gusty sigh: "Pop came home drunk from lodge meeting. I veritably couldn't sleep, with them fighting. He hit the lid lifter against the stove just to make a noise, busted it to hell square off, frankly you wouldn't believe the things I put up with, frankly . . ."

"Look, Sharon—that Billy Kell. I think he did hurt your hand. You could tell me about it."

"I couldn't permit you to beat him up. Frankly I couldn't take the responsibility."

"I don't beat people up, but I might scare him a little."

"He don't scare, anyway I'm not afraid of him. He didn't really push my finger back, just pretended he would." She had no real resources of deception; I took advantage of that, by simply waiting. "Well, he was trying to make me say—something I wouldn't, was all. About me and Angelo. Billy can go drown. He is a mere phenomenon, Mr. Miles. . . ."

"And the finger?"

"Honest, it's all right. Look, this is how you play a scale." She demonstrated, on the floor. I saw, not only that her hand was unharmed, but that her thumb already knew how to pass under the fingers in clean precision. After only one lesson. Slow, of course,

48

but right. You yourself, Drozma, have spoken kindly of my ability as a pianist. But I know that we can never equal the best human players, and not merely because our artificial fifth fingers are dull. Do you think it might be because human beings live only a little time, and remember this in their music?

"I'm puzzled, Sharon. This morning Angelo said something about Billy Kell. As if they were friends, or so I thought."

She said with adult bitterness: "He does think Billy's his friend. I tried to tell him different, once. He wouldn't believe me. It's because he thinks everybody is good."

"I don't know, Sharon. I don't think anybody who wasn't would fool Angelo very long."

Well, that was good doctrine, and seemed to make her feel better. She again changed the subject delicately: "If you want to, we could make Amagoya a space ship. I do that sometimes."

"Sound idea."

There was nasty furtive scampering somewhere in that dead kitchen. "Think nothing of it," said Sharon. "You see, when I leave here I cover up everything with that other box, to keep off the phenomenons. . . ."

Handsomely dressed, Angelo met me on the front steps when I returned from the space ship, and transmitted an invitation to stop downstairs for a little coffee. Feuermann was already there. Rosa's idea of a little coffee included pizza and half a dozen other items, all tempting. Rosa herself, in Sunday clothes, looked wilted from something more than the heat of the morning. She reminded me ruefully: "You wanted peace and quiet, Mr. Miles."

"Oh, call me Ben." I tried to relax without losing the primness of Mr. Miles—which had never had a chance to get established, with Sharon. We kicked around the question of photograph albums, Feuermann returning obsessively to the main point: what could a burglar want of them?

"We aren't missing any down here," Angelo said. "I looked."

Later Feuermann said hesitantly: "Angelo, Mac told me he'd—well, dig a place. In the yard. If you want him to."

49

Angelo choked on a mouthful. "If it'd make *him* feel better."

"Dear," Rosa muttered. *"Angelo mio*—please——"

"Sorry, but can't somebody tell Mac I don't wear diapers nowadays?"

"Why, son," Feuermann said, "Mac just thought——"

"Mac just didn't think."

In the raw silence I suggested: "Look, Angelo—have patience with the human race. They try."

He glared across the pretty kitchen table, hating me. The hatred softened and vanished. He seemed only puzzled, perhaps wondering who and what I was, what place I had in his secret widening world. He apologized with not much difficulty: "I'm sorry, Uncle Jacob. Glad to have Mac do that. I was mad because I can't manage a spade with my damned leg."

"Angelo, don't use those words—I've asked you——"

He turned beet-red. Feuermann intervened: "Let him, this time, Rosa. I would too if Bella'd been mine. A damn never hurt anybody."

"Sunday morning," Rosa whimpered, "only an hour after Mass . . . It's all right, Angelo, I'm not cross. But don't do it. You don't want to sound like those tough kids down the street."

"They aren't so tough, Mama." He fooled with his food. "Billy Kell puts on a show but it doesn't mean anything."

"Tough talk makes tough thinking," said Feuermann, and Angelo seemed not to resent that.

When I made my manners Angelo followed me to the basement stairs and asked without warning: "Who are you, Mr. Miles?"

His way, to fetch up the hardest questions—and I don't mean I was worried about the Martian angle: I wasn't. I disliked having to fence with him. "A not very exciting ex-teacher, as I told your mother. Why, friend?"

"Oh, you sort of understand things, maybe."

"Don't lots of people?"

His Latin shrug dismissing that was desperately mature. "I dunno. . . . I met an old man in the park, month or so ago. Maybe

50

he did. He said he'd lend me some books, but then I never saw him again."

"What were the books, remember?"

"Somebody named Hegel. And Marx. Well, I tried to get Marx out of the public library, but they threw a whingding."

"Said mere children don't read Marx?" He looked up quickly, with some incredulity. "I could get those for you if you like."

"Would you?"

"Those and others, sure. You can't study out a thing for good or bad if you don't go to the source. But look, Angelo: you scare people. You know why, don't you?"

He flushed and scraped his shoe tip on the floor like any small boy. "I don't know, Mr. Miles."

"People think in fairly rigid patterns, Angelo. They think a twelve-year-old boy is just thus and so, no argument. When one comes along who thinks ahead of his age, well, they feel as if the ground shook a little. It scares 'em." I put my hand on his shoulder, wanting to say what words could not; he didn't draw away. "It doesn't scare me, Angelo."

"No?"

I tried to imitate his very fine shrug. "After all, Norbert Wiener entered college at eleven."

"Yeah, and had his troubles too. I read his book."

"Then you know some of what I was trying to say. Well, other books. What do you *like* to read?"

He abandoned caution and said passionately: "Anything! Anything at all. . . ."

"Roger!" I said, and squeezed his shoulder and started upstairs. I am not sure, but I think he whispered: "Thanks!"

4 Early that afternoon I had my feet up in my own room, frustratedly trying to guess what Namir's next move might be. Feuermann wandered in, spruced up but not solemn. He said he had a date with his wife. At his age I suppose one needn't be portentous about a Sunday afternoon visit to the cemetery. He was taking Angelo along for the drive and invited me to join them.

His "jalopy" was a '58 model. I marveled at the swooping lines of some '62s and '63s that Angelo pointed out as we purred down Calumet Street. He and the old man talked automobiles, somewhat over my head. I was the only one who noticed a gray coupé sticking behind us as we worked through town and out on a splendid country highway. "The cemetery isn't in Latimer?"

"No, Susan's people were Byfield folks. She wanted to be buried out there. About ten miles. Susan Grainger she was—been Graingers in Byfield since 1650, they say. My papa, he came over on the steerage."

"So'd my grandfather," said Angelo. "Anybody care nowadays?"

Feuermann glanced at me over the small brown head and drooped an eyelid and smiled. I said: "One world, Angelo?"

"Sure. Isn't it?"

"One world and a good many civilizations." He looked bothered.

"Well now," said Jacob Feuermann, "I kind of like the idea of one world government."

"I'm afraid of it," I said, watching Angelo. "Too easy for it to turn monolithic, for individualists to kill individualism without knowing it. Why not seven or eight federations corresponding to the major civilizations, under a world law recognizing their right to be unaggressively different?"

52

"Think we could ever get such a world law? And where's your guarantee against war in that, Miles?"

"There can't be any except in human ethical maturity. A sensible political structure would help enormously, but there's going to be risk of war so long as men think they can justify hating strangers and grabbing for power. Human hearts and minds are basic— the rest is mechanics."

"Pessimist, huh?"

"Not a bit, Feuermann. But scared of the wishful thinking I sometimes do myself. In politics, wishful thinking just gives the wolves a license to howl."

"Mm." The old man squeezed Angelo's bony knee. "Angelo, you figure Miles and me are old enough to sweat out these things?" Angelo might have disliked that gentle sarcasm from anyone but Feuermann. He chuckled and flung a make-believe punch at Feuermann's shoulder, and we pushed it around on that more comfortable level all the way to Byfield. That gray coupé stayed behind us and I didn't mention it. This was a well-traveled road. My imagination could be overheated. Still, Feuermann drove with slow caution and many other cars whooshed by us impatiently. When we pulled into a parking lot near the cemetery the gray car speeded up to hurry past, the driver bending down with averted face.

Angelo had been here with Feuermann before. I would have gone all the way with Jacob to the grave, but Angelo shook his head and led me to a green bank overlooking the most ancient part of the graveyard—quite ancient in the American-human sense, for some of the crumbling stones dated from three hundred years ago when I was a boy. Angelo pointed those out to me, not snickering as most youngsters would have done at the labors of a long-dead stonemason who symbolized angels by eyed circles with a few gouges for hair. "Guess all they had was that sandstone or whatever it is."

"Yes, marble would have done better by a few centuries."

"Sure." He did laugh then. "Sure, what's a few centuries?" He sat on the bank, chewing a grass blade, swinging his feet. Jacob

53

Feuermann was fifty paces away, seeming on his island of contemplation more distant than he was, full of stillness, with sunlight on his white head. He looked down at whatever truth he saw in that modest swell of earth, and then away toward summer clouds and eternity. In a younger man it might have appeared morbidly sentimental, at least to human beings, always swift with labels for the quirks of others. But Feuermann was too solid, too tranquil inwardly, to worry over labels. Later he sat on the ground, chin in hand, unconcerned about dampness or creaky aging joints, and Angelo murmured to me: "Every Sunday rain or shine. Sure, even if it's raining, though maybe he doesn't sit on the grass then. Winter too."

"I suppose he loved her, Angelo. Likes to be here where nothing much comes between him and the thought of her." But I was losing myself in shadow. My mind smelled chloroform, saw that blank-faced young Hercules looming over Sharon in the doorway, glimpsed a gray coupé that should not have hung behind us. Small things. Nothing ugly had happened except Bella's death; the warm sweetness of this day made it seem absurd that any more ugliness could happen. But even in a sunlit hush of jungle you may see some distant fluid motion of black and orange stripes in the grass, or hear the whisper of a leaf no wind disturbs. I produced a yawn and hoped it sounded comfortable, lending a phony casualness to my question: "You go to church, Angelo?"

"Sure." Though mild, his face became too watchful. Probably he knew the question was not casual, knew I was groping for his thoughts and wondered whether to grant me the right to any such exploration. . . . "I even sang in the choir last year. Kid in front of me had ears like an aardvark. Threw me off pitch." He hummed, a clear contralto with a curious effect of distance: *"Ad Deum qui laetificat juventutem meam——"* he spat out the grass blade and smiled off at nothing.

"And has he made your youth joyful?"

Angelo chuckled. "Now you sound like that man I talked with in the park. He said religion was a fraud."

54

"I don't consider it a fraud, though I happen to be agnostic myself. Matter of individual belief. You should go anyway, if only on your mother's account—at least I suppose she's devout, isn't she?"

He sobered quickly. "Yes. . . ."

"Tell me something about Latimer." I watched his feet swinging, the finely shaped one, the twisted one with the brace. "Keep thinking I might decide to settle here."

He spoke doubtfully: "Well, there isn't much. People say it's kind of gone to seed. I dunno. Lot of empty houses. Nothing much ever happens. The country's nice, like here, when you get out in it—— Cheepus, I wish I could! You know: just walk all day, climb hills. I go a mile and then it's pain up the back of the leg, have to quit."

"Think I'll get a car. Then we could go out in the country a bit."

"Cheepus!" He lit up from inside. "Spend a whole day in the woods maybe? I could go for that. . . . You know, that painting, the one in your room, it wasn't any place I ever really saw. I've seen places like it—birches—Uncle Jacob takes me for drives sometimes. But when I want to get out and walk he has to come along and worry about my leg instead of letting me worry about it and quit when I'm ready to. . . . I like animals. You know? The little things that—I've read, if you sit still in the woods a while they'll come around and not be afraid."

"That's true. I've often done it. Most of the birds don't mind if you do move a little, in fact they prefer it, looks less suspicious. I've had orioles come pretty close. Red-wing blackbirds. Fox almost blundered into me once. I was sitting in one of his favorite paths. He just looked embarrassed and made a detour. . . . Met a friend of yours, by the way. At the delicatessen. Sharon Brand."

His mind was still in the woods. He said absently: "Yes, she's a nice kid."

"You sort of grew up with her?"

"Sort of. Four-five years anyway. Mama—doesn't like her too much."

"Oh, why? I think she's swell."

He picked a fresh grass blade. He said carefully: "Sharon's people aren't Catholics. . . ."

"Is Billy Kell Catholic?"

"No." He looked puzzled. "Billy? When did I——"

"This morning, Angelo. When we found Bella. You said: 'Billy Kell might know. . . .'"

"Oh. Did I?" He sighed uncomfortably. "Cheepus . . . !"

"You said something about the Diggers too. What are they? A gang?"

"Yeah."

"Round about your age?"

"Yeah. Some older."

"Tough?"

He grinned in a way I hadn't seen, as if he were trying out toughness to see how it felt. "They think so, Mr. Miles, to hear 'em bat the wind."

"Sounds as if you didn't like 'em."

"They're a bunch of——" He stopped, weighing me, I think, and wondering if I'd tolerate an obscenity from a twelve-year-old, and deciding against it. He said mildly: "Nobody likes those bastards."

"What all do they do?"

"Oh, they fight dirty. Some stealing, I guess, fruit-stand jobs or stuff off the back of a truck. Billy says some of the older ones are muggers, and some of 'em carry shivs—knives, I mean." I didn't like his smile: it was a dissonance in the character I thought I was beginning to know. "Most of 'em come from the sh—the crumby end of Calumet Street, the south end. . . . Got a cigarette?"

I gave him one, and lit it for him. Feuermann wasn't looking, and I suppose I could have argued it with Feuermann anyway. "Don't the Diggers have any competition, Angelo?"

He hesitated, only a little. "Sure. The Mudhawks. That's Billy Kell's gang." He was smoking casually, inhaling without coughing. "You know, I saw Billy crack a walnut once, just putting it against

his biceps and closing his arm. Nobody tangles with Billy Kell."
He said as if trying to convince himself of something that mattered:
"The Mudhawks are all right."

"Can you talk with him? With Billy Kell?"

He knew what I meant, but said uneasily: "How do you mean?"

"When I first saw you, yesterday, you were reading the *Crito*.
I just meant, things like that."

He said evasively: "Books aren't everything. . . . He's good in
school, straight A's all the time."

"How is the school? Pretty fair?"

"It's all right."

"But you have to put on an act, is that right?"

He rubbed out the cigarette against a stone. He said presently:
"They play around an awful lot. Maybe I do. Some of the time. I'm
no good in mathematics. Or manual training—honest, you should
see a birdhouse I tried to make, looks like a haystack in a blizzard."

"What are you good at?"

He made a face at me, enjoying it. "The things they don't teach.
All right—like the *Crito*, Mr. Miles. Philosophy."

"Ethics?"

"Well, I got a college text on that, out of the library. I didn't
think it got down to cases very much. They've got Spinoza there.
I didn't try it."

"Don't." I took hold of his good ankle and hung onto it a moment. "You're way ahead of your class, my friend, but you're not
ready for Spinoza. Not sure I ever was myself. If you can take him
all in at one gulp, I suppose it's good, but let it wait. . . . History
was my subject when I used to teach school. How about that?"

"They just don't teach it, not to say teach. Formula stuff. They
tell you one thing, and you get something out of the library that
says just the opposite, so who's right? I mean, the teacher dishes
it out the way he sees it, and then you're supposed to wrap it up
and give it back to him the same way. Or you're wrong: E for effort.
Schoolbook says we broke away from England in 1776 because

57

British imperialism was strangling the colonies economically. Declaration of Independence says we did it for political reasons. Really both, wasn't it?"

"Those were two of many reasons, yes." I can never be reconciled to our deception, Drozma. How I should have loved to tell him that afternoon of the way I saw the French fleet come into the Chesapeake before Yorktown! I remember the early autumn storm too, that came up when the poor devils of redcoats were trying to get across the river—I suppose I might not have wanted to describe that to him completely. Or I might, I don't know. . . . "History frustrates all teachers," I said, "simply because it's too endlessly big. There has to be selection, and the best of teachers can't escape his own bias in making that selection. But of course they ought to keep reminding you of that difficulty, and I suppose they don't."

"No, they don't. The Federalist Papers don't explain everything with economics either. I said I'd read 'em. Wasn't supposed to. I don't mean she gave me hell or anything. She said it was fine that I should make such an effort, only she was afraid they were a little over my head. And besides, although the Federalist Papers were 'quaint and interesting,' they weren't part of the course, and wouldn't I try to be a little more attentive in class and show a better all-around attitude?"

"You mean, Angelo, some days it just don't pay to get up?"

He liked that, and blew out a grass blade in a puff of laughter and pulled another one to chew. "Level bevel, Mr. Miles." In the teen-age argot of 30,963, that means you're all right. Angelo uses that cant very seldom, being far more at home in the precision and beauty of normal English than any adults I have met on this mission.

"Are you a member of that gang you told me about? Billy Kell's? Not that it's any of my business."

He looked away, all pleasure gone. "No, I'm not. I guess they want me to join. I don't know. . . ." I waited, which was not easy. "I couldn't let Mama know about it if I did."

58

"Joining would mean agreeing to a lot of things, wouldn't it? It usually does."

"Maybe so." He got down off the bank, lounging with his hands in his pockets. I didn't see again that flash of phony, half-experimental toughness. But I did realize presently that I had intruded on a matter in which he would accept no counsel, and that he wasn't going to answer the unspoken question. He had taken on a look not distant but almost sleepy; he was hidden in the thousand-colored privacy of a mind I'd never know, yet not far away. At that moment and at others I remember, he reminded me of that slumbrous creature of heaven who leans on the shoulder of another in Michelangelo's "Madonna, Child, St. John and Angels." (I bought a fair print of that painting and still have it; sometimes it seems more like him than a snapshot, which is supposed to tell the truth.)

"Any car I get," I said, "will have to be a jalopy. How were the '56 Fords?"

"Good, I guess." He smiled brilliantly, thinking of my promise, and held up circled thumb and forefinger in that American gesture which appears to mean that everything's jake. "Any old wheeze-on-wheels, you won't be able to get rid of me." He limped to the nearest of the graves and rubbed a finger on the eroded carving. "Here's a guy who 'sought his reward August 10, 1671, a servant of Christ.' Name of Mordecai Paxton. Must've figured he was pretty sure what reward." He started to brush a cobweb from the slanted, half-submerged stone, but his hand fell. "Nah, she'd only build it up again, and besides . . ."

"She and Mordecai get along. Might even be descended from a spider who knew Mordecai personally."

"Might be. Other people are neglecting Mordecai though." Angelo picked a few saucy dandelions and tucked them around the stone. "Him and his whiskers." He glanced up with shyness. "Kind of thing Sharon's always doing. Looks better, huh?"

"Much."

"Gaudy whiskers, I'll bet."

"A caution to the heathen." We pushed Mordecai around. I said ginger whiskers, but Angelo claimed Mordecai was roly-poly, with black cooky-brushes, and had been tempted by Satan in the form of a pork chop. We quit when Feuermann returned, not that the old man would have minded laughter.

I thought I saw that gray coupé behind us on the way home. It shot by, again too quickly, when we stopped at a roadstand, where Angelo consumed a forbidding quantity of pistachio ice cream. Back in the car, he burped once, said: "Ah, hydrogen chloride!" And fell asleep.

I was in danger, since he drooped against me. But his head was not directly on my chest; he was too sound asleep to notice that my heart beat only once in sixty seconds. What are we, Drozma? More than human, when we observe them; less, when we batter our wings against the glass.

5 The following week is, in my mind, a kaleidoscope of small events:

Waking late, when Sharon and Angelo were installing a bit of paving stone to mark Bella's grave in the back yard. If I had not witnessed Angelo's earlier resentment I should have thought he was enjoying it, until he happened to step behind Sharon and his face abandoned pretense, becoming patient, puzzled, tender like that of any adult watching make-believe, himself remembering the forests and plains and deserts of maturity. Later they strolled down Martin Street into the city's jungle. . . . Sitting empty-brained before my typewriter, deciding at length that Mr. Ben Miles would be convincing enough as a guy always on the point of writing a book but never doing it. . . . Visiting EL CAT SEN with Angelo

60

(Tuesday that was) and finding not Sharon but a harassed little chap, Sharon's father, who became determinedly hearty talking baseball with Angelo; he didn't look like a smasher of cast iron. . . . Meeting Jack McGuire in a bar after his day's work at a garage. We started with the burglary but wound up with Angelo. "Ain't healthy," Mac said. "Nose all the time in a book. Couldn't ever be an athalete with that bum leg, but all the same it ain't healthy, irregardless. He'll grow up lopsided or queer. Soon put a stop to it if he was my kid, but what can you do?" I didn't know. . . .

Nothing that week made me suspect the presence of Namir.

I saw Billy Kell again, from my window, playing catch with Angelo in Martin Street, and I wondered if my bad first impression of him could have been distorted. Had Sharon been at fault too? He had been tormenting her, but maybe she had goaded him to it. In that ball game Billy was a different person. He was throwing so that Angelo would not have to run much, yet he contrived to make Angelo work for it. There was no air of condescension or pulling punches, nothing patronizing in Billy's shouted comments. He was taking a lot of unboyish trouble to give Angelo a good time. When they tired of it they sat on the curb, blond head and dark in some amiable conference. It was all casual: Billy did not seem to be urging or arguing anything. When Rosa called him in for supper, Angelo exchanged some parting gesture with his friend— turn of the wrist and upraised palm. I remembered that Billy Kell led the Mudhawks. But Angelo had also said that he hadn't yet joined the gang. . . .

I had Thursday evening dinner with the Pontevecchios, the old ladies present. Rosa's cooking was from the heart. She was light on her feet in front of the stove, or bringing a dish to us. I wondered how much of her tiny income was lavished on that sort of thing. It was not waste: Rosa was a giver, hospitality as necessary to her as oxygen. When she could break out a fresh handsome table-cloth and stuff her guests with kindness, Rosa came glowingly alive, and then I saw not a tired worried fat woman but the mother of Angelo.

Mrs. Doris Keith, majestic with white hair, gray silk, amethyst brooch, tended to glare—daring me to remember that when I first met her she was in several yards of cotton nightgown and screeching. She stood six feet and must have been rugged when she was on the warmer side of seventy. Mrs. Mapp would always have been soft and poky, in youth a charming valentine. Yet it was Mrs. Mapp who had once taught school—she "gave" art and music at a girls' finishing school—while Mrs. Keith had never attempted any career but housewifery and rather defensively told you so. When their husbands quit the struggle years ago these two had worked out a symbiosis plainly good for the rest of their lives. I hoped they'd be lucky enough to die at the same time. "Angelo," said Mrs. Keith, "do show Agnes your latest work."

"Oh, I'm not doing much of anything."

She labored graciously to treat him as an adult. "One can't advance without expert criticism. One must avoid getting in a rut."

"I just horse around." But he was petted and hectored into bringing two paintings. On his way to get them the little devil winked at me.

Three mares in a high meadow, heads lifted to the approach of a vast red stallion. Colors roared like mountain wind. A meeting of wind and sunlight, savage and joyful, shoutingly and gorgeously sexual. Angelo should have been spanked. The other painting was a mild dreamy landscape.

I had to admit to myself that the ladies were desperately funny as well as pathetic, in their painstaking comments on everything but the obvious. "The color," said Mrs. Mapp daringly, "is—uh—quite extravagant."

"Yes," said Angelo.

"This leg is a trifle long. You lacked a model, I presume."

"Yes," said Angelo.

"Masses. Learn to balance your masses, Angelo."

"Yes," said Angelo.

"Now *this*——" Mrs. Mapp took up the landscape with enormous relief. "This is—uh—not bad. This is lovely, Angelo. Very lovely."

"Yes," said Angelo.

Rosa laughed. Totally unaware of embarrassment because there was none in herself, full of nothing but warmth and admiration, she couldn't keep her hands out of his curls as he took the paintings away. Nor was she much aware of them as paintings: just as Angelo's books were unknown country, so Rosa could not imagine that a twelve-year-old's work might have meaning for the world outside, or that his almost contemptuous virtuosity had achieved what most adult painters only struggle for. The shield of her kindly ignorance could have its uses.

While those two helped Rosa with the dishes, Angelo showed me his room. I did not try to stay angry with him, or to explain that dazzling and shocking little Mrs. Mapp was a shabby victory. He knew it, and was already sick about it.

The room was a tiny oblong, one grudging window at the level of Martin Street, hardly space for more than his cot bed, a bookcase, an easel. It was also the studio which had produced certain triumphs that were undervalued even by himself. He selected another painting from a stack against the wall. It was simple, technically unfinished, but he was right in not wanting to do any more with it. A hand curved to shelter what it held, and what it held was a tiger, fallen, mouth curled in a snarl of uncomprehending despair at the javelin in its side. "Evidently you do believe in God, Angelo."

He looked annoyed. "Hand could symbolize human pity, couldn't it?" But it seemed to me that his mind abandoned the picture in the moment when I offered my half-baked interpretation. He slumped on the cot, chin in hands, woebegone. "I better apologize?"

"Not necessarily."

"How d'you mean?"

"Might just embarrass her worse. Why not let it go? And remember for the future that nice old ladies and randy stallions don't mix too well. Matter of empirical ethics." I watched: old man

63

"empirical" didn't worry him. He knew the word without even finding it unusual.

He thought it over and sighed: "Okay." Relieved but not satisfied. It went on bothering him. I suppose that was why soon afterward he gave the soft landscape to Mrs. Mapp with sentimental flourishes, and took it like a gentleman when she kissed him and thanked him too much.

The next Sunday came in with warm persisting rain. I spent the morning reading the Sunday paper. It was difficult to evaluate the news when I so badly needed more light myself. After a week I had no plan worth the name. I knew something of the environment; something of Rosa and Feuermann and Sharon, scarcely anything of Billy Kell. I had shopped around for a cheap used car the day after our talk in the cemetery, but found nothing safe, so I put through a call to Toronto. A justifiable expense, Drozma, if only to let Angelo discover the woods—at any rate I have been in most of the temples and cathedrals of the world, and the peace I sometimes found in them was never more than a small substitute for what there is under the arches of the leaves. I had no clue to Namir's whereabouts and intentions. With the stolen photographs, scent-destroyer, and Martian skill in disguise, he might be planning a masquerade. Or did he only want to make me afraid of that, so that I would distrust Feuermann and others, wasting my strength in pointless suspicions? To make me turn my own ignorance and weaknesses against myself, to make me stumble from my own blindness, to make Angelo do the same—that would be Namir's way, and his pleasure. In intelligent life, human or Martian, maybe there has always been a genuine division between those who honor the individuality of others and those who are driven to control and pervert it. A shifting division, I admit, since some of us, confused, may have a foot in both camps at times, and some spirit-killers may reform, and some of the generous may be corrupted.

From the front page I deduced that the new government of Spain would join the United States of Europe before long. That could be of profound human importance, but I let the paper sag on my knees, contemplating Angelo's birch tree and the other painting, the wounded tiger, which he had blandly given me. I read, too, about the projected satellite station. In 1952, said the article, it had been thought that ten years would do the job—ten years and some small change amounting to four billion dollars. It seems it will take a mite longer than that, and a billion or so more. Exhaustive tests simulating conditions of outer space had hinted at possible long-term damage to the human system, which early briefer experiments could not reveal. Nothing too serious. Candidates would have to be even more critically screened, that was all. Nineteen hundred and sixty-seven, maybe, or '68. We could have told them a little, from our ancient history, but I recognize the wisdom of our law: we must let them alone with their technological problems. It was all right to help some of the early tribes find the bow and arrow the way we did, but times have changed.

In the afternoon Feuermann came in to see me. He was visiting the cemetery again. Rain was still gray and whispering, and I spoke of it. He smiled at wet window glass. "Sun's up beyond it some-where."

"Jacob"—we were on first-name basis now—"do you know any-thing about this Digger-Mudhawk business? Hate to see Angelo mix into that."

"Kid stuff, I guess. Hard to get him to talk about it."

"Seems the Diggers include older boys, some of 'em tough."

"So?" He was concerned, but not seriously. "I figure a boy's pretty much a wild animal. They work it out of their systems. Not that I'd favor it for Angelo. But that Kell kid seems to be all right."

I still wondered. "Where does he live, do you know?"

"South Calumet Street neighborhood somewhere, the crumby section. I believe his parents are dead. Lives with a relative, guess it's an aunt." Jacob had found my discarded newspaper, and was forgetting Billy Kell. "Or some woman who adopted him, I don't know. They get sort of casual in the south end. He's in Angelo's class in school, supposed to be a good student, so I hear. . . . Hey, did you see this? Max is in jail again."

65

"Max?" I recalled a front-page item. It was a New York City paper, with the usual random mass of political maneuverings, speeches, oddities, personalities, disasters. One Joseph Max had been arrested for causing a near riot with a handful of followers at a meeting addressed by some senator. There was a write-up on Max himself, but I had not followed its continuation on an inner page.

"An heir of Huey Long." Feuermann was reading intently. "Missed my paper this morning. Long, and Goat-gland Brinkley, and the Ku Klux, with a dash of communazi to flavor the brew. . . . Ach, they never die!"

"One of those? Don't think I've heard of Max before."

"Maybe the Canada papers didn't bother with him. All he needs is a special-colored shirt. He turned up first in 1960, I think, with —now wha'd he call it?—Crystal Christian League, some damn thing, made capital of the word 'Christian.' Christian like a snapping turtle. You know how the freak parties always emerge in a presidential year. Froth on the pond."

"Yes, they thought Hitler and Lenin were froth, for a while."

"Well, I tell you, it's the damn human way, not to look at what scares us. Max dropped out of sight for a couple years, started making headlines again a year ago. 'Purity of the American race.' It says here. We never learn."

"That's Max's line?"

"Yeah, but it looks as though he'd chucked some of the fantastic stuff. He's formed something he calls the Unity Party. Claims a million of the faithful, nice round number. 'Right will prevail!' says he on his way to the clink after busting a few heads. Hope they don't make a martyr of him—what he wants, naturally."

(I believe it might be worth a full-time Observer, Drozma, if one has not already been assigned.) "You think he might become big-time?"

Feuermann sighed. His good engineer's hands knotted and relaxed in his lap. "I sit around too much, Ben, and think too much. I'd give an awful lot to be out on the rails again; 509 and me, we were sort of friends"—he was shy about that—"you understand? Active all my life, hard to get it through your head you're old. Maybe I imagine things. Sitting around . . . No, likely Max is just froth. Ought to be enough common sense in the country to sort of disinfect him before he gets a-going. Wouldn't you think, all the time we've had, troubles we've seen, we could do a little better, Ben? Use more love and less pride? Hang onto your own self but treat the other guy like he had one too? Do unto others . . . Care for a drive to Byfield?"

He was lonely, but I declined, blaming the rain. He left me, with a characteristic, openhearted smile on his face that I never saw again. . . .

The rain ended in late afternoon. I found Angelo and Billy Kell on the front steps, lazy in the moist warmth. Probably the quality of their talk altered when I appeared and fussily spread a newspaper on the top step to sit on. It was my second face-to-face meeting with Billy. Angelo introduced us formally, and Billy gave no open sign of remembering me. He was polite, as a fourteen-year-old can readily learn to be. Ironically, I thought. He offered a skillful imitation of grown-up small talk—Canada, baseball, this and that. He had an unlimited fund of it, and I couldn't isolate any one part of it to call it mockery.

Sharon appeared on the other side of the street in what I believe was a new pink dress. She looked small and lonesome as well as starchy in the waning sunlight, studiously tossing her red rubber ball on its elastic string. Angelo called: "Hey, kid! C'm'on over!" She turned her back. Angelo poked Billy's ribs. "One of her moods."

"Deep bleep," said Billy Kell. A teen-age formula, I guess.

Having made her point, Sharon did approach. She marched up the steps with no recognition for the boys, and addressed me in brittle dignity: "Good evening, Mr. Miles. I wondered if I'd find you here."

I gave her some of my newspaper to sit on. "The steps are still damp, and that looks to me like a new dress."

"Thank you, Mr. Miles." She accepted the paper with absent-minded queenliness. "I am glad to know one's efforts are not wholly unappreciated."

Angelo's ears turned flame color. I was in the cross fire and saw no way to get out of it. Billy Kell was enjoying it. Angelo mumbled: "Time for some catch before supper—huh?"

"I oughta be on my way," said Billy Kell.

"Mr. Miles, have you ever noticed how some people are always persistently changing the subject?"

I attempted sternness: "I might change it myself. How have the lessons been going this week, Sharon?"

That reached through her thin-drawn politeness. She talked of the lessons with pleasure and relief, not forgetting, of course, to use the conversation as a saw-toothed weapon, but nevertheless enjoying it. The lessons were terrific and getting terrificker all the time. Mrs. Wilks was going to give her a real piece to memorize Monday. She could almost stretch an octave, Sharon said—anyhow by rolling it a little; it was true that her fine fingers were long in proportion to her size. Angelo suffered in silence, and in spite of his remark Billy Kell was lingering. At length Sharon ran down and began to repeat herself. Angelo turned, not smiling at all. "Sharon, I'm sorry." He put his hand on her shoe tip. "Now tell me, what should I be sorry for, huh?"

She ignored her own foot, allowing it to remain where it was. She addressed an imaginary Mr. Miles somewhere on the rooftops across the street: "Mr. Miles, have you any idea what this child is talking about?"

"Oh, bloop," said Angelo, and Billy Kell guffawed. I sought myself for a change of subject, asking whether Mr. Feuermann usually stayed in Byfield as late as this.

Angelo pulled his mind from the exasperations of the eternal feminine. I'm not entirely sure what Sharon was mad about that evening, besides his failure to notice the dress. I think it was Billy's mere presence when she wanted Angelo to herself: a grown-up jealousy in a ten-year-old frame that could hardly bear it. Angelo began to be puzzled about Feuermann too, and worried. "No, Ben —no, he doesn't."

Billy murmured: "Isn't that his car now?"

It was. The white-haired man waved as he drove around the corner, headed for a garage down Martin Street. Angelo was still having woman trouble when Feuermann returned on foot, swinging his door keys, smiling at the children, noticing me and nodding— stiffly. Something was wrong with Jacob Feuermann. He halted on the bottom step and said, apparently to Angelo: "Nice out there in spite of the rain." His voice was tense.

I needed to hear that voice again. I said as if idly: "Doesn't seem to've cooled things off much."

He would not look at me, and he spoke with a note of sober slyness not natural to the Feuermann I thought I knew: "Doesn't ever get this hot in Canada, I guess?"

I thought then: Namir has met him. Namir has dropped a whisper, to make him think I am not what I seem. Of course. Namir would know all the uses of scandal and innuendo and half-truth. Strange weapons, so easy to take up, the stain indelible on user and victim. I had tried to foresee other methods of attack, and stupidly overlooked this one, so natural to any creature who believes that the end can justify the means. Now I would have to find out somehow what the whisper had made of me—Asiatic spy, anarchist, escaped criminal. It could be anything: the whole field was open, and when I traced down one lie to kill it, another would replace it. I said: "Why, yes, sometimes it does. Not apt to be as damp as this, inland."

"That so? You remember it pretty well?"

Angelo looked merely puzzled, Billy Kell blank. And Feuermann had parted with me in such a friendly way only a few hours before! "Not very long since I was in Canada."

"No? Your mother in, Angelo?" Not waiting for an answer, he went around to the basement entrance. To avoid passing near me.

6

The money came from Toronto the following day. I acquired a pretty fair one-lunged '55 job with a cauliflower fender, and during the next two outwardly quiet weeks Angelo learned a little about the woods. Or perhaps a great deal, because there was no need to teach him how to listen. He met the living quiet of the woods with a wonderful receptive quiet of his own, and we didn't trouble much with words. Under the trees his normal boy's restlessness disappears: he can sit still, and wait, and watch, so rather than make any stuffy effort to teach him about what he saw, I kept quiet and let the earth speak for itself. We had four such expeditions, about thirty miles out of town into the piny foothills of the Berkshires—two full days and two afternoons. Since talk would have been intrusive, I can't say that it advanced my knowledge of him, but that doesn't matter: he was happy, and learning things with all five senses that Latimer could not show him. Rosa trusted me, and seemed glad to have him with me.

Not so Feuermann. On the evening of that rainy Sunday I visited his room. He was unwilling to face me, brusque to my small talk; he dreamed up an outside errand for himself to get rid of me. I didn't comment on the change—humanly speaking, I didn't know him well enough. But there was a false note in it. Reading this far unbiased, Drozma, you have probably seen the truth. I didn't, then. I only thought that if he suspected something ugly about me the Feuermann I had known would have investigated, or put his suspicion in open words. Sulky withdrawal wasn't properly in character.

It was nearly two weeks after that day when Rosa bared some of her worries to me. She was cleaning my room, on another muggy

70

morning. Her color was poor, her breathing labored; when I urged her to rest, she took the armchair gratefully. "Aie!—if I can ever get up again. . . . Ben, when you were a boy, did you ever get into one of those, you know, kid gangs?"

I by-passed my own youth. "I don't think Angelo will do that."

"No? . . . You've been good for him. I appreciate it." I remember thinking it strange that she was still friendly, if Namir was using the poison knives of whispers. "Well, I almost married again, just on account he needs a father so bad. Wouldn't've worked, I can see now." She mopped her kind face, round, sad, shining under the towel she used to guard her hair. "He sure enough told you he wouldn't join up with Billy Kell's gang?"

"Well, no. But maybe the gang isn't so bad, Rosa."

"It's bad. They get into fights, I don't know what all. And I *never* can figure out what's best for him. All I can do to add up a grocery bill. How'd I ever come to have such a boy? Here I'm common as mud——"

"Far from it."

"You know I am," she said, and not coquettishly. "Well, Father Judd (he's dead now) he christened him Francis, that was Silvio's idea. For, you know, the blessed Francisco di Assisi, so that's really his name, Francis Angelo, the Francis never stuck. When he wasn't a year old yet he looked so—so—anyway I had to use the name *I* picked. . . . Ben, would you sort of talk to him, about not joining that gang? You could say things that I—that I——"

"Don't worry. Sure, I'll talk to him about it."

"If he joins maybe I won't even *know*."

"He'd tell you." Her face said bleakly that there was much he never told her. "By the way, Rosa, is Mr. Feuermann sore at me?"

"Sore?" She was astonished, then adding two and two in some private hurried way. "Oh, it's the hot weather, Ben. He feels it bad. Hardly seen him myself all week." She pushed herself upright and finished her work. . . .

That afternoon I took out my car—Angelo and I had named it Andy after Andrew Jackson because it's always quarrelsome with body squeaks—and drove past EL CAT SEN when I knew Sharon would be on her way to a practice hour at the empty school. She accepted the lift with gracious calm. "Seems to me you ought to have your own piano at home, Sharon."

"Mom has Headaches," she said politely. "And besides . . . It's a good piano at the school. Mrs. Wilks told 'em they hadta. Mrs. Wilks is terrific. I love her beyond comprehemption."

"Like to meet her sometime."

"She's blind. Looks at your face with her fingers, all kind of feathery. I memorized the first piece in two tries, no mistakes."

"That is terrific."

"I get terrific sometimes," said Sharon, preoccupied.

At the school we were admitted by the janitor, a dim-eyed ancient who took my word for it that I was a friend and shuffled off into his forest of cold steampipes: no protection there. The piano was in the assembly hall—too big a place, too empty, but in a yard under the windows teen-age basketball practice was going on, and I noticed two young women working in an office we passed. I shoved aside the worried parent in me, and paid attention to a half-expected miracle.

Not music, naturally: beginner's stuff, the five-finger, the scale of C major, a kindergarten melody with plimp-plump of tonic and dominant in the left. That didn't matter. Touch was there, and a hunger for discipline and self-discipline. Left hand and right were already partners, after a scant fortnight of lessons. Yes, touch. Call it impossible: I heard it.

I tiptoed down into the auditorium and slumped in a seat with my mouth open. A shaft of sunlight was making her brown hair luminous in a haze of gold. Certainly she was the Sharon of Amagoya, of the red rubber ball on a string, but I could see the woman too. I saw her as beautiful, even if she retained the pug nose—likely she wouldn't. The gown for her debut ought to be white, I thought, and she would not be really tall, but would seem so, alone under the lights, a massive black Steinway obedient to her.

72

It was real to me. For her, there should be that transitory dazzling of crowds they call fame; there should be the greater achievement to which contemporary fame is a thin echo. But even if the end was in black frustration, Sharon was a musician and could never escape it. I would have to meet blind Mrs. Wilks: we could talk.

I ought to have heard the soft opening of the door at the back of the hall, but I was intent on Sharon, and on shutting out the basketball squeals, until I caught faint motion at the edge of my field of vision. I was slouching in shadow; he must have been unaware of me until I jerked up to look around. Then he was retreating quickly, face averted, head low. Even with a glimpse of yellow hair I could not be certain it was Billy Kell. The door clipped shut gently. He was gone.

I could try to dismiss it. Some boy wandering in, not knowing the assembly hall was in use. Some harmless playmate of Sharon's who became shy at seeing an adult. But the hurried retreat had been furtive, ratlike. I felt that coldness in the throat—the human equivalent is what they call goose flesh.

From one of the windows I studied the basketball crowd. I didn't see Billy, and he didn't rejoin the handful of spectators down there. But that meant nothing.

A glance at my wrist watch amazed me. Sharon had been working a full hour. Perhaps I was partly in Martian contemplation but I don't think so. I think it had been a one-way communication, her toiling fingers holding me, compelling my mind to share the effort, the promise, the small but mighty victories. She had stopped now, and was observing me out of her sunshine. "Heck, do you play?"

"Some, honey. Want to rest?" She gave me her seat, and I did as well as I could. For a school piano it wasn't bad, though it hardly reminded me of the three Steinways we so painfully brought and reassembled for Northern City a few decades ago. It was more like an elderly Bechstein I once played in Old City. They like things mellow in Old City, and the voicing of this school piano was over-mellow, the bass tubby and disagreeable. But it would serve. I played as much as I could cleanly remember of the Schumann "Carnaval." Sharon had no objections, but asked for Beethoven. I suggested "Für Elise."

"No. Mrs. Wilks's played me that. Something bigger."

Heaven forgive my stupid fifth fingers, I played the "Waldstein." I may have hoped (in vain) that by associating the sonata with Sharon I could displace a deep memory. Drozma, perhaps you recall my tour of the Five Cities in 30,894? For me the "Waldstein" must always create again the auditorium in City of Oceans, its windows dreaming into the heart of the sea, windows fashioned with such effort, so long ago—they told me there that some of the builders' names were lost. It is hardly strange that our people in City of Oceans were always a little different from the rest of us. When I played there that year, honestly I believe I approached the level of the modern human masters, and if so, the reason was in City of Oceans itself, not in any new virtue of my hands or heart. The long motion of the seaweed beyond those windows, always and never the same, the flicker and change and passing and returning of the fishes in scarlet and blue and green and gold—I see that now, and cannot help it. And of course everyone there was more than kind to me. They listened from within the music, and treated me as though they had wanted my visit for a century. It was later, as you know, that the study of human history became my necessity. The necessity is genuine and enduring; but the reason why I shall never make another tour is that I would remember City of Oceans too much. Drozma, what hideous blindness of chance, that our far-off ancestors should have chosen an island so near Bikini! Well, at least it was ours for twenty thousand years, and we must be glad there was warning enough so that some of our people could escape. And there may be another City of Oceans in some century after Union is achieved. . . .

Sharon was a nearby buzz, suggesting: "Now some Chopin?"

"Oh, darling, I'm tired. And out of practice. Some other time."

"By the way, I love you beyond comprehemption."

And that really broke up the meeting so far as I was concerned,

74

though I was able to bumble something or other from behind the façade of Mr. Miles. She was tired too and we adjourned.

The door had been opened again, harmlessly, by those office workers who wanted to hear my thunderings. I was suitably flattered. Sharon went on out to the car while I had a word with them. I spoke of someone sneaking in while Sharon practiced and hurrying out at seeing me. I suggested the hall was too lonely. Probably just another kid, but—etc. One of the girls wanted to practice sweet eyes on a real live pianist, but the other caught on, and promised me that henceforth the janitor would find a way to keep busy in the corridor during the practice hour. The bothered parent in me was soothed.

Partly. Until, after letting Sharon off at EL CAT SEN, I saw a familiar blond head down the street, not hurrying exactly. I crawled a block in the car, and parked when I was out of Sharon's sight. Then I followed Billy Kell on foot. Mainly, I told myself, to find out how much I remembered of the difficult art of shadowing. Oh sure.

Small streets branch off from the southern end of Calumet, twisting like cowpaths. The houses are mostly detached, old frame buildings stooping from neglect. The district may have been better before so many families moved to the country, abandoning what had never been much loved. There were still children, cats, dogs, pushcarts, a few drunks, but these scarcely lightened the burden of desertion and loneliness. In spite of the still clustering life there was the smell of desolation. Boarded windows, or unboarded windows broken and gaping like missing teeth in an abused face. Litter. Broken glass and grayness. A rat watched me with pert lack of fear before oozing through a crack in a foundation wall. Human beings have never been very adult about cleaning up after themselves. A panhandler put the bite on me for a dime and got it. That was on the side street that Billy Kell had taken, turning off Calumet, and when I was rid of the beggar I saw Billy cross that street rather abruptly, a block ahead of me.

Half a block beyond Billy there was a junk-wagon horse hitched at the curb—ribby, scabby, drooping in the heat. Automatically I crossed the street myself to avoid walking near him, although my scent-destroyer was fairly fresh. It ought to have occurred to me then, to wonder why Billy Kell had done the same thing; perhaps I may be excused, for without scent-destroyer no Martian could have passed in that narrow street without scaring the poor old plug into a tantrum. Even as it was, with my scent suppressed, the horse tossed his head when I passed and cleared his velvet nostrils in discomfort.

Farther on Billy Kell stopped to chat with a group of ten or twelve youngsters who were lounging against the fence of a discouraged-looking churchyard, perhaps waiting for him: he had the air of a leader or counselor. I found a handy empty doorway. They were giving Billy the flattery of shrewd attention, admiring stares, laughter at his jokes. Boys and girls both wore that cocky tam-o'-shanter which seems to have replaced the zoot suit as a teen-age badge. The voices were squeaky and vague and loud, using a gabbling argot of transposed syllables and made-up words—I could not follow much of it. When Billy left them I saw again that motion of turned wrist and raised palm. . . .

He took several turnings in those patternless streets and at length entered a frowzy two-story shack, but just before that I learned what I should have understood earlier. I was half a block behind him, strolling, my hatbrim lowered. As he mounted the shabby steps a breeze lifted and dropped a scrap of wastepaper near me. I barely noticed the slight sound; but Billy, half a block away, heard it. His head snapped about with the speed of an owl's. A swift stare identified the source of the noise and swept over me, whether with recognition or not I couldn't tell. He passed indoors, unconcerned.

I have seen human beings with muscular responses as rapid as ours—Angelo's are extremely rapid at times. I never knew one whose hearing approached our Martian acuteness. I had to remember then: Namir has a son. As I write this, I still have no definitive proof. He could have turned his head for some other reason; his avoidance of the horse could have been accidental, or caused by a human aversion for the animals. But I think I am right: other Observers ought to be warned.

There was no good place for me to hide and linger, nor any reason why Mr. Ben Miles shouldn't wander in this sorry region if he chose. I walked past the house, as a storm of squalling abuse broke out in there. A woman's monologue, so blurry with drink that I caught only a few words: "No-good jerk"—a gust of whining profanity—"try 'n' be a mother to you, what's the use—get out! Don't *bother* me! I ain't well. . . ."

I glanced back in time to see Billy come back out, after the smash of a bottle splintering on wood. He ambled around a corner without haste. On impulse I returned. I pounded on the door until I heard dreary cursing and a shuffle of slippers. I said: "Fire Department survey."

"Yah?" She blocked the doorway with beefy arms. She was blinking, red-eyed, vague, not really old—fifties perhaps—and not badly dressed. Hostility in her face dissolved in a silly simper, and her breath was fearsome. Over her shoulder I saw a dingy front room filled with dressmaker's gear. She was certainly human—after all, a Salvayan practically can't get drunk. I think that sober she might have been quite different, perhaps grimly respectable and hard-working—the dressmaking equipment looked professional. The drink would be an addiction, an escape from smothering hardship and frustrations, and the years of it had beaten her down like a disease, leaving her frightened, peevish, isolated, old: so much was written on her face in coarse print. The bottle (empty) had crashed against the doorframe, scattering shards everywhere; I guessed that Billy would have been safely clear of it before she let it go. "Had lil accident," she chuckled. "It's the hot weather, I ain't well exactly." She struggled with a wandering strand of gray-brown hair. "And what have I the honor do f'you, mister?"

"Routine survey, ma'am. How many live here?"

She lurched away from the door. "Me and the boy is all."

"Oh—just you and your son, ma'am?"

" 'Dopted—that be any damn business yours? I pay taxes, no offense of course, 'm sure."

"Just routine. May I look over the wiring?"

She waved and patted her lips. "Anybody stopping you?"

I left her making futile passes at the broken glass, and took a swift trip through the house, unopposed. There were only two rooms upstairs, the neat one obviously Billy's; sorry and rather ashamed, I did not linger in the other bedroom. Billy's room told me nothing, unless the very absence of boy's trinkets meant something. A military-looking cot, a pile of schoolbooks noticeably unmarked, though Feuermann and Angelo had said he was supposed to be a good student. If there was any Martian scent it was so faint I could not separate it from my own; but the absence of it would not be negative proof, for Namir had stolen enough destroyer to take care of two users for a long time. At any rate Billy could not be Namir himself, since even the Abdicator's skill in disguise could not make him convincingly square-bodied and a foot shorter.

The woman was painfully apologizing as I left. Hot weather, she said. She'd offer me a lil drink only there wasn't a thing in the house, though ordinarily she liked to keep some on hand for her digestion, so's the food wouldn't all the time rift up on her. We parted friends.

If I am right about Billy Kell, I suppose he talked and charmed his way into some makeshift unofficial relation with this woman, playing on her loneliness and thwarted maternity, to give himself a temporary name and a screen of human association. In calling him "adopted" her manner had displayed truculent fear of authority. Legal adoption, I believe, is hedged about with formalities that neither he nor she could have satisfied. When her usefulness to him is ended, no doubt Billy Kell will vanish—without conscience or pity or any debt of loyalty if he is the son of Namir.

7   Back at the lodging house, I wanted to make good on my promise to talk with Angelo. More reason than ever now, after seeing the human background of Billy Kell. But there were difficulties in any direct approach.

Angelo was fond of me, I felt sure. He listened if I spoke. The interludes in the woods were a delight for him: he wanted to say so, and managed to do it, with an adult's command of words and a boy's shyness. I had bought books for him, and drawn others from the library. He was very handsome with his thanks for that too. (One was *Huck Finn,* which he had disgracefully never read.) Somehow we got into no really satisfying discussion of those books. He wallowed in Mark Twain and Melville; I knew he was startled by Dostoevski, and amused by the thin wind of fallacy that blew through the unsanitary beard of Marx. But there were reservations: whole regions of his thought and feeling blocked off by invisible signs: NO TRESPASSING. He didn't seek me out in unhappy moments, though I knew he had many. So—grandfatherly advice against joining the gang, such as Feuermann might already have given him? The gentle barrier of Angelo's humor made that absurd. Stern advice then? When actually I go in fear of his sleepy smile? If he were Martian I might have known what to do. I notice men themselves have never invented a god capable of understanding them.

I slouched tired in the warm hallway, still seeing the bloated, vulnerable face of Billy Kell's "adopted mother," presently hearing Feuermann's voice behind the closed door of his room. Its meaning reached me slowly. "Any experience is useful. Maybe the Mudhawks are tough—can you get anywhere in this world without

79

toughness? You have to fight back. Can't afford not to, with your intelligence. People hate intelligence, didn't you know?"

"Depends on what it does to 'em, doesn't it?"

"Not so much, Angelo. Dream up a new gadget, they'll be grateful for a while," said Feuermann's voice. "It'll be only the gadget they love, not the brain that made it—that they fear. They may have enough superstitious dread to worship it—devil-worship—but never will they respect it except superstitiously. I haven't talked to you this way before because I wasn't sure you could take it. But I guess you can." I heard a thing like Feuermann's kindly, wheezy laugh. "Of course, the superstitious awe of your brains that people will have—that can be used."

"How d'you mean?"

"Oh, that'll take care of itself." I heard an old man's sigh. "Anyway, remember it's gadgets they want. Gadgets, simple ideas that seem to explain but leave basic prejudices untouched. They'll pay a price if the gadget or idea is shiny enough. I know 'em, Angelo." It just wasn't Feuermann. Feuermann wouldn't have spoken disparagingly of gadgets. In his sober way he was as much a gadget-lover as any other American of the '960s. Hadn't most of his life been spent in service of a mighty gadget that altered the face of the earth? "No, you have to fight all the way, all the time, with any weapon you can grab. I'm old, son. I know."

"Oh," said Angelo lightly, "I can battle my way out of a damp paper bag. But if you don't go for fighting for the sake of fighting——"

"Then you lose. Sometimes you must even do evil—oh, so that good may come of it, but it's all tooth and claw, devil take the hindmost."

So I began to know, Drozma, that Jacob Feuermann was dead.

I knocked and entered. Hardly prepared at all, driven to intervene as some human beings are, when they sense danger to those they love. I recaptured Mr. Miles in time to close the door peacefully and light a cigarette. It was only Mr. Miles whom Angelo saw from his lazy perch on the window seat. I did not care what was seen by that other in the room.

He was in the armchair with his feet on the hassock which Feuermann had worn threadbare. He was even smoking the horse-head meerschaum. That added illogically to my wrath: I may have made one of those human identifications with the inanimate which we are warned to avoid. "Hope I'm not intruding," I said as I intruded. "Had a hankering for the consolations of philosophy." I couldn't have cared less about philosophy. "Throw me out if the spirit moves." I straddled a chair near the window. He would have had to throw chair and all, and he couldn't have done it. It was at least some comfort to have no physical fear. "That's a beautiful meerschaum, by the way. You must be a fancier of horseflesh, is that a fact?"

I saw his eyes. When a human being is startled, the pupils may dilate, never the whole iris; I believe the entire structure of the eyeball is subtly different. My last doubt was gone. He said careless-carefully: "Oh yes, in a way. . . . Philosophy, huh?"

"Ah, philosophy!" Angelo chirped. "Here's where we dish it out, Ben. Step right up, ladies and gentlemen, and state your problems in words of less than one syllable. Feuermann and Pontevecchio, brought here at enormous expense, will solve it in the merest flick of a hysteron proteron: they walk, they talk, they crawl upon their bellies like a rep-tyle. For a nominal fee, they look into the past, the future, even the present, your money back if not satisfied. Why, ladies and gentlemen, it was these seers, these incomparable counselors of the unseen world"—he was warming to it, and as friendly as a puppy chewing my shoe—"who recently unscrewed one of the most inscrutable riddles of suffering humanity, namely, who put the overalls in Mrs. Murphy's chowder."

I asked him who did.

"Divil a soul," said Angelo. "They fell in when she lost her temper, and Mr. Murphy entirely in them at the time."

The image of Feuermann didn't speak or smile. I said: "Try the future, Prophet. Andy's got valve trouble, or maybe it's the car-

81

buretor. So, how long before petroleum gets so scarce we go back to—horses?" Under my breath I added the Salvayan word for "horses," so seldom used among us and always with the jar of indecency. It is onomatopoetic enough so that to Angelo it must have sounded like throat clearing. Namir's Feuermann-face remained frozen in calm.

I cannot evade blame for that stupid error, Drozma. I might well have hidden the fact that I recognized him. I tossed away that clear advantage because of an anger for which no Observer can be excused.

"Now that's a very good question," said Angelo, and fingered an imaginary beard at his round chin. "I would say, sir, that the extrapolated eventuality will eventuate in the due course of events, not before." I tried to listen to his nonsense, knowing that somewhere a warmhearted, harmless old man must be lying dead— hidden; buried, I supposed—solely because his death was useful to one who hated his breed. I wondered if Namir still possessed the dissolution-grenade he must have had when he resigned so long ago. Even the old style is quiet enough, and I know of no reason why it wouldn't disintegrate a human body as easily as one of ours. If Namir had used that, human law would never catch up with him. And it must not, as I knew. What had seemed almost funny at the time of the burglary was so no longer. Americans are not casual with prisoners, who must submit to physical examinations and are autopsied after execution, I believe. Human criminals occasionally obliterate their fingerprints by surgery. From where I sat I could see that Namir had not done so: his fingers were, Martianly speaking, normal; that alone would start a blaze of curiosity, the moment our unlooped angular ridges appeared on a police record. And if he were cornered—Drozma, I cannot share your feeling that he would be deeply inhibited against betraying us.

He has become like a creature of no race, a law to himself, past reach of reason, loyalty, or compassion. What other sort of being could have gone through with the murder of Feuermann? (At the time I write this I have proof. I had none that afternoon, but a sickening certainty took the place of it, and proof, when I did find it, was only a bloody period to a sentence already written.)

I tried again to listen to Angelo, who was bubbling merrily along like a little fountain in the sun: "—and this invention, this crowning triumph of the Feuermann-Pontevecchio genius, is a simple, simple thing. Allow me to sketch the reasoning which led to the blinding consummation. Earthworms love onions. They are alliotropic, a term derived (as every schoolboy knows) from *Allium,* the botanical genus embracing the common or garden onion. Alliotropic —five dollars, please. We propose therefore to design light carts— ain't flat-out done it yet on account we ain't got the capital—for hitching to the rears of a calculated sufficiency of earthworms (*Lumbricus terrestris*). An onion will be supported on a pole in advance of the worms, which crawl in pursuit of it, applying traction to the cart. In the event of a halt one need only jump from the cart (assuming it is not moving at excessive speed), dig a hole in the ground, lower the onion into it. The worms will then go underground after it, but their harness will be so contrived that they can never reach it, thus obviating any replacement of the onion—but of course a good team of worms must be properly fed and cared for at all times. And whereas their strength will be insufficient to pull the cart underground, their efforts to do so will provide a gentle braking action and the cart will eventually come to rest. Why be old-fashioned? Why wear yourself out with uneconomical, unreliable, dangerous horses? Why suffer from horsemaid's knee, when a trip to your nearest dealer will put you in possession of the streamlined, fur-lined, underlined, air-conditioned, trouble-free Feuermann-Pontevecchio wormobile?"

"Have you incorporated?"

"Not yet, Ben. We could let you in on the ground floor with a very nice proposition—and where've you been all day?"

"Listened in on Sharon's piano practice. She has talent, Angelo."

"So?" Sharon had been nowhere in his thoughts. "Can you tell?"

"The way she goes at it. The touch. She seems—dedicated. There aren't so many things that call for that. The arts, the sciences.

83

Politics, though not by the man in the street's definition. Religion—again only if you have an intelligible definition of it." Namir-Feuermann was deep in abstraction, the pipe gone out. "The study of ethics."

"Dedication to the study of ethics," said the old man's voice. "Sounds like a formula for the care and feeding of prigs."

"Why?" said the boy.

Namir faked a cough, and in the breathy noise I heard a whispered Salvayan word, the one best translated by the more polite English "Get out!" Then the image of Feuermann was smiling in kindly deprecation. "You're not far enough along, Angelo. Wouldn't beat my brains too much if I were you. Likely to make yourself introverted." Namir was making a mistake there, and I could rejoice at it, seeing Angelo's face veil itself in the resigned quiet that said: *Okay, sonny, I'm twelve.* "Get around more, Angelo. Enlarge experience. As I was saying a while ago, everything is struggle. You'll need to be out there in the middle of it more and more, not locked up in an ivory tower." Well, the old railroad engineer had probably been familiar with that phrase. I decided that Angelo was not bothered by the change in him because conversation with the real Feuermann had probably never been very penetrating. The real Feuermann had offered undemanding affection and tolerance, but could hardly have treated Angelo as a mental adult. Now the old man's attitude would seem to Angelo to be only a grown-up shift of mood. The physical disguise was perfect of course: trust Namir for that. He had even reproduced a tiny white scar at the hairline which few human eyes would ever have noticed.

I asked Angelo: "Would you say Beethoven was fighting anybody when he wrote the 'Waldstein'?"

"Not prezactly." Angelo was off his perch. "Grocery errand—the mighty brain just remembered." I got up too, nodding politely to the one I intended to kill.

I justify this intention by the law of 27,140—"harm to our people or to humanity." I needed only proof of Feuermann's death, then I could act. I would find a means to draw Namir away from

84

human surroundings, and would use the extra grenade Supply gave me. Afterward I would sleep well. So I thought. I allowed myself no backward look as I closed the door and caught up with Angelo, expecting to find him still full of fun and unworried.

He wasn't. He had started downstairs but came back before I spoke, and glanced at my door uneasily. "Could I stop in a minute?"

"Sure. What's cooking, friend?"

"Oh, just ham and eggs." But there wasn't any laughter in him. He fidgeted around my room. In a comic way he had, he pulled down his upper lip with thumb and finger and pushed it from side to side. "I dunno. . . . Maybe everybody feels like two people, sometimes."

"Sure. Two or more. Many selves in all of us."

"But"—he looked up, and I saw he was genuinely frightened— "but it shouldn't be—sharp. Should it, Ben? I mean—well, there in Uncle Jacob's room, it was like——" He fussed with trifles on my bureau, to hide his face maybe; added miserably: "Wasn't any errand at the store. I just wanted out. . . . I mean, Ben, there's a me that likes it here—everything: living here, Sharon, Bill, the other kids, even school. And—well, especially the woods, and—oh, talking with you, and stuff. . . ."

"And the other one would like . . . ?"

"Chuck everything," he whispered. "Just every damn thing and start fresh. In there, in that room, I was like—like cut down the middle. But that's whacky, isn't it? It doesn't make any sense. I don't really want to go anywhere else. If I could . . ."

"I think it'll pass," I said, finding no better words than these weak ones that could hardly help him.

"Oh, I guess." He started to go.

"Wait a minute." I took the wrapped mirror from the back of a bureau drawer. "Something you might like to look at. I brought it from Canada. When I taught history, Angelo, it was ancient history mostly. This thing was given me by a friend who knows his archaeology, who——" Drozma, I think I had been afraid of that mirror. That may be why I had never unwrapped it until this poorly chosen moment. Is it a product of accident or a lost art? Some subtle distortion in the bronze that compels many truths to cry aloud? I saw the young Elmis, the almost-good musician, the scatterbrained youth whom you taught so patiently, the persistent student of history, the absent-minded lover and husband, the clumsy Observer, the inadequate father. How can this be, in a poor frail artifact of the long-dead Minoan world? At other shifts of the mirror—oh, let that escape words. It is one thing to know, with the mind only, that one will be old, that one has different faces for victory, shame, death, hope, defeat; another thing to watch it brilliant in the bronze. I was lost there, seeking for what I was once at City of Oceans, when I heard Angelo say: "What's the matter?"

"No, nothing." I did not want to show it to him now, but it was passing from my silly fumbling fingers into his innocent brown ones, and I went on talking somehow: "It's Minoan—anyway, came from Crete, likely made before Homer lived. You see, the patina's been kept away—I mean, taken away, polished off, so it's still a mirror as it was——"

He wasn't hearing me. I saw him shaking, his face crumpled and twisted as if in nightmare. "Here, let me take the damn thing—I hadn't looked in it before, myself. I didn't know, Angelo. But it's nothing to be afraid of——"

He twitched it away when I would have taken it, forced to stare in spite of himself. "Cheepus, what a——" He started laughing, and that was worse. I took it out of his hands then and flung it on the bureau.

"I ought to be kicked. But, Angelo, I didn't know——"

He pulled away from my hand. "Look out—I'll prob'ly erp." He ran for the stairs. When I followed, he glanced back up out of the well of darkness and said: "It's all right, Ben. I get whacky, that's all. Forget it, will you?"

Forget it?

8　　　That night I could neither sleep nor enter contemplation. I heard humanlike sounds from my enemy next door. If Namir had gone out I would have followed him. If the grenade's disintegration were complete, I might have destroyed him that night, in his room. But there would have been some noise, even if I caught him asleep. There would have been the stains, the purple glare, the reek of gases, handfuls of rubbish to clear away.

I did not go to bed but sat dressed near my window, and was rewarded by a moonrise I could not enjoy. At midnight a copter-bus thundered, the last until six in the morning. Smaller human sounds persisted: late footsteps, a girl laughing behind a curtained window, a few cars whispering by on Calumet Street but none on Martin, which ends blindly at a lumberyard three blocks east. A baby fretted till someone hushed him. Past one o'clock I heard the Chicago–Vienna jet liner, far and high and lonely.

The opening of the door in the back-yard fence was a ghost of noise. The moon had climbed; no light touched my face. It was near two in the morning. I watched him slip in, fog-footed, pale-haired, dangerous. He had to pass through moonlight, then scratched on the kitchen screen delicately as an insect's wing. He was aware of my open windows, but I was in darkness.

Angelo came out. They did not talk. They faded across the yard, Angelo moving in spite of his lameness as softly as Billy Kell.

I let them gain some distance down Martin Street, then eased the screen out of a window and jumped. Only fifteen feet, but I had to be cautious of sound. They did not look back. I found moon shadow, and they were stealthy in that shadow too, gliding toward the lumberyard like embodiments of a mist that was making damp-

87

ness on the walks, aureoles around the street lamps. From my window I had hardly noticed the mist. Now I breathed it. It was all around me, wandering, melancholy, less bewildering than the cloud in my mind. Earth can weep too, my planet Earth.

As I sneaked into the lumberyard after them I heard suppressed muttering of a dozen voices, most of them treble, a few mature like Billy Kell's. A tall stack of two-by-eights loomed black in front of me, and I knew the gang was on the other side of it. With luck I could climb that stack in silence and look down. The voices became individual. I heard Billy Kell's: "You passed all the other tests, you won't fluff this one." And some small excited whiny voice encouraged: "He's nothing but a damn dirty Digger, Angelo." A shuffling of feet lent me a covering noise. I mounted the stack and wormed across it to peep over.

A thin lad was tied by the waist to a timber of the next stack. His hands were bound behind him, his shirt hung in rags over the cord at his middle, his face and chest were begrimed. He was the only one facing me. His head drooped forward; even if he looked up he might not see the blot of my head against the greater dark. He was cursing mechanically, sounding rugged, contemptuous, and not in pain. I supposed I could jump down if I had to and break it up in time to prevent major disaster. Meanwhile I had to try to understand.

Billy Kell was embracing Angelo's shoulder, urgent and coaxing. He drew Angelo away from the others and near to my hiding place. The cricket-voices of the other boys ceased to exist for me. "Angelo, 'tisn't as if we were going to do him any real harm, see?" Billy Kell's whisper was smooth and soft. I could watch him smile. "Look——" and he was showing Angelo a knife, turning it to catch the wan light, which gave me Angelo's face too, a dim battlefield of terror and excitement, fascination and revulsion. "Just a five-and-dime gimmick," said Billy Kell. "It's plastic. Look." He jabbed the knife at his own palm, so realistically that I winced before I saw the blade curl harmlessly at the tip.

"Just scare the pants off him, that it?"

"Sure, Angelo, you get it. Poke it to him without touching, see, and then a jab—oh, at the shoulder or somewheres. But listen: the other guys think you think it's a real knife, see? I'm giving you a break because, hell, you're my friend, I know how you feel. You couldn't use a shiv. I understand, see, but they don't. So put on an act for us, huh?"

"I get it. And that other thing you told me about him——"

"Oh, that was real. He did the burglary all right. We been giving him the works. He squealed. He sang, fella. He did it on a dare from the Diggers, had to take something from each room, only he went chicken about the money, just took a little and then grabbed the pictures and stuff instead—chicken. He was supposed to keep away from your apartment too. Know why? To make it look like you'd stolen from the tenants."

"Oh hell, *no!*"

"Fact, kid. And he killed the pup. We made him sing, I'm telling you. He chunked her a bit of hamburg and busted her neck. . . ."

"Mr. Miles didn't lose anything, and that was the room——"

"May say he didn't. Listen, Angelo: one of these days I'll tell you a couple-three things about your Mr. Miles."

"What d'you mean? Miles is a good guy."

For this relief much thanks. . . .

"Think so? Never mind—later sometime, kid. Here, take this." And Angelo reached for the knife. There was fumbling. Billy dropped it, and stooped, searching in the dark. Then they were moving away from me, and Angelo had the knife in his hand, and the others crowded close to watch, a rabble of goblins in a confusion of troubled night. So I blundered again, Drozma. I ought to have guessed.

Angelo's voice was thin now, thin to the cracking point: "You killed my dog? You killed my dog, you dirty Digger?"

The thin boy spat at Angelo's foot without answering. But his nerve was crumpling, and he whimpered, watching the blade. He cringed as Angelo's little hand lashed out with it. But he was not the one who screamed when that knife bit flesh—I saw it—and blood jumped from the bony shoulder to splash Angelo's fingers. It was Angelo who screamed. Screamed and flung the knife away; ripped a handkerchief from his hip pocket and tried to stop the blood before the others had done more than gasp and giggle. "Damn you, Billy—damn you——"

"Shut up, kid—what's a little blood?" Billy shoved Angelo away. Swiftly and competently, Billy untied the thin boy, motioned two others to hold him, and wiped the wound to examine it. "A scratch," said Billy, and that was true, in a way. The wounded one was Angelo.

I saw Angelo nauseated and shivering. His stained hand made abortive motions toward his mouth, and dropped. Dreamily he groped for the handkerchief Billy had discarded, and made feeble efforts to clean his fingers with it, and threw it down, and retched.

Billy twitched the captive around and kicked him. "You ain't hurt. Now run, Digger, run! Run and tell your drips we've burned the wax."

The thin boy reeled away from him, clutching a fragment of his shirt against the cut. "You wha-at?"

Billy chuckled. "We burned the wax. We'll meet your guys any time."

The thin boy ran. The goblins snickered. Billy Kell grabbed Angelo's wrist and held it up. "A full member of the Mudhawks! And is *he* all right?"

"He's all right," they said. A spooks' chorus.

"Listen, studs, you know what? He switched knives when he guessed the other was a phony. He didn't wanta, but he did, because he knew it was right. Now there's a *real* Mudhawk. *I* knew it, when he put his blood on the stone for the first test."

They swarmed around then, with hugging and jittery laughter and naïve obscenities and praise for Angelo, who took it all with a sick smile, with submerging shame and hidden contempt and swelling pride, with unwilling acceptance, as if now he were making himself believe Billy's lie. Because the lie was good politics? I couldn't know. "Well," said Angelo, "well, he killed my dog, didn't he? Cheepus . . ."

Fog was swallowing Billy Kell's covine one by one, with turned wrist and raised palm. Too deep a fog: I can't pretend to understand these children. I wish I were old enough to remember four or five hundred years ago.

There is a lost quality, a vagueness in them, which I did not find in the gangs that I studied a little when I was in the States seventeen years back. The gangs of that day were, on the surface, much more vicious and noisy and difficult, motivated more by wordless resentment of the grown-up world and by obvious material hungers —sex and money and thrills. These waifs (in a sense, they are all orphans) have reverted to more primitive fantasies. Their witchcraft—in some modern dress and slanguage but still witchcraft— suggests that the mental and moral desertion by their elders has progressed to the stage of genuine indifference. It may or may not be due to the decay of the cities. South Calumet Street is a backward eddy in the stream, and I might find matters very different in the suburbs or the countryside—I don't know. But it is hardly strange that this desertion, this adult delinquency, should occur, in a culture which has not yet learned to replace the antique religious imperatives with something better.

It is transition—I think. The force of the ancient piety was lost in what they call the nineteenth century, and millions of them, in the hasty human fashion, tossed out the baby with the bath. Such concepts as discipline, responsibility, and honor were discarded along with the discredited dogmas. With the prop of Jehovah removed, they still don't want to learn how to stand on their own feet; but I believe they will. I see twentieth-century man as a rather nice fellow with weak legs, and a head in bad condition from banging against a stone wall. Perhaps fairly soon he will cut that out, get sense, and go on about his human business, relying on the godlike in himself and in his brother.

Billy and Angelo were the last to leave. I followed them back to No. 21. Before Angelo went in I saw him bend his wrist and raise his palm, a full member of the Mudhawks. I dreaded for him the pain that would assume shapes of unclean horror in his dreams, if

91

he could sleep. I shadowed Billy Kell down Calumet Street. When he was a block beyond EL CAT SEN I overtook him and swung him around. I spoke in Salvayan: "Son of a murderer, are you proud?"

He watched me with a baby-face human stare, undismayed, then permitting a human fear to show. Naturally or by calculation? He stammered in English: "Mr. Miles, what the hell, you sick or drunk or something?"

I said wearily in English: "You understood me."

"Understood? Thought you was choking. You taking H on the main line or something? Get your hands offa me!"

I had grabbed his shirt. I knew my intention. I intended to rip his shirt away, and though that fog-blind moonlight would not have been strong enough to show me the tiny scent glands on his lower chest (if they were there) I could have ground my hand across them and smelled my hand. He knew it. Or else he was human, terrified in a human way. "Where did your father find surgery for you? The Abdicator Ronsa had the art—is *he* still living, for his sins? Answer me!"

He wrenched his shirt free—he was strong—and stumbled back from me. "You cut that out! Let me alone!"

But I went on, in Salvayan, quite slowly and plainly: "By tomorrow night I shall have proof of what your father did. Finished, child. He'll have to die, I think, and I know that you will be taken— by other Observers if not by me—for judgment and help to the hospital in Old City——"

"Goda'mighty, you're *really* high! Want me to call copper? I will if I got to. I'll yell, mister."

And he would have. (But would a human hoodlum have made that particular threat? To a menacing adult, yes, maybe.) He could have roused the neighborhood and brought police on the double. Then I would have been an ugly, outsize, not very well dressed man, accused of roughing up a defenseless boy. Rather, before that could happen, before the prowl car was abreast of me, I would have had to pull the key on my grenade. There would have been the brief purple flare, the heap of trash on the sidewalk, the nine days' wonder in Latimer—my mission over, Angelo deserted, undefended against those who seemed to be his friends. I snarled in English: "Oh, go to hell!" I walked back up the street as swiftly as I decently could.

When I was passing EL CAT SEN, and heard a whispered "Hey!" above me, I had to glance back and make sure that Billy Kell had gone, before I dared look up to the pale flower that was Sharon's face in a second-floor window. "Hello, honey—too hot to sleep?"

"Yeah, heck." I could see her arms on the sill, and darker flowers that would be her eyes. "The moon was all smoky round the rim, Ben. Well, I might come on down the rainspout, but frankly I haven't got anything on, frankly."

"Some other time."

"Were you chasing Billy?"

"Was that Billy? I didn't notice. No, just out for a breath of air. Maybe you'd better go back to sleep in time to wake up."

"Think I better? By the way, I drew a keyboard on my bed table, only I couldn't fix anything to make the black keys stand higher."

"I'm going to figure out something better than that."

"Huh?" It was the blank puzzlement of a child not accustomed to expecting much unqualified good from anyone. Having met her peevish little father, I wondered how even the money for the lessons had been forthcoming. Some probably transitory pressure from the mother with Headaches, I guessed: it wouldn't see Sharon through, on the steep road I knew she had to travel. I made up my mind, and found comfort in doing so.

"I'm going to talk with Mrs. Wilks. I think I can arrange better practice time than you can get at the school. . . . Ter?"

"Rif," Sharon sighed. "Can you? Oh, rif!"

I did not see Angelo that morning or afternoon. I went downstairs in the late morning, but Rosa told me he was under the weather; she was keeping him in bed and thought he was asleep. A cold, she guessed. She was not worried: he had them rather often. That alone informed me that he had said nothing to her about the gang. A *cold!*

In the afternoon I did accomplish one thing. I have committed us, Drozma, to an obligation which I think our little department of finance in the Toronto enclave will be pleased to honor. The money required is not much, and I can think of it as something good achieved even if my mission should end in failure. I went to see Mrs. Wilks, who used to be Sophia Wilkanowska, and as I had anticipated, it was not difficult to establish a meeting of minds. She is a genuine teacher—that is to say, a lover of her own kind, uncorrupted by the pressures of every day: they beat upon her as they do upon everyone, but without destroying her spirit.

She is tiny, porcelain-pale, with a deceptive look of fragility. She lives on a quiet street just barely on the right side of the tracks (I have sent the address to the Toronto Communicator) with a sister who has scant English but is not blind. They manage. Sophia's English is adequate. When I spoke Polish she was happier, and friendship was easy from that moment on. These two escaped from blighted captive Poland in 30,948, when Sophia was already fifty, her sister forty-eight; I thought it better not to ask how Sophia's husband died. They both dye their hair brilliant black, and they have a few other gentle vanities, and music is in Sophia like the fire in a diamond, indestructible.

We talked about Latimer, which is not indifferent to music in this fairly leisured decade. Prematurely, because there were many other pressures on my mind, I suggested expanding their studio into a small school. They said: "But—but——"

"I'm an old man. I have money—Canadian securities, other resources which I can't take with me. What better monument?" I pointed out that the house next door to them was vacant. There could be a partnership, perhaps, with one or two other Latimer teachers—and free practice rooms for promising students like Sharon Brand. Sophia Wilkanowska was not displeased to notice that cat coming out of the bag. She knew what Sharon was: if she had not, she would not have been the teacher I wanted for the child. I would buy and equip the house, I said, my part in it strictly anonymous. I would deed it over, guarantee upkeep for ten years;

the rest was up to them. For an hour or so I let the idea develop in their disturbed, not quite believing, but essentially practical minds, as we sat about and talked Polish and drank wonderful coffee from tiny transparent cups which had somehow made that dark journey with them fifteen years before. Sophia was pleased to call me a good pianist after I played a Polonaise to her restrained satisfaction. I was an expansive, eccentric, aging gentleman, vaguely Polish-American with money in the background, who wanted a little unlabeled monument for himself. It made sense gradually. More to me than to them, but at length I "confessed"—told them I had happened to get acquainted with Sharon and hear her practice. I had learned that she could not have a piano at home and I was angry. I loved her, I had no children of my own, and anyway I still wanted that monument.

They took it from there. "It is dangerous," said Sophia, "to have that little one's hunger. Before her first lesson I had thought my own hunger was—do you know?—hammered away under the fingers of little brats who—never mind. But what is there for her, Mr. Miles? School or no school? In this world or any other?"

"Trial. Victories, defeats, maturity. The worst cruelty would be to protect her from the pain of struggling."

"Oh, dear God, true enough. And we accept your offer, Mr. Miles."

This much is done.

9

I finished that chapter a week ago, in my stuffy room, the evening after meeting Sharon's teacher. I was waiting there for the gradual coming of summer darkness. Tomorrow I shall not be dead, but Benedict Miles will be. I am writing now in haste, Drozma, to complete my report, to convey to you a resolution from which not even you, my second father, can swerve me.

When darkness came that evening I took Andy out of the garage on Martin Street—seeing there the neat car that had been Feuermann's—and drove to Byfield. I parked off the highway, cut through a small patch of woods, clambered over the cemetery fence. Moonrise had not yet come.

I could always find peace among the human dead. They are surely our kindred here at least: our five or six hundred years make no more ripple in eternity than the comic hurry of a second hand. I found the bank where Angelo and I had waited on Jacob's ritual, and fumbled at Mordecai Paxton's headstone for traces of the dandelions. They were still somewhat more than dust. I went to the grave of Susan Feuermann.

It was ten days since Feuermann had gone to Byfield and only an image of him returned. That had been a day of rain; none had fallen since. They are tender of their memorials here. The grass is trimmed; I saw fresh decorations on many stones. There are other places, away from this modern part, where nature has been allowed to shelter the fallen in her own fashion, and grass is tall, with here and there a few of the unimperious flowers that men call weeds.

I searched for signs of a tragedy darker than any of the deaths commemorated here: Jacob Feuermann had died not from age, or chance, or in the witless attack of illness, or through any fault or quality of his own, but, like a child in a bombed city, had been arrogantly shoved out of life in a conflict not of his making.

In ten days the grass had fairly righted itself, patiently following its own privilege of life, but still leaned enough for me to discover where something had been dragged to an area of lower ground behind a screen of willows. In that hollow Namir had covered his traces casually: it might cheat the uncritical eye of whatever attendant cared for the graveyard. On this ever-shaded ground the turf was thin and mossy. Namir had rolled some of it back, scattering surplus earth with scant effort at concealment. Replacing the turf, he had joined the edges: I could find them.

96

Kneeling in the unremembering dark, I could look across ten days and see that rain-drenched afternoon as it must have been. Feuermann had said: "Sun's up there somewhere." Few would have thought of that. No human being at all would have visited this small cemetery on such a weeping day, except the old man. He did. He stood in the rain for whatever harmless consolation it gave him, and the thing came on him out of the grass.

I ran my thumb through earth where there should have been a network of grass roots and was not. Behind me—oh, moonrise was still far off—behind me, Namir said: "He's there. You needn't undo my grubby work."

He watched from the higher ground, a killing animal with the face of Feuermann and glints of our blue night-fire in his eyes. You reminded me, Drozma, that he is a creature always in pain. He seemed so, tight-mouthed, head thrust forward on wide shoulders. But I think the pain of those who live with evil becomes something other than pain. I think they come to love it, as a victim of heroin bitterly loves his affliction. How else explain the desperate recidivism of so many criminals, the persistent fury of a fanatic with the black dog of one idea on his back, the mountain of corpses around a Hitler? It was no simple hysteria when the witches of other recent centuries boasted of coupling with the devil.

His very pose was tigerish. But a tiger is innocent, merely hungry or curious at the wriggling of smaller life. I said: "Do you care to tell me how you justify it to yourself?"

"Justify? No."

"Explain, then?"

"Not to an Observer. Some will honor what I am, in the future."

"You have no future. But you still have a choice."

"I make my own choices." I saw the simple long-bladed knife come into his hand. "Sometimes with this." He did not see the round stone I took from Feuermann's burial place before I stood.

"Is that how Feuermann died?"

"Yes, Elmis, if you want to speak of anything so definite as death after the mean half-life of his tribe."

"He had no chance to defend himself?"

"Should he have had? Why, Elmis, he even smiled. He said: 'Here, you don't want to do that, I haven't done you any harm.' You see? His small mind simply couldn't imagine that anyone could regard his life as of no importance. He said: 'What's the gag?' And held out his hand for the knife as if I were a naughty boy—*I!* Then he saw that his face was already mine, and it confused him. He said: 'Does every man have another self? I'm dreaming this.' So I ended the dream for him, and now for you."

"Nothing to you, that my blood on the grass would be orange blood?"

"Nothing. Why let it worry you? If they find you in time for autopsy, you'll be back on page three as soon as there's a livelier murder with a sex angle."

"You're only a small devil, Namir. Back of me there are thirty thousand years on Earth, my planet Earth."

"Then defend yourself with your thirty thousand." And he came down the slope, stumbling in haste, panting as if he suffered. The stone caught him on the cheek, jarring the true skullbone under his artificial flesh, half stunning and toppling him. The knife leaped away into the dark. He rose immediately and closed with me, hands at my throat and mine at his, his face straining toward me as if he loved me but loved the thought of my death a little more. I broke his clutch on my windpipe and gripped his shoulders over the subclavicular nerve clusters where a Martian should feel pain, but he was hard to down.

We swayed and struggled so for a longer time than I can measure. It may have been only seconds, since the moon had still not risen when it was over. Once I heard him gasp: "Do you yield, Elmis? Do you *now?*" Later, when I had forced him back to the broken turf of Feuermann's grave, he choked on other words, sensing the shadow of his own death as a weasel might know the shadow of sudden wings: "I am old—but I have a son. . . ." He felt uneven ground under him, and raised his knee to foul me with it, but I had been waiting for that. My foot wrenched his other leg and he went down at last on the soft ground; his arms were straws and with his body he ceased fighting. He groaned: "I am one of many. We live forever."

I found his knife and slipped it under my belt. "There's still a choice. The hospital in Old City, or this." I showed him the grenade. "I have another. Perhaps you still have one of your own you'd rather use?"

"Little snot-nose cousin of the angels—no, I have none."

"When was yours used?"

"In Kashmir." He fumbled aimlessly at the grass, his eyes a blue blaze of memory and some laughter. "Maybe a century ago—want to hear?"

"I must."

"Oh yes, your precious duty. What a milky vanity! Well, there was a little chap with something of the Buddha in him. Rather like Angelo. I taught him a while, but he abandoned me. He might well have been another Buddha. I had to dispose of him. He'd already begun preaching, you see. I didn't want his body turned into holy relics, so I used the grenade in such a manner that he is still a vaguely remembered *devil*, Elmis, in two or three illiterate villages. Peace, he was saying; magnify the inner light by honoring the light of others—dreadful stuff, you know the style, and he only a beginner. He liked to quote the last words of Gautama, and other fools had started to listen. 'Whosoever now, Ananda, or after my departure, shall be to himself his own light, his own refuge, and seek no other refuge, will henceforth be my true disciple and walk in the right path——' and so on and so on, with little additions of his own."

"And for that you found it necessary to destroy——"

"Yes, give me credit for nipping at least one tiresome religion in the bud. I was fond of him, too. He was quite like Angelo, who was sneaking down toward South Calumet Street, by the way, when I left the house to follow you——"

"How's that?"

"South end. War, you know." He smiled up at me, not looking

99

at the grenade. "The Diggers are meeting the Mudhawks tonight. Angelo and Billy Kell—that's quite a boy, Billy." He could not quite control the slyness with which he glanced away, and that may be one more grain of proof for what I suspect about Billy Kell. "Well, they had a council of strategy, on which I eavesdropped. Angelo had some very sound ideas. One in particular, making use of rooftops, appealed to me. The Mudhawks will occupy the roofs on Lowell Street, where the Diggers have to pass on their way to the prearranged engagement, which is to be in Quire Lane. I believe both armies use what they call gleep-guns. Instead of bullets they shoot twenty-penny nails, variation of the arbalest. You might get the best view from the corner of Lowell and Quire Lane, if it isn't all over when you get there—*don't* let me detain you!" Some of his laughter may have been genuine. "Ah yes, the choice! Elmis, I wish you could know how funny you look. You imagine *you* can destroy me?"

"An instrument of my people and others. Hospital or grenade?"

"Grenade of course." And he ceased laughing.

"Only twelve Salvayans in all history have died by execution. They took the grenade with unbound hands. I'd like to respect that tradition, if I thought I could trust you. . . . Do you respect it?"

"Of course. A signal honor: No. 13." He stretched his arms above his head and spoke with real sorrow, although I heard no overtone of regret. "I am Salvayan too, Elmis. Also old and tired."

I set the grenade at his waist and stood back.

He taught my foolish mind, then, what 346 years had never quite taught me: there is no such thing as hearing truth from those who despise it. He snatched the grenade and flung it in a great arc. It missed me, struck a willow, filled the graveyard with a second's purple brilliance as sap and new wood of the lower trunk dissolved. The treetop plunged toward me in a long whispering and rushing. I had to jump like a fool to save myself. Namir's high laughter snarled back from among the graves: "Explain *that* to your adopted people!"

I could not assume that what he had told me of the gang war

was a lie. I cleared the fence behind him, though not pursuing him now. Seeing his knife in my hand, he swerved into the woods, his one backward look a mad smile. I shall see him again, if I don't die first of my own hesitating stupidity. His car—Feuermann's car—was parked behind mine. I slashed its front tires, and drove in my own car back to Latimer.

I parked Andy well beyond No. 21. After killing the motor I could hear something, a distant squealing, more like steam in a kettle than anything else. The dark clutter of houses muffled and shut it away. The moon had risen at last while I was driving back from Byfield, but gave poor help as yet in these blind-faced streets. Lowell Street branched from Calumet two blocks beyond EL CAT SEN; I did not quite know Quire Lane. The houses on Lowell Street were not detached but all one mass, making the narrow street resemble a New York City canyon. When I turned the corner the vicious clamor was no longer far off, but doubled in volume. A breathless running man bumped into me. "Hey, mister, don't go that way! The gangs——" He caught my arm to steady himself. "Sent for cops, ain't come, damn it, always the way when you *want* 'em—thought I'd try 'n' find the beat cop on Calumet——"

"Anybody hurt?"

"Kids with busted heads—there'll be worse. Mister, you better——"

"I'm all right. I live down that way."

"Well, stay inside, I'm telling you. Little bastards chunking rocks off the roofs, right here on Lowell. Hit a little girl—she wasn't with 'em, just running after 'em——"

"Where? Where is she?"

"Huh? Oh, some woman grabbed her, took her into a house——"

"My daughter——"

"My God! Don't borrow trouble, bud, could be any kid. Anyway, she wasn't bad hurt, wasn't even knocked out, see, and this woman——"

"*Which house?*"

101

"Other side, second from the next corner."

I squeezed his arm for thanks and ran.

A stone hit the pavement behind me. Just one (Angelo's idea?) and the bang of its fall was nearly drowned by the yelling from what must be Quire Lane ahead. My mind declared it could not be Angelo who threw it—not now, not at a single grownup, after the Diggers had already passed by that block. Part of me still insisted on that as I burst into the house.

It was Sharon. They had her on a bed in the front room, two women, one cleaning the gash on her head, the other fluttering. Sharon stopped whimpering when she saw me. I abandoned all Observers' Rules, kissing and scolding her. "What were you trying to *do?*" I suppose my irises were gray soup plates, but she wouldn't have noticed. It was all right, as people say: the bleeding had nearly ceased, and Sharon's rescuer had the wound properly cleaned. "Sharon, Sharon, what——"

"I wanted to make them stop it. Will you make them stop it?"

"Sure, I'm on my way. It's all right, Sharon."

She relaxed partly, and sighed, and wiped her nose with an angrily competent sweep of her whole arm. "Frankly, Ben, you always turn up when I want you, frankly."

"It's all right, Sharon. I'll make 'em stop it." The women crowded me away then, one of them wanting to know what I meant by letting my little girl run around in the streets. I escaped by saying she wasn't mine, damn it, I just knew where she lived, and would come back presently and take her home. I ran out in search of a war, and found it.

Quire Lane was a foul alley, a dead end, bordered by two warehouses, ending at the blank rear wall of a third. Later, from the police, I learned what the Mudhawks' strategy had achieved. The Diggers had stormed up Lowell Street, expecting a prearranged fracas in the relative seclusion of Quire Lane. The idea was simply to see how much mayhem could be dealt and received before the sirens sounded off. Probably the Diggers didn't exactly understand, when the rocks fell in Lowell Street. They themselves had gone to the trouble of smashing the street lamp at Lowell and Calumet. One boy was killed outright. Police found another afterward, in an areaway, with a broken shoulder. The dead child must have been somewhere in shadow when I was running down that block. . . . After passing the shower of stones, the Diggers sighted a small detachment of Mudhawks who staged a phony retreat into Quire Lane. Then the main force of Mudhawks closed the trap, swarming out of their hiding places in doorways and up the street, reinforced by the stone throwers from the roofs—by all but one of them, that is. Billy Kell has not been seen since, by myself or by the police, and he was not in the brawl in Quire Lane. Careful of his orange blood?

It seems to be necessary for me to believe that Billy Kell was alone on the roofs after the Diggers had gone by.

The Mudhawks forced the Diggers back to the blind end of the alley, with fists, stones, knives, gleep-guns. By the time I reached that smeared corner of Quire Lane and Lowell, the Diggers understood matters very well and were fighting back with total fury. A certain loathsome moonlight had reached the alley then. I could see plainly.

I could not find Angelo.

Some of the boys had flashlights that shot a writhing illumination when they were not being used as clubs. While I was yelling futile things that nobody heard, a Mudhawk—I knew him by his black tam-o'-shanter—dashed by me with a thing that looked like a wooden gun. I glimpsed the elastic bands, the nail in the slot, and tore it out of his hand. He glared foolishly, covered his face with his arm, and ran.

I could not find Angelo.

But now at last there was the thin imperative wrath of a siren, somewhere off on Calumet Street. The boys heard it too, and their stampede began, a stampede of those who could move at all. At least three were lying still at the rear of the alley.

I saw him now. He jumped up from nowhere. He jumped on a box near the clogged mouth of the alley, his shirt ripped away from flailing pipestem arms, blood and dirt all over him, his face beautiful, defiled, insane, and he was screaming: "Get 'em *now!* Don't let 'em break away! What are you—chicken? It's for *Bella*——"

Few heard him. The sirens were louder and spoke in clearer terms. The boys were all trying to get free of the alley, Diggers and Mudhawks in common panic, blundering into the warehouse walls, into me as I tried to plow my way through to Angelo. Then two patrol cars squealed into place, shutting off retreat, the sirens' question ending in the affirmative of a growl. Angelo heard that. He leaped off his box before I could catch him—I don't think he knew me then—and ran unseeingly straight into the grabbing arms of Patrolman Dunn. "One anyway!" said Dunn, and struck him on the ear.

In the next few howling moments they rounded up six or seven besides Angelo. Three of the four policemen were trying for arms or shirt collars instead of using their clubs, but some of it had to be frantic and dirty work. There was an ambulance beyond the patrol cars. I was cursing Dunn root and branch, but I stopped that, and don't know if he heard it. While he still gripped Angelo's arm I yelled in his ear: "Dunn! You can't take him to the station, it's going to kill his mother if you do."

"His mo——" It might have been only then that he recognized Angelo. Gore, mud, gravel marks on a mask of anguish—it wasn't strange.

I pressed my small advantage: "Her heart, man—you can't. The kid's only twelve anyhow. He was sucked into it, I happen to know —tell you later. Take him home, Dunn. Don't book him."

"Who're you?"

"I live there. Saw you when we had that burglary."

"Ah, yah. . . ." He shook the boy, not roughly but slowly. Angelo swayed at the end of his arm, and spat blood from a cut lip. "Jesus, kid! But you was always a *good* boy—never in no trouble before, what the hell?"

Angelo asked quietly: "Is that true? I don't exactly know."

"Huh? You never done nothing like this before."

"I have," said Angelo drowsily, and his head drooped and I could scarcely hear him. "Yes, I have, in my dreams. They come like clouds. Which is the sky: the clouds or the blue?"

"Now, boy, now. What kind of an answer is that? You're highsterical is what it is. Pull yourself together. You see that ambulance? You see what's going into it, huh, Angelo?"

"Take him home, Dunn. Take him home."

"They all go to the station, mister. But you could be right. I won't book him, maybe. I'll get him home. Understand, Angelo? A break. On your mother's account, not on yours, believe you me. And if there's ever a second time, no break, no break at all. Now come on——"

"Ben! Ben—ask them to clean me up before they——"

"In with you. In with you now. . . ."

Those women had given Sharon a sleeping pill. (It is increasingly a sleeping-pill culture, Drozma. Seventeen years ago I don't think a respectable woman in a poor district would have had a supply of barbiturates, much less given one casually to a child without even a doctor's word. It could be a small symptom of the many forces that may make fools of us and our hope of Union within five hundred years or so. Yet I don't blame them too much. Life in its growing complexity nags and bedevils them: rather than learn the uses of simplicity, they reach for sleep.) I carried Sharon to my car, and home, cutting short the startled mooings of her parents with some ill-tempered noise of my own. It wasn't their fault, in a way—to make her frantic effort, Sharon had slid down the rainspout when they supposed she was in bed. It was another playmate, a seceding Mudhawk, who had let slip word to Sharon of what was planned. So Sharon told me a day or two later. I must finish this report quickly, Drozma.

Namir as Feuermann had not returned to No. 21. I did not think he would. (As I write this, the body of Feuermann has not been found. There was an item about "mysterious summer lightning" destroying a tree in Byfield; the damage done by the falling top may have canceled out the marks of the shallow grave. If the old man is ever found, I suppose his motiveless murder will become a popular mystery to addle the experts.)

No. 21 was gently quiet. I found Rosa sewing in her basement living room, unconcerned, mild, too far from the war in Quire Lane to have heard its crying, comfortable in the belief that Angelo was asleep in his room with a bit of a cold. It was too much for me. I don't understand either the strength or the fragility of human beings, as I see them sometimes bending viably before enormous pressures, sometimes snapping at a touch.

Rosa knew from my face that something was wrong. She put her sewing away and came to me. "What is it, Ben? You sick?" Still unhurt, still safe behind her unreal shield of love and security—the house quiet, Angelo surely in his room—she could be sorry for me, and anxious to help. "What *is* the matter, Ben? You look awful."

So I gabbled. "Nothing serious, but——"

I might have succeeded somehow in preparing her for it. I don't know. I was hopelessly human in my stammering hunt for words that might warn without wounding. While I stammered, Dunn came in. Through the basement door, without ringing, holding Angelo by the arm. Yes, they'd tried to clean him up a little, but couldn't hide the cut lip or the gash over his eye. They'd washed his face, but couldn't wash away the shame, the glaze of withdrawal, the agony.

I saw Rosa's hand leave her wobbling lips and clutch at her left arm. I could not reach her, nor could Dunn, in time to check her fall.

There was no rising. Only the choking, the brief struggle, and the relinquishment. Even after her face turned cyanotic I think she was still trying to see where Angelo was, or perhaps say something to him—that it was all right, not his fault, something like that. . . .

"May I go and get Father Ryan?"

That blank whisper made Dunn remember him and turn to him. "Why—she's gone, boy. She's gone."

"Yes, I see, I know. I did that. May I go and get Father Ryan?"

"Of course."

He never returned, Drozma. The priest came quickly, but Angelo was not with him. Father Ryan said Angelo had run on ahead of him.

In the week since then, the Latimer and state police have done everything possible. There is an eight-state alarm, everything else that human intelligence can devise. They are looking for Feuermann too, the worthless rumors like the haze that hangs on after forest fire. Since it seems that he ran into night, and night took him, I will go into night myself, and look for him there.

A word about Sharon. I saw her last in Amagoya, but she knew its magic had perished, as well as I knew it, and it was unavoidable that we should talk like grownups. I told her that of course Angelo would be found, or more likely come back by himself when he could. I told her that I was going away alone to look for him. It was hard for her to accept the obvious fact that she could not come with me. She did accept it. I have never been so dangerously close to revealing what we must not, as I was there in Amagoya when she said: "You know everything, Ben. You *will* find him." So I know everything! She was a woman, Drozma. Even her mangled big words weren't funny, they weren't funny at all. I made her promise to do what she already knew she must—stay, stay with her music, grow up, "be a good girl"—we found we could laugh some at that last, nevertheless knowing what it meant.

If I end this here, I have time to make myself a passable new face before dawn. As soon as there has been time for this report to have reached you I will call through the Toronto Communicator and learn your orders.

Whatever they are, I cannot return to Northern City if it means abandoning this mission. I will yield no such victory to Namir and his kind. We are a little less than human, Drozma, and a little more.

part two

In our barbarous society the influence of character is in its infancy.
> —RALPH WALDO EMERSON, *Politics*

1 Drozma, tonight I am racked by an old malady, a love for the human race.

I have searched more than nine years. As you know from my reports, I have not found him. If living, Angelo is twenty-one. You have been kind, to support me with money and counsel. With the Russo-Chinese War reeling into a third dreary year and the rest of the world in a frenzy of indecision, I know you cannot spare other personnel to aid me, but I must go on searching. I will send this journal later in place of a formal report. A few hours ago something happened which will be a pleasure to record, but otherwise I have little to tell: frustrations, false clues, dead-end journeys. I have come here to New York and taken an apartment, because of a newspaper photograph that made me think of Billy Kell.

It was a picture of that fellow Joseph Max being interviewed by some journalist. Behind Max was a face alertly blank like a bodyguard's, enough like Kell to excite my wondering. Namir (and his son?) may have been searching for Angelo as persistently as I. In the nine years I have had no more hint of their whereabouts than of his. I was in Cincinnati when I saw the picture a week ago. I had gone there because one of my hobo friends slipped word to me that someone resembling my "grandson" was hanging around the river docks. Nothing in it. One more dark-haired bum with a limp; a face like a woodchuck. The world's full of dark young men with lame left legs. The tramps and prostitutes and petty criminals who try to help me are not people who know how to describe a face. When I make contact with them I am a crazy old coot hunting a grandson who might have died long ago or (they think) never lived. They try to be kind, supplying rumors to keep

111

the old man going, partly for laughs. I have no good reason to suppose that Angelo sank into the shadows of the underworld: it's only that those shadows are easier to explore than the endless multitudes of the respectable. Quite possibly some decent family gave him shelter and another name. I go on. I can't mingle in any crowd without sooner or later seeing some dark youth with a limp. Once I saw one who not only resembled Angelo but had a scar over the right eye, as Angelo must have. That was on the copter-bus from Sacramento to Oakland. I trailed him home, watched him a few more times, made inquiries in the neighborhood. Nice kid, not even Italian, lived in Oakland all his life. Some hopes won't die.

No doubt you have Observers keeping track of Joseph Max and the antics of his Unity Party. I shall be another, at least until I satisfy myself about Billy Kell. Maybe I can turn up something interesting as a by-product. Hell's a-brewing around Joe Max. And by the way, what is there about his party to attract a man of the stature of Dr. Hodding? At risk of repeating what other Observers may have told you, this is the Hodding story as I saw it in the papers two years ago: Jason Hodding was director of the Wales Foundation (biochemical research and very good), and startled the world out of its pants with a propaganda blast for Max's party in the congressional elections of '70; supposed to have helped elect that freak Senator Galt of Alaska. Then Hodding quit the Foundation (or was fired?) and dropped out of sight of the public. Lives prosperously on Long Island, "retired"; said to know more about virus mutations than anyone else at large. . . .

Max calls it the Organic Unity Party now. He no longer yelps in public about racial purity, though some of the whispers against the Federalists' Negro-Indian candidate must originate with Max. In public he approves of human brotherhood: there are votes in it. He'll make a try in the fall election, shouting for America to rule the world. "Clean up Asia!"—a banner with that legend decorates his headquarters on Lexington Upper Level, and nobody laughs. We must go in and reform Asia (for its own good of course)

112

while the Russian and Chinese giants are (apparently) gasping their last. Maybe they are: everything Max says carries the virus of half-truth. The techs say, and Satellite observations are supposed to confirm, that no atomic explosions have taken place in Asia since last summer. I give the Satellite Authority credit for resisting the pressure a year ago to solve everything with a few hydrogen jobs. That took courage, up there on the Midnight Star, since the humanitarian opposition was, as so often, tiptoeing by on the other side. As of March, 30,972, we don't know—frantically, elaborately, diplomatically don't know. If you believe Satellite Authority communiqués (I do, more or less) there must be idiotic trench-and-outpost warfare all along the north-and-south backbone of Asia, Siberia remaining the darkness it always was. Now and then the Authority says plaintively that it really can't collect social and economic data from 1075 miles up. Drozma, tell me when you write whether Asian Center is still safe. I had friends there.

Here, only the Organic Unity Party appears to have no doubts.

Nobody laughs at Max. That frightens me. The public is hardened to seeing his fanatic puss on the front page, telescreens, newsreels, always a bit sallow and sweat-shiny when they catch him without make-up, a bad animated caricature of John C. Calhoun with nothing of Calhoun's honesty or personal gentleness. When, last year, Max developed a flopping cowlick—damn the thing, nobody laughed. He saves his juiciest venom for the newly formed Federalist Party. I haven't made up my mind about them. Seems to be nothing disingenuous in the movement and much sense, if they'd tone down the doctrinaire certainty of their one-world members. They sometimes lose sight of their own good premise, that difference-within-union is the essence of federalism. Toward the Democrats and Republicans Max has only contempt—he says they are on the way out and that's that. They make the mistake of paying him back in his own coin or trying to ignore him out of sight. The Republicans have been fresh out of ideas since '968, when the Democrat Clifford got in (and how wrong I was about '64! Would've lost my shirt, only I'm not the type.) Rooseveltian splash

113

followed by Wilsonian bubbles. Nice chap, Clifford. Progressive, they tell me. I sometimes wonder if he knows his aspirations from his elbow.

A word about the Philippines, Drozma. Watch that Institute of Human Studies. Founded in '968. I have a hunch the personnel is earthquake-proof, same as the buildings, which I hope I'll live to see someday. Not just another inflated foundation. It has the quiet sort of courage behind it. I like their prospectus: "To collect and make accessible to all the sum of available human knowledge"— large order, but they mean business. "To continue research in those studies most directly related to the nature and function of human beings." And they explain that the use of the term "human beings" instead of "Man" is deliberate—that would naturally appeal to my cantankerous bias. Point is they're thinking in terms of centuries and not scared by next week. You remember how Manila ought to have been one of the world's greatest centers of trade and culture, if European rule-and-grab hadn't smothered it in what they call the eighteenth century and later. I don't know why it shouldn't be the Athens of the twenty-first. When my mission is ended one way or another, I want to go there before returning to Northern City.

Tomorrow morning I shall visit Organic Unity Party headquarters and pose as a snarky old man with money. My new face suits me. I may have used a bit too much heat when I raised the cheekbones, but that merely makes me apple-cheeked, cute as hell, six feet two of short-tempered Santy Claus, talking slightly daown-East, and I've practiced a deadpan stare that comes in handy. I mean to be a potential angel for the campaign fund, not quite convinced but open to indoctrination. They'll lay down some kind of carpet. If Billy Kell is in there I'll smell him out.

Now I can turn to something that has lightened my 355 years.

After I left Latimer, to follow up a rumor that someone had seen a kid hitchhiker twenty miles out of town, I knew that the police were not uninterested in Benedict Miles. I had my new face, and it seemed best to inform Mrs. Wilks, through Toronto, that Miles

114

had died, leaving the school provided for in his will. Less harassed and hurried judgment might have produced something better than that, but once it was done I couldn't undo it. Mrs. Wilks wrote faithfully to the Toronto "trustees" until two years ago, and the Communicator sent her letters on to me when possible—often I had no address. Two years ago Sophia's sister died. Sophia turned the school over to a successor, and took Sharon to London, feeling that her own teaching could carry the girl no further. Sharon's family wasn't mentioned in that last letter. I have not been too severely distressed by my separation from the child I loved, because I have known that, chance permitting, I would hear of her again. When I came to New York last week, Sharon's debut was in the announcements. This evening she played, in Pro Arte Hall.

It is a new auditorium, part of a splendid development along the Hudson. You wouldn't recognize New York, Drozma. I almost didn't, for the last good view I had of it was back in 30,946. I have passed through a few times in the nine years, but with scarcely a chance to pause.

In the '960s New York decided to make its waterfront beautiful instead of hideous. A great Esplanade runs from George Washington Bridge to Twenty-third Street, with tall buildings at intervals, some set back among the lower structures on the inner side of the Esplanade, others rising sheer from the river. They tell me the railroad still rumbles down below. Dock facilities have actually been expanded, but it doesn't look so: to come in on a ship or ferry is to enter an archway in a gleaming cliff. When I have time, think I'll go over to Jersey in order to come back on one of the chubby Diesel ferries and see for myself. The heavy automotive traffic on the second level is not felt up on the Esplanade, as you don't feel it when you walk on the upper levels of the north-and-south avenues. On the Esplanade you have only the sky, the graceful buildings, human beings, and the Hudson River wind that now seems not hostile, gritty, and snarling but a refreshing part of the city's majesty. It was difficult to have any patience with New York in the old days. Times change. Hell's Kitchen was wiped

115

away long ago; blest if I know what they did with Grant's Tomb but I'm sure it's tucked in down there somewhere. This waterfront was planned soon after they snatched the city from the politicians and tried the manager system. They have kept out catchpenny concessions. On the wide Esplanade itself not even bicycles are allowed, though children are everywhere.

The city's resident population has gone down by about a million, with corresponding increase in the huge arc of the metropolitan district. There's revival of the old proposal to make the district a separate state. Civic groups kick the idea around. One in particular is gathering petition signatures and doing spadework in Congress. They want the new state to be named Adelphi. I've got no objections.

Pro Arte Hall is high up in one of the buildings rising directly from the river—clean-shining steel and stone and glass. Conditioned as we have been, Drozma, to the hidden life, we'll never quite know how they do it. These buildings are wholly human, artifacts of their complex science, yet married to nature also, to wind and sky, stars and sun.

The auditorium itself is severe. Cold white and self-effacing gray. Nothing irrelevant to tickle or distract the eye, only an uncomplicated stage and stern classical dignity of the piano. (But it was good, during intermission, to go into a lounge and find, beyond its glass west wall, an open space from which one looked down to the river. How far down I don't know. A bright liner passing downstream was a playroom toy. In spite of the March chill I was happy to watch it until the bell rang for the second half of Sharon's miracle.)

Few in the audience knew anything about her, I think. Just one more New York debut. I had a case of nerves, my heartbeat shaking me each minute. I read the program a dozen times, and knew nothing of what it said except that the first number was the Bach G Minor Fugue.

Then she was there. Slim, slight, seeming tall—oh, I'd known that! In white. I'd known that too. Her corsage was a tiny cluster

116

of blue scillas and snowdrops, absurdly modest. She still wore her brown hair shoulder-length, misty with strange lights. She didn't find it necessary to smile. Her bow was almost perfunctory. (She has told me she was totally petrified, couldn't bow deeper for fear of going over flat on her face.) I remembered Amagoya.

She seated herself, touched her palms with a handkerchief, adjusted the long skirt to clear her ankles. Dimly I knew she was still sort of snub-nosed. Somewhere there must have been a red rubber ball on a string. . . .

Then I had to pay her the best compliment: forgetting her. The fugue took hold with clear-cut authority. What unreal and therefore eternal cities did Bach know, to create his architecture out of the marble of dreams? Was the G Minor written after his blindness? I don't remember. Not that it matters: his visions need no common eyesight. It was as if Sharon had said (to all of us): "Come here with me. I can show you what I saw." No other way to play Bach, but who at nineteen is supposed to know that?

In spite of the fugue's enormous ending there was not the usual burst of excitement killing the last chord. Instead they gave her some seconds of that enchanted silence all human performers pray to receive (an experience I can't quite share, since Martian audiences grant the silence as a matter of course, for music's sake). When the crash came it was not prolonged, for Sharon did smile then, and the shy grimace touched off sympathetic laughter, a way of saying they loved her, and the applause broke off short at the merest half turn of her head back to the piano.

The rest of the first half was all Chopin. The sonata; three nocturnes; two mazurkas; the F Sharp Minor Impromptu, which I think is the extremest distillation of Chopin, a union of ecstasy and despair nearly unbearable. Sharon thinks so, played it so. Even with that still burning inside us, we demanded an encore at the end of the first half, a thing unheard of nowadays. When the shouts were unmistakable, she gave us the little first Prelude, as she might have tossed a flower to a lover who deserved it but wasn't too bright. Pianissimo all the way through, disregarding the

117

conventional dynamic marks: like opening a window on a waterfall and closing it before you can guess what the river is saying. I never played it like that. Frédéric Chopin didn't, when I heard him in 30,848, but I don't believe he'd have minded. I can't fathom the phonograph-intellects who insist on "definitive interpretation." You might as well insist, when a friend gives you a jewel, that only one facet may be looked at, world without end. You might as well ask for a definitive moonrise. Sharon grinned after that tour de force—not a definitive grin either, a big human one. She ran off. The lights went up.

It was an uncommonly long program, especially for a debut. A newcomer is still expected to be humble before tradition. A chunk of Bach for the critics, a chunk of Beethoven, maybe some Schumann to fill in the cracks, Chopin to prove you're a pianist, finally a scintillant gob of Liszt for bravura and schmaltz. Sharon had paid her respects with Bach all right—what Bach!—but only because she wanted to. My mangled scrap of program told me the second half began with a suite by Andrew Carr, an Australian composer not known till a year ago. And it ended with Beethoven, Sonata in C, Opus 53.

Realization came slowly. I'm not in the habit of thinking in opus numbers, but it came through then to my dazed intelligence that 53 is the "Waldstein." I think that was what made me reach one of those impulsive, wholly emotional decisions which I don't expect to regret. I scratched on the rumpled program: *Not dead, had to change face and name to help me hunt for A. No, dear, I haven't found him. May I see you? Alone, please, and don't tell anyone about me yet. You're a musician. I love you beyond comprehemption.*

I found an usher, a girl who promised to get my note to Miss Brand. I wandered outside. I watched that ship going downstream in the open night. After a while, as I've told you, I was quite happy. When I went back the popeyed usher located me, pushed a slip of paper in my hand, and whispered: "Hey, know what she did when she read your note? Kissed *me!* Well, I *mean* . . ."

I bumbled like Santy Claus. The lights had already dimmed, but I could read the huge scrawl: *Blue River Café 2 blox down Esplan riverside wait for me lounge escape earliest poss O Ben Ben* BEN! ! !

She may have tried to see me in the audience, though I had mentioned a changed face. There was a blind look about her. I knew terror, fearing I might have upset her and hurt the second half of the concert. But then she was resting her fingers silently on the keys, as if the towering Steinway had its own will and could communicate, soothe, clear away confusion and leave her free. I needn't have worried.

The Andrew Carr suite is excellent. Complex, serious, young; perhaps too heavy, too immense, but with a cumulative passion that justifies it. Likely a greater maturity will teach Carr the value of the light touch. In the program notes, I remember, he acknowledges a major debt to Brahms. All to the good, especially if it means that composers of the '970s have finally buried the I-don't-really-mean-it school of the '930s and '940s. Carr has learned more from the young Stravinsky than from the old; Beethoven glances over his shoulder; he needs more Mozart in his system. . . .

I won't play the "Waldstein" again. Anything else, yes—I don't despise my own talent. Not the "Waldstein." For anyone else it would have been bad programming to let the sonata follow the shattering climaxes and nearly impossible athletic demands of the Carr suite. Not for Sharon. She wasn't tired. She made it a summing up, a final statement to throw the colors of a thousand flames on all the rest.

Maybe I've heard the opening Allegro done with more technical finish; never with more sincerity. In the melancholy of the brief Adagio I was lost. I don't know all that Sharon meant; Beethoven's meditations are not altogether ours at any time. She took the gentle opening of the Rondo more slowly than I would have done, but she was right, and the acceleration of the A Minor passage became all the more a terrifying flash, a blaze of longing abruptly revealed.

. . . The sonata's conclusion was blinding. No one looks at that much light.

I don't recall much about the ovation they gave her: we were all hysterical. I don't even remember what all her encores were. There were seven. We let her go at last only because she put on a small comic pantomime of exhaustion.

You could not imagine, Drozma, the first thing she said when she slipped into the Blue River Café, astonishingly small, shy, a mousy gray wrap over her gown—slipped in and knew me somehow through all my changes, caught up the clumsy skirt to run like a child and throw herself at me and bury her snub nose in my shirt. She said: "Ben, I fluffed the Prestissimo, I *fluffed* it, I went too fast, I scrabbled it—where, where have you *been?*"

"You never fluffed anything." I must have muttered more such stuff while we struggled for calm.

We found a booth, with a window overlooking the river and the night. Tranquil and civilized, that restaurant, mild lighting, no fuss, hurry, or noise. It was past eleven o'clock, but they produced a hero-size dinner for Sharon, who admitted to fasting before the concert and now looked with pathetic astonishment at the lobster, saying: "Could I bodaciously have ordered *that* in my madness?" She ate it though, with all the fixings, and we grinned and mumbled and made groping reaches for the unsayable. Then the lobster was gone, coffee and cognac were with us; Sharon squared her little shoulders and sighed and said: "Now . . . !"

If there was anything in the nine years I failed to tell her it was either an unavoidable part of our Martian deception or too small to remember. I am "Will Meisel" at present. She found it difficult not to call me Ben. My departure from Latimer had been, in a way, cruel—I knew it at the time. She did not reproach me for it, or for the false message of my death—not directly. But once she took my fingers and pressed them against her cheek and said: "When Mrs. Wilks told me—you see, until Angelo went away I'd never lost anybody—and then you——" But rather than let me flounder and beg forgiveness she went on quickly: "Your hands are the same, just

120

the same. How was it possible to change your face so much? I saw you recognize me, or maybe I'd've known you anyway, but——"

With careful vagueness and wholly genuine embarrassment, I lied about having suffered a serious face injury, years before my time in Latimer. I hinted that part of my facial structure was prosthetic, under a successful skin graft, and that I could play tricks with it. I conveyed too that I was sensitive and didn't like talking of it. "Nine years' aging too, Sharon, and the white hair is natural."

"Ben—Will—why was it necessary? But, darling, don't tell me unless you want to. You're here. I'll get used to it sometime. . . ." I told her that my going away had made the police suspect me in connection with the disappearances of Angelo and Feuermann. She confirmed that Feuermann had never been found. My search had to be unhampered, I said, so I juggled personalities and faces, burying an old identity. It was all too far from the human norm and I don't think it satisfied her, but it was the best I could do. She too remembered Amagoya. She hasn't a suspicious heart. Sharon at ten had been somewhat sheltered from grown-up speculations and rumors, missing the real and unreal implications of that disaster in Latimer. Music and Mrs. Wilks had held her steady when the loss of Angelo and myself had shaken her world. Soon there had been time, and adolescence. I had foolishly not quite grasped the vast difference between nine of my years and Sharon's nine between ten and nineteen. . . . I told her too how I thought Angelo might have been swallowed by the underworld—joined the hobos, something like that—or even suffered amnesia because he felt lost and condemned himself for his mother's death.

"Why did he mean so much to you?"

"I felt responsible, perhaps. I ought to have kept him out of trouble because I knew he was supernormal and vulnerable, and I didn't do it." She wasn't satisfied. "And I came to think of him as like a son." There was too much truth in that. "I should have been a better guardian, because I don't think anyone else saw the dangers." Not for the first time, she started to ask another question,

121

but held it back, frowning into her cigarette smoke, cherishing my hand. "How well do you remember him, Sharon?"

"I don't know." She has developed a number of vivid little mannerisms, none of them posed. A trick of leaning forward suddenly, shoving both hands up into her hair and keeping them there, while a tiny frown-crease comes and goes in her smooth forehead; pouting her big sweet mouth without knowing it; smiling so fleetingly you can't be sure afterward that she smiled at all. "I don't know. I know *that* I loved him pretty terribly. Ten years old is such a *long* time ago, Ben. . . . Afraid I don't even know much about the famous male sex. It's been—you know: technique, not parties—Czerny, not boy friends. And worth it, too—I haven't minded that."

"Plenty of time."

"Oh—time. . . . I suppose I began to feel he was dead, after Mother Sophia—I'm sort of in the habit of calling her that, she likes it—after she told me that you were. I never forgot him, Ben, I just had to let it go into the past, like a station on a train. I didn't finish high school, by the way. My mother died when I was thirteen, and Pop remarried—oh well, make way for Cinderella, I couldn't stand the stepmother and she sure-to-God couldn't stand me, so Mother Sophia took me to live with her—all I could've prayed for. I—hear from Pop now and then. Stiff little letters. Exceedingly grammatical."

"He wasn't there tonight?"

"Ah no, he"—her wonderful fingers were gripping my hand hard again—"he doesn't get around much, as the jellyfish said to the sea serpent. Means, translated, that while the heller he married runs the store, he goes down to the corner. Got it in all its beauty, darling? He's Brand Anonymous. And little daughter can no more reach him than—oh, the devil with it. He writes only when he's sober, about once in two months, Ben——"

"Will."

"I'm sorry—Will, Will. I've thought so much about *Ben.* . . . Well, he wrote that he would like to come to the recital but was very busy and not well. Could be the lady dictated it. She knows he still loves me, in his fashion, that's her cross. People are so . . . so . . ." She gave it up.

We were both silent too long. I said: "Oo ill i owioffsh?"

For some reason that made her cry, but even while she groped impatiently for a handkerchief, and snatched mine, she was saying: "O. Ah ery ush. But I could go another cognac. . . ."

"And Mother Sophia?"

"Splendid." She was still annoyed at her eyes, wiping them, and repairing make-up. "Immortal—my God, if only she were! I didn't know what to say, about coming away tonight. Lousy liar. Said I had a whim to be completely alone an hour or so, guess she didn't mind. She'll sit up for the press notices and not sleep, so can't I take you home to see her?"

"Not this time, dear. Later." I had saved that newspaper photograph, and presently showed it to her. "The man just behind Max, on his left. Remind you of anything?"

"Heck, it almost does." She held it at different angles, then leaned back, closing the veils on the ocean-blue, opening them widely. "Billy Kell!"

"Just could be. Old Will Meisel has to find out."

She stared awhile, darkly perplexed, not distrusting me but perhaps hurt by her certainty that I was withholding too much. "Will —what *for?* Do I sit quiet and play the piano while you butt your head on a stone wall? I have you back just in time to see you get hurt."

"Angelo is alive, somewhere."

"Faith," she said gently. "But, Will darling, I just never have seen any of the mountains they say it moved. Well, you think if Angelo's alive he might be in touch with—that fellow?"

"It's possible."

"I do remember Billy Kell, and a nasty piece of work he was, not that he ever actually did anything to me. He *would* grow up to be a Unity Party job, wouldn't he! I've got to say it: what if you're just breaking your heart over something that—I mean, it was *so long ago!* And *none* of it your fault anyway. Why, Ben—Will—the

123

police must have looked, good and hard, it's what they're for and they have the means, they wouldn't've let it drop. But you—look, if he's—if he died, you probably wouldn't ever even know it. Would you? Or maybe by this time he's a bank teller or a physics professor or some ghastly thing, and you—I could shake you."

"I'm old," I said. "I have money. I could help him. Now that I know you're a big girl, there's nothing I want to do more."

"Then I'll eat my words. If it's what you have to do. . . ."

"It could mean a lot to you, if I find him. Couldn't it?"

"Darling, to be filthily honest: how do I know?"

2

New York
Thursday, March 9

Today and yesterday make an ending and a beginning. *Drozma, I am nearly certain Angelo is alive.* I'll fill in some background.

Damn the Organic Unity Party, at least it doesn't hide itself. It occupies the first floor of an office building that went up when Lexington was remodeled as one of the two-level avenues—the others are Second and Eighth, a triumph of the Gadget. Lower levels are only for cars equipped with electronic controls; no wheeled traffic on the upper levels except busses in narrow center lanes; overpasses for crosstown traffic.

My apartment is in a plush downtown development near the ghost of the Bowery. I started early this morning and walked above Second Avenue Upper Level for the fun of it. There is a game for the young on those airy overpasses: you can't climb the guard fences, but through the mesh you can register an occasional hit on a bus top with wet chewing gum. I don't know what scoring system is used.

I took a bus on Lexington Upper Level. Organic Unity Party

headquarters is uptown near 125th. And Harlem is not as you remember, Drozma. Negroes live anywhere in town, or almost anywhere: still some plague spots of white supremacy, but these are dwindling and unimportant. Harlem is merely another part of town, with as many pale faces as dark. I didn't find any dark faces at the Organic Unity offices. . . . Prosperous place. Saving the world for the pure in heart is profitable. Always was, I reckon.

The receptionist blonde had glassy perfection like a rhinestone. She assessed my good clothes, turned on welcome—Smile, Standard B-1; semiautomatic; Sugar Daddies, for the control of—and waved me through a frosted glass door labeled DANIEL WALKER. He's a synthetically jolly endomorphic mesomorph softening with fat in his thirties. Just a greeter, one step up from the blonde. I took my time and got a cigar out of it. Nothing too blatant about Walker. His gaze is carefully candid; he speaks with the odd hollow noise of a man whose every word is a quotation. "I'm interested," I said. "You don't seem to be getting a good press."

"You're from a newspaper, Mr. Meisel?"

"No." I looked shocked. "Retired. Used to be in real estate."

"Never worry about the press," he quoted. "Joe doesn't. It's all reactionary. Doesn't Express the Organic Unity of the People." He talked in capitals while I nodded and looked grim and wise. "In the Larger Sense, we do get a good press. They hate us, that makes talk, and talk brings us Intelligent Inquiries like your own." I bridled: a durned old goat. "What interests you most about The Party, Mr. Meisel?"

"Your Sense of Purpose," I said. "You're not afraid of Stating an Aim." I lit the cigar with a lighter that cost me forty-eight bucks —lingeringly, so that Mr. Walker's candid eyes could price-tag it. (I'll bring it home, Drozma. It has a pop-up white-gold nude half an inch high who whangs the flint with a hammer and kicks up behind. Aesthetic value about a nickel—the kids might enjoy it.) "When you're Alone in the World——" I sighed. "Frankly, Mr. Walker, I feel the Party might give me a Sense of Purpose of my own." I told him the world was dangerously drifting. Internationalist delusions. Losing touch with the Eternal Verities. Skepticism rampant. Speaking as a skeptic myself, wonder if it *could* ramp? Think maybe it could.

"Yes indeed," said Mr. Walker kindly, and pumped me for autobiography. I let it be dragged out that I was from Maine, widower, no children. Used to be a Republican of course. Not now, by God. They were Reactionary: didn't understand the inevitability of taking steps in Asia. No Sense of Purpose. I was good and cross about the Republicans.

"They're on the way out," Walker quoted. "Don't give 'em a thought. Have you wondered why we call it the Organic Unity Party?" He didn't wait to hear. "Here's something confidential, Mr. Meisel. You notice the word 'unity' has one inconvenience. Can't call ourselves Unionists or Unitarians—heh-heh. Nor Organists for that matter. The word, Mr. Meisel, is *Organite*. Something the Leader gave us only a few days ago, so it isn't in the literature yet, but I'm sure you get the point. Soon it will be on everyone's tongue. On the tongues of our enemies too, who will make fun of it." He pointed ten manicured fingers at me. "Let them! We profit by that too." That was the only moment when true masochistic fanaticism peeked from behind the mask of this soft athlete. "Now! Why Organic? Because it's the *only* word that expresses the Nature of Society and the Basic Needs of Man! Society is a Unitary Organism. Now! What must any unitary organism have? Simple, isn't it? Means of locomotion. Means of satisfying hunger, of reproducing. Sense organs. Certainly a unitary nervous system. Now! What, for instance, is Society's means of satisfying hunger?" Under his busy hands, his desk leaked pamphlets and throwaways till my pockets were full.

"Agriculture and its workers," I said, having seen some of the pamphlets and memorized the patter for these ideas, ideas so old and stale that human beings had begun to be hypnotized or repelled by them at least five thousand years ago.

"And what is the nervous system of Society?"

"Well naow, that right there, that bothers me some, frankly.

126

Everybody wants to be part of the nervous system, seems as though."

"No, friend, there you're wrong—you don't mind my saying it? Not everybody. The man in the street, Mr. Meisel, *wants to be ruled.* Don't forget, Democracy must be defined as the greatest *good* for the greatest number. Ask yourself, sir, how many people know what's good for 'em? The man in the street, Mr. Meisel, is in need of Enlightened Re-education. He must find, understand, and accept his appropriate place in the Organism. Or accept without understanding, sometimes. Now! Who's to tell him? Who *can,* except an elite body of the well informed, the natural rulers, in other words the nervous system of Society?"

I attempted to look as if I'd just thought of something bright and shiny. "Seems as though that's where the Organic Unity Party might come in." I had let the cigar go out, so that the forty-eight-dollar nude could flip her lid again. I puffed, looking so pleased with myself that I am still queasy at the memory. Walker was pleased too. Nor was I mistaken about the glimmer of contempt I saw in him, swiftly hidden as a weasel peeping over a rock pile.

"You put it very well, Mr. Meisel."

"Doesn't the Forward Labor Party have kind of a similar idear?"

That may have been a slip, a question slightly too intelligent for Old Man Meisel. Walker grew more watchful. He said quietly: "They have several good ideas. Better understanding of Society than the old parties. They see, same as we do, where the greatest danger is."

I tightened my tough old Martian neck, to make a flush appear in my well-made cheeks. "I guess you mean those damn Federalists?"

It was the right noise. I think he was reassured. He said, still softly: "Worst traitors to America since the Civil War. Yes, of course. . . . Have you had any connection with Forward Labor, Mr. Meisel?"

"Oh no." So far as I can tell, Drozma, he was reassured.

He made up his mind. "Like you to have a talk with Keller.

Wonderful guy, you'll like him. If you have any doubts about what we're doing, what we stand for, he can clear them up better than me." Studying me sidelong as if I were a work of art, he boomed into the telephone: "Bill? How's it?" My throat was cold. This was what I came for. Bill Keller. Billy Kell. . . . I strained my wicked Martian hearing, but the voice at the other end was only a wiry squeak. "Uh-huh, Bill. . . . Like you to meet him when you get a bit of time." Code, I guessed, for "allow time to check on the sucker." Presently Walker covered the mouthpiece to ask me affectionately: "Going to be free this afternoon, latish?" I was free.

He was easing me to the door. He didn't put an arm over my shoulder because I am three inches taller; he did everything else to make me feel like the Grand Old Man of the Kennebec. "Confidentially, Bill Keller is *very* high up. Don't misunderstand—just as democratic as you and me. But you see, a Leader like Joe Max, all his responsibilities, worries, he can't give as much time to everyone as he'd like. Has to rely on a chosen few." Walker showed me crossed fingers. "Bill Keller is right *up* There!" He patted my back. Old Man Meisel marched out, squaring his shoulders with a Sense of Purpose.

I didn't think they had anyone tailing me; didn't care much. They had my address and could smell around if they chose. I wandered all morning. Had lunch I forget where and wound up at Central Park Zoo. That March day was like a little girl fresh out of her bath, cool, sweet, ready for mischief. I could respond to it now. We're almost human, Drozma: if you can't find the one you love maybe an enemy is the next best.

The bears were restless with spring. An old cinnamon patrolled the front of his enclosure in neurotic pacing, ten steps left, swing of the head, ten right, talking dolorously to himself. The only other watcher at the moment was a brown-faced boy who acknowledged my presence after a while with a bothered inquiry: "What he moaning about?"

"Doesn't like being in a cage, specially this time of year."

"Would you turn him loose, mister? If you could?"

128

"No—too fond of my own skin."

"Bet he'd chaw us plenty. Wouldn't he?"

"Uh-huh. Couldn't blame him."

"Naw?"

"It was people like us who put him in there."

"Yeah. Gee!" He strolled off, frowning at it.

It was past four when I returned to the Organic Unity offices. The lounge was crowded. Walker was busy. I sat for a quarter hour watching the coming and going of Organites. Sad, strained, introverted faces, many of them; others had the power-hungry look. Several were shabby, several prosperous. Only one clear common denominator: they all wanted something. And between a little chap with a placating smirk who probably sought a job sealing envelopes, and a lean paranoid with some brand-new design for the universe, I couldn't find a great deal to choose.

Walker at last escorted me down complex lanes between desks to an office in the rear. Big. They measure rank as Mussolini did, by the amount of carpet between door and desk. When that door opened . . .

Drozma, the Martian scent was thick enough to slice.

Yet I would have known him without it, that heavy figure looming like Il Duce. He had altered his face only in the direction of maturity. Thicker cheeks; a practiced, half-genial scowl. He waited impressively before rising to greet us. An underling certainly—there's no doubt in my mind that the grimly human Joseph Max is the fount of authority—nevertheless William Keller was bloated with power and loving it.

I had renewed scent-destroyer in a pay toilet, and my new face is good. True, Sharon had known me. But Sharon loved the memory of me, and saw my look of recognition before she ran to me. In Billy Kell (I must learn to call him William Keller) there was no recognition. He came solidly around the desk, shook hands, grandiosely tolerated Walker's backslapping introduction, dismissed Walker with an eyebrow.

Keller didn't spout ideology. He made me stiffly comfortable, and expected me to talk. I did. I used the lighter; I gabbled autobiography interlarded with Party catchwords. I couldn't afford to be as crass as I had been with Walker. At length, contriving to be severe and yet respectful of my white hairs, he said: "I'm interested to know what brought you to us, Mr. Meisel. The Party's greatest strength is among young people. We wake their crusading spirit, give them something to believe in—that's why nothing can stop us. People with your background are more apt to be hostile. Or tired or discouraged. I'm happy you're here, but tell me more about what made you come."

I wondered: "What if I go around that desk and strangle you into telling all you know?" It was a moment of grueling loneliness, the full weight of nine bad years settling on me. I managed to say: "I think your Leader's personality was a deciding factor, Mr. Keller. I've followed Joseph Max's career—radio, television—and then, well, one morning I woke up wanting to *do* something. . . . I've studied his book. . . ."

He nodded after stern reflection. "The bible of the movement. Can't go wrong if you go by *The Social Organism*—it's all there. And you do seem to have a grasp of the theory—actually not theory: plain social fact. What I want to be sure you understand: this is serious business. We don't play at it, got no patience with dabblers, no time for 'em. . . . There are two types of Party membership: associate and sustaining. Associate membership is for anybody who cares to pay the dues and sign a card. Sustaining is something else again, given only after a period of study. And examination."

"Seems reasonable. Don't know if I could qualify for anything like that. But I do feel I belong at least among the rank and file of the"—I smiled most humbly—"of the Organites."

He asked too softly: "Now where did you hear that word?"

"Why, Mr. Walker said it was to be used in the literature soon."

"Oh. . . ." His mask was cold as a funeral. "It happens he shouldn't have said that." Keller's fingers drummed on the desk. "Since he did, I'm obliged to tell you—that word is *not* going to be used. Some of the Leader's minor advisers considered it at one time. Inappropriate, too open to ridicule. Naturally Max saw the objections at once. I suggest, Mr. Meisel, that you never heard it."

Damn all calibrated jokes. These people are as humorless as the communazis. I stammered pathetically: "Well, of course—I didn't realize——"

"Quite all right. You couldn't know."

"Mr. Keller, would it be possible for me to meet—Him?"

He watched secret meditations, shrugged, and nodded. He looked tired now, in almost a human, sympathy-stirring way. "Sure. Could be arranged. This evening if you're free. Max—by the way, he avoids the Mister: just Max when you meet him the first time—Max has Thursday evening open house for friends of the Party. Take you up myself if you like." He waved away thanks. "Glad to. Another thing—among other members of the Party he does like a certain formality. I think of it as a quirk of greatness. Don't care a damn myself, but when we go there we call him Max and use the Mister for each other, you see?" I nodded reverently. "Drop by at my apartment about eight-thirty if you will. Green Tower Colony, last apartment building up the Esplanade short of the bridge. If you're going back downtown now, a taxi on Eighth Lower Level is the best way to get back uptown to my place. Tell the driver to set the rob for Washington turnoff." He reached for his telephone. "See you then." As I left I heard him ask for Walker's office.

I took wrong lanes among the clattering desks and ran into a snafu of dead ends from which I was rescued by a stenographer. It used up a few minutes. When I reached the lounge Walker was outside at the water cooler. His hyperthyroid gray eyes peered at me blindly, perhaps without recognition. Would a trifling error in the routine of Party terminology have made his big hand quiver so badly he couldn't hold a paper cup?

I wanted to telephone Sharon. But after that interview with the cold and secret thing that used to be Billy Kell I was in a bad reaction, a foul temper. I would have snarled, and scared her, or said too much. I promised myself a talk with her after meeting Max, if

131

it wasn't too late in the evening. I ate a dull dinner alone, then trusted my fortunes and my sacred honor to a taxi driver who whisked me across town and into Eighth Lower Level. In a single-lane entrance radiant with white tile, the motor died of itself; the driver pressed a coin into a wall slot. A panel on his dashboard bloomed in orange light; he touched a tab on it marked *W*. The motor woke without his guidance and the taxi rolled into a mystery of humming and radiance. My driver lit a smoke with both hands off the wheel. "What the hell?"

"First time, bud? Never get used to it myself." He slid to the right, to rest both arms on the back of the seat and face me companionably. By the speedometer, we were doing 120. "Uptown traffic ain't heavy this time of evening. All done with this here Seeing Eye. It ain't human. But you know, bud, it ain't that I'm used to it, but I'm getting so all I think is, hell, here's a chance to stretch. Got a little shocker on the wheel, don't hurt, just reminds you to keep your hands off of it." He yawned.

I watched a blur of lights and pillars. "Ever have any accidents?"

"Not a one, they say. It's the scanner. Gives a once-over, the second you drop in your four bits. I got snagged that way once—points was bad, I hadn't known it. Robbie shunted me over into repair yard just inside the entrance. Repair man's *plenty* human—cost me three bucks and you know what? My fare wouldn't pay it. Sulked. Well, it was a dame with a date to meet. Funny thing, they still get a few folks that think the lower level will take any old car. Got a cop at each entrance to weed 'em out. Damn fool out-of-towners mostly. . . . Here comes the turnoff."

"Already?"

He chortled. We hummed through a subterranean clover leaf and up to an exit, where he sighed and took over the wheel. "Thing of it is," he said, "it ain't human. . . ."

Green Tower Colony is in soaring modern design. Whatever the surfacing material may be, the effect is of green jade with a muted shining. The tower dwarfs the uprights of the bridge, without diminishing the airy pride of a structure now thought of as very old.

Keller's apartment is on the fourteenth floor immediately above the twelfth.

Keller admitted me, absently friendly, tired but not relaxed. At his doorbell two other names were listed: Carl Nicholas and Abraham Brown.

As I entered the elaborate foyer I heard piano practice softened by closed doors. Someone was trying to make sense of the eighth Two-Part Invention of Bach, with fingers and brain by no means ready for it. The same left-hand blunder was repeated twice as Keller took my coat and steered me into a solemnly expensive living room. The player knew the error but hadn't learned that only slow practice could correct it. Though muffled, it created a maddening background of frustration, impatience goaded to futility. "Scotch?" said Keller. "Still a bit too early to go up there."

"Thanks." He busied himself at a fantastic little bar. Something nagged me, besides the stumbling music. Not the lavish evidence of money: I already knew that Max's type of messianic enterprise is a gold mine. The legions of the lonely, the mentally and emotionally starved, the bewildered and resentful, the angry daydreamers—who of them wouldn't chip in five or ten dollars to buy a substitute for God, or Mom, or Big Brother, or the New Jerusalem? It wasn't that: it was something the corner of my eye had noticed as I entered the room and then lost. I rediscovered it while Keller fussed with the drinks. Simply a painting near the arched entrance from the foyer. I had to drift toward it, and stare.

There was a background of melancholy darkness deepening to black. A mirror, and perhaps some light was felt as coming impossibly out of the mirror itself. A young man looked into it. Of him you saw only a bare arm and shoulder, part of an averted cheek; these alone were enough to speak, and poignantly, of extreme youth, whereas the face in the mirror was bitterly knowing with many years. There was in it no grotesque, no exaggeration of age. Taken alone, that sorrowing outward-gazing face might have belonged to a man with thirty or forty difficult and disappointing years behind him. I suppose any imaginative artist might have hit on such a conception, and while the technical skill was great, so is that of a thousand painters. But . . .

"Like it?" said Keller idly, coming behind me with my drink. "Abe gets the damnedest ideas sometimes. Not everybody cares for it."

I put my face in order. "Rather startling work."

"I guess so. He doesn't really work at it, just tosses 'em off."

"Abe—oh, Abraham Brown? I saw the name on your doorbell."

"Uh-huh." He was without suspicion: Will Meisel is quite functional. "Friend of mine, shares this apartment with my uncle and me. He's practicing now, don't like to bust in or I'd introduce you."

I thought: *Your uncle?* "Some other time," I said. "Is he—uh —interested in the Party too?"

"More or less." Keller sat down with his drink, sighed, waved smoke away from his face in a human gesture. "Not really politically conscious. Just a kid, Mr. Meisel. Hasn't found himself. Only twenty-one."

I had to change the subject or betray myself. "Max live near here?"

Keller smiled tolerantly; his eyes said I was a little slow with the drink. "Right upstairs. Penthouse. . . ."

Angelo is alive. I finished my drink, not obsequiously but fast.

A gorilla searched me politely in the penthouse foyer, and Keller apologized for not warning me about it. It's fortunate the grenade fits flat to the skin. Joseph Max was already in a chattering crowd. Keller ran interference for me through a forest of arms, bosoms, cocktail glasses. My mind was downstairs with "Abraham Brown." I believe my foggy abstraction was mistaken for the tongue-tied veneration I was supposed to feel in the presence of a Great Man.

At close range the resemblance to Calhoun ends with the jaw. The rest of the big sallow face is blurred and puttyish under a graying mane. Hyperthyroid eyes like Walker's and with the same weak look, almost of blindness. He probably avoids glasses out of vanity, but of course Max is anything but blind: he had Will Meisel weighed, taped, card-indexed in one smiling glance. I saw in him,

134

Drozma, something of the paranoid intensity of Hitler; not very much of the peevish intellectual fury of Lenin and his mirthless bearded schoolboys; plenty of naked power hunger, but very little of the genuine ruggedness we associate with Stalin or Attila or Huey Long. Max is in the tyrant tradition, but there's a weak core. His first major defeat may be his last—he'll shoot himself or get religion. But the machine he's built won't necessarily crack when he does.

"Mr. Meisel! Mr. Keller spoke of you today. Fine to meet you, sir. Hope you'll want to work right along with us." He has charm.

I said: "This is a great year for America."

Thought that one up all by myself. The large eyes thanked me. I watched him testing the words for a campaign banner. A bright platinum girl blazed a smile at me. Glasses went up in a toast to something or other. At a directive glance from Max, Platinum took me in tow, provided me with a drink, and clung. Miriam Dane, and a smoldering bundle she is.

Vividly, self-consciously female. Her mouth is unhappily petulant when she forgets to smile. She has an air of listening for something that might call her any moment. She was practicing little-girl awe at anything that fell from my lips. I guess I'm into the Party, Drozma, if I choose to play it that way. But now that I know *Angelo is alive,* all bets are off. I have no plan beyond tomorrow morning, when I shall go to that apartment after Keller should have left for his office.

Miriam was watching for someone, and presently asked: "Abe Brown didn't come up with you and Bill, did he?" Her hand wandered toward a solitaire diamond on her finger as she spoke.

"No, he was practicing. I didn't even meet him. . . . Honey, I'm a horribly observant old man." I beamed a Santa Claus look on the diamond. "Abe Brown?"

There was something wrong with her little act of cute annoyance. It was acting twice removed: meant to look like pretty irritation hiding pleasure, what it hid was not pleasure but some sort of confusion. "You don't miss much, Mr. Meisel—can I call you Will? Yes, that's how it is." And then she was introducing me here and

135

there. I shook something moist and unappetizing that belonged to Senator Galt of Alaska, and he brayed. Has a hirsute fringe like William Jennings Bryan.

And Carl Nicholas. Yes, Drozma. Max's big room was so full of smoke and women's perfumes that I did not distinguish the scent from Keller's until Miriam took me over to meet him. Gross, ancient, pathetic. His Salvayan eyes are far down in morbid flesh. The nine years have brought him into our change of old age, Drozma. And whereas you, my second father, accepted the change graciously as you accept all inevitable things, and spoke of it once in my presence as your "assurance of mortality," this Abdicator, this Namir—why, he's a bottle imp, irreconcilable, locked up in fat and weakness and still aching to overturn an uninterested universe. He wheezed and touched my hand but hardly looked at me, intent on Max's performance. Nevertheless I was worried and escaped quickly. Miriam said under her breath: "Poor guy, he can't help it, gives me the creeps though. Know I shouldn't feel that way. He's done a lot for the Party, Max thinks everything of him." She patted my arm. "You're nice. Silly, aren't I?"

"No," I said. "You ain't. Just young and slim." She liked that. "You're—full time in Party work, Miriam?"

"Oops!" She round-eyed her lovely face at me. "Didn't you know? Little me, I'm secretary to—Him." The eyes indicated Max's gaunt grandeur and misted over. "It's wonderful. I just never get used to it." After a pause resembling silent prayer (no, I don't dislike Miriam: she's funny and pretty and I think she's going to get hurt) she took me to see Max's famous collection of toy soldiers.

They have a room apart: broad tables, glass-covered cases. Red Indians, Persians, Hindus on elephants, Redcoats, Dutchmen of the Armada. Some are old; one set resembled some I saw at the Museum in Old City—French medieval. They say Max plays with them when he can't sleep. A quirk of greatness? That room was dim when we entered. Miriam turned on overhead lights, disturbing a muttered conversation of two men in shadow at the far end. Miriam ignored them, leading me from case to case. One of them

136

was Daniel Walker, and his smooth round face was ravaged, desolate. The other—old, white-haired, taller than I, absurdly cadaverous—was far gone in drink, glassy-eyed, holding himself upright with silly dignity. As we left, Miriam whispered: "The old man, that's Dr. Hodding. . . ."

Same Hodding, Drozma. Late of the Wales Foundation, and evidently still with this crowd. I don't get it. May have a chance to dig up something.

Max was showing fatigue, darkness under the eyes, when I shook hands for good night. Interesting, being near enough to a Great Man to notice the bad breath. But what I saw at that leave-taking was not a Great Man but a scared child, the kind who's just put an iron pipe on a railroad track. For that matter I met a really great man once. It makes a difference, a greater ease in meeting malign pygmies such as Joseph Max. I visited the White House in 30,864. One doesn't forget.

New York
Friday afternoon, March 10

3   Through the thick apartment door I heard limping footsteps, and turned my changed face away, though I knew I would never be any readier to look at what nine years had done. The door was opening. It was after ten-thirty; I assumed Keller would have gone to work. Namir? To hell with him.

The boy's no taller than Sharon. I realized I was staring at his shoes. No brace; the left sole is thickened. "Mr. Keller home?"

"Why, no. He's at his office." He has a good voice, mature and musical. I had to meet his eyes, which haven't changed. A V-shaped scar over the right one. No recognition. "He left about an hour ago."

"I should've phoned. You must be—Mr. Brown?"

137

"That's right. Phone him from here if you like."

"Well, I . . ." I blundered in past him, a confused and silly old man. "Think I left something here last night. Stopped in for a drink before he took me upstairs to meet Max. You were practicing, I think."

"Left something?"

"Think so. Can't even recollect what—lighter, notebook, some damn thing. Ever have your memory go back on you? Guess not, at your age. Only had a couple of drinks at that. Name's Meisel."

"Oh yes. Bill spoke of you. Look around if you want to."

"Hate to bother you. If I did leave something, guess Mr. Keller's uncle wouldn't've noticed—no, he'd already gone upstairs."

"Mr. Nicholas? Hate to wake him. He's not well, sleeps late——"

"Heavens no, don't bother him. . . . Smoke?"

"Thanks." I used the fancy lighter. While he was intent on the flame I managed for the first time to look directly at his face. The angel of Michelangelo has hurt himself, Drozma. "I'm always forgetting things too," he said. Yes, even at twelve he had that sort of tact.

"Just my eighty-year-old memory playing tricks."

"You don't look eighty, sir." Sir? Because I'm old, I guess. It's an almost obsolete courtesy.

"Eighty just the same," I said, and dropped in an armchair with a grunt. "You have another sixty to go before they call you well preserved."

His beginning smile vanished as he cocked his young head at me. "Haven't we met somewhere?" I couldn't answer; before my eyes found the painting near the foyer entrance, I glimpsed fear in him. "It's your voice," he said. Fear, and defiance too. "I can't place it though."

"Maybe you heard me when I stopped in last night with Keller." He shook his head. "I don't hear anything when I'm practicing." Yes, that dreadful Bach. . . . "Going to music school?"

"No, I—— Maybe next fall. I don't know."

But why was he afraid? "I heard a fine recital Wednesday. New-

138

comer. Sharon Brand. Audience went nuts and no wonder."

"Yes," he said with too much control. "I was there."

So much for our celebrated Martian sixth sense! He was there, re-membering Sharon. Perhaps even near me on that balcony, seeing the gleaming downstream passage of that ship as I saw it. Near enough to touch. And because his mind must have been full of Sharon, perhaps he even remembered me too, now and then—a ghost, a moving shadow. "Splendid talent," I said. "She must've given up everything else for it, to get so far at nineteen. Well, I happen to know she did. Known her since she was a little girl."

I still peered stupidly at the painting, knowing the hand with his cigarette had stopped halfway to his mouth. He said with desperate politeness: "Oh . . . ? What sort of person is she, off the stage?"

"Very lovely." I wanted to yell at him. He should have been bursting with a need to say: *"So have I! So have I!"* "Mr. Keller told me you painted that."

"He shouldn't've hung it there. Most people don't care for it."

"I suppose. . . . Still, why not?"

"Too gloomy maybe. I was trying to find out how Rembrandt made a heavy background mean so much. Unfortunately I'm not an artist, Mr. Meisel. I just . . ." *Not an artist, Angelo?* "Look, I could swear I've heard you speak somewhere, sometime."

I gave it up, Drozma. A revulsion against all pretense. I know: that's the medium in which we Observers must live. Yet if I didn't have that vision of Union within a few centuries I don't think I could stand this swimming in lies. The superimposing of a human lie on our inevitable Martian lie was too much for me, that's all. I slumped back in my chair and watched him helplessly. I said: "Yes, Angelo."

"No . . ." He started toward me. He gazed foolishly at his ciga-rette fallen on the carpet, and did not bend to retrieve it until a feather of smoke was curling upward. "No," he said.

"Nine years."

"I can't believe it. I don't believe it."

"My face?"

139

"Well?"

I shut my eyes and talked into reeling darkness: "Angelo, when I was middle-aged, years before I met you in Latimer, my face was badly injured. A gasoline explosion. I'd been a lot of things before then—actor, teacher (as I told your mother), even a sort of hobo for a while. Shortly before that injury I'd struck it rich—invention, happened to catch on. So I had money, took a chance on a surgeon who was working out a new technique. Prosthetic material I don't begin to understand myself. Unfortunately he had success in only about a third of his attempts, and it raised hell with the failures. Never publicized. He had to give it up. Died a few years ago, knocked himself out trying to develop a test that would eliminate the sixty-odd per cent who couldn't use it. But I was one of his successes, Angelo. What it amounts to: the stuff is malleable under heat; I can alter the cheekbones if I like, and that changes the whole face." A smaller lie anyway: one that needn't cloud our relation—if we were to have any relation. "I did that, when I left Latimer. Took on a new personality, as most people can't readily do. There was a possibility the police would think I had something to do with your disappearance, and Feuermann's. Do you remember Jacob Feuermann?"

"Of course," he whispered, and I could look at him. "What—what became of Uncle Jacob?"

I wobbled on the edge of forbidden truth. "Disappeared, same night you did. All we ever knew. Tried to find you maybe. As I have."

"Find me. . . . Why?"

I didn't even try to answer that. "Do you believe I'm Ben Miles?"

"I—don't know."

"Remember the headstone of Mordecai Paxton?"

"Mordecai . . . Why, yes."

"Ever tell anyone, who might have passed word to me (whoever I am), that you put dandelions around that headstone?"

"No, I—never did." And Namir was somewhere close by—sleeping? The doors were closed, our voices very low.

"Did you ever tell anyone about that mirror?"

"Oh! No, never." He sat on the floor by my chair, his head on his knees. "You must have had better things to do than look for me."

"No. I still have that mirror, Angelo."

"Abraham. Abraham Brown, please."

"All right, it's a good name."

"I had—reasons, for taking it in place of my own."

"Well," I mumbled, "what's a self? I've lived a long time and don't know. . . . Glad to see me?" A stumbling human question.

He looked up and tried to smile along with his muttered "Yes." A smile of confusion.

"What do you want to do, Abraham? Music?"

"I don't know." He stood clumsily and walked to the painting, his back to me; lit another smoke as if cruelly hungry for it. "Bill got me a piano a year ago. I—oh, I work at it."

"Mm. Billy Kell."

He didn't look around. "So you recognized him too."

"Newspaper photograph. Looked him up on the chance he'd be in touch with you. I'm pretending to be interested in the Organic Unity Party."

"Only pretending, huh? You never liked Bill, did you?"

"No. . . . Look at me, Abraham."

He wouldn't. "Bill Keller and his uncle have done everything for me. They saved my life, really. A chance to start over, when——" He stopped.

"I met your fiancée last night, at Max's." He just grunted. "Keller and his crowd didn't buy your brain, Abraham. You know that gang of power-hunters isn't your dish. You can't look at me and say it is."

"Don't!" He choked on it, but wouldn't turn around, and somehow there was little force in his protest. "My brain! If you knew— if I had a good one, would I be——" Again he couldn't go on.

"How long have you been Abraham Brown?"

"Ever since I was picked up in K.C. for breaking a window."

141

"What did they do with you?"

"Home for the homeless. Reform school—we weren't supposed to call it that. The court was my legal guardian. Unfortunately it was a jeweler's window, though I hadn't noticed it."

"Kansas City—that was soon after you left Latimer?"

"Soon? I guess." He spoke as though suddenly indifferent whether he relived this dream of the past or not. "Latimer—I simply walked away. Junk yard, patch of woods, think I slept there. Didn't eat anything for two or three days. Later I happened on a rail siding, couple of hobos gave me a hand up. Kansas City. They wanted me to stick with them, but I didn't belong—not with them or anywhere——"

"Wait a minute——"

"You wait a minute. I've never belonged anywhere. I wasn't even a good hobo, so I walked out on 'em." He faced me at last, quickly as if to catch me off guard. "I didn't want anything. Can you understand that? Can you? Twelve years old, hungry, not a cent, but I did—not—*want* anything! Oh, Christ, there's not a worse God-damn thing in the world—well, all right, I saw that plate-glass window—late at night—nice half brick in the gutter, so I thought: '*Here!* Suppose I do that, maybe it'll make me interested in something'—like a nightmare—you try to wake yourself up by hurting yourself. . . ."

"Was it interesting?"

"Made a hell of a fine smash. . . . I graduated six years later."

"Never told about the real past?"

"I did not." He grinned savagely. "History's a process of selection, remember, Mr. Miles?"

"I met some of your mother's relatives after her death. Nice people."

"They were nice people," said Abraham Brown. "At the school I told three or four different stories. Safer than faking amnesia. They followed up the first two or three, you see, and then decided I was a pathological liar. K.C.'s a long way from Massachusetts. Homeless kids a dime a dozen."

"Are they, Abraham?"

"That was the impression I received for six years."

"And it was important not to go back to Latimer?"

"Do you understand *your* mind?"

"No. But you're still the boy who was interested in ethics——"

"Oh, Ben!"

"And you're still blaming yourself for your mother's death: I want you to stop that."

He stared blindly, but not without understanding. "Who else——"

"Why blame anyone? Dunn maybe, for hauling you in there without warning and looking like the wrath of God, but he was merely doing his job as he saw it. Why blame anyone? Is blame so important?"

"Yes, if it reminds me that I'm capable of spoiling anything I touch—reminds me never to love anyone too much, or care too much——"

I scrambled up and caught hold of his wrists. "That's one of the worst damn-fool monkey traps in the world. And there you are, with the biggest mind and heart I'll ever know, running circles inside the trap with your tail in your teeth. You think nobody ever got hurt before? You've got life, and you're saying: 'Oh no, there're flies on it, take it away!' "

"I'll live," he said, and tugged at his wrists a little. "Miriam, for instance, she's just my size, a nice brassbound decorator's job with her heart in the right place and I don't mean her chest." I guess he was trying to hurt me with words thrown back in my face. "Just bitchy enough so I don't have to care whether I'm in love with her or not——"

"Nuts! She's a harmless little woman who could be hurt like anybody else. I think you got engaged to her because Keller and Nicholas and maybe Max planned it that way."

"What!"

"Yes. . . . What happened after you graduated?"

143

He stopped pulling at his frail wrists. "Oh, I—saw Bill on a telecast. Hitchhiked to New York. That's all. What did you——"

"Three years ago?"

"Two."

"After a year of what, Abraham?"

"What did you mean about—Keller and Nicholas——"

"Skip it—I could be wrong, if I am I'm sorry. Tell me about that year after you graduated, Abraham."

"I—oh, I'd never make a good criminal, I'm simply one of the school's failures. Matter of fact I was a good boy. Grease monkey in a filling station for a month, till they missed something out of the cash register. Hadn't taken it, but there was the record. Couple of dishwashing jobs. Not good at that either. Often wondered if I'd make a good flagpole sitter——"

"Why not stop whipping yourself?"

"Ever sleep in a barrel, Mr. Meisel?"

The doorbell rang. "Abraham, you must promise me never to tell Keller or Nicholas or anyone about knowing me in Latimer."

He looked up with his wounded, half-cruel smile. "I *must* promise?"

"If anything connected me with that ancient history, it could mean my life." His anger vanished. "Like you, Abraham, I'm vulnerable."

He asked softly with no wrath at all: "Outside the law?"

The bell rang again, long, urgently. "Yes, in a way, and I can't explain it. If you ever spoke of that it could be a death sentence."

He said with immediate sincerity: "Then I won't speak of it." I let go his wrists. He limped into the foyer, where I heard him exclaim: "Hey, take it easy! Are you ill, Dr. Hodding?"

He looked ill, that old man, so ill and changed that without hearing his name I might have failed to recognize him from the evening before. He had been drunk then, fish-eyed drunk. Now there were fires in his cheeks; his necktie was under one ear, his silvery hair wild. He lurched past Abraham as if the boy were intrusive furniture. "Walker—let me see Walker——"

144

"Dan Walker? He isn't here. Haven't seen him for days."

"Well, damn the thing, boy, you know where he is."

"But I don't."

I stepped forward. Hodding looked frantic enough for physical violence. But then he shuddered and collapsed in the chair I had abandoned. "Not at the office," he said, and fumbled at his wrinkled lips. "I called." He noticed me and croaked weakly: "Brown, who the devil is that?"

"Friend of mine. Look, *I* don't know, haven't heard any-thing——"

"You will. You will if you don't find him. You'll see——"

One whose voice I remembered said: "Hodding, cut that out!"

He stood in the silently opened doorway, massive and sodden. His bulk was wrapped in a huge black and orange dressing gown almost hiding the wobbling columns of his ankles. His artificial hair is appropriately white; it was rumpled from the pillow, not much whiter than bloated slabs of cheek.

He still has power. He glanced unconcernedly at Abraham and me. He walked—not a waddle but relentless rolling motion—to stand over Hodding with a mountain's calm. Hodding was choking. "Ten years. Ten stupid years ago, that's when I should've died——"

"You're hysterical," said Nicholas-Namir.

"That strange?" Hodding groaned. "You people bought me—I didn't bargain much, did I? Damn the thing, I was sincere, too. I thought——"

Nicholas slapped him. "Get up, man!"

Hodding stood, weaving like a dry weed in the wind. "You've got to find Walker. He's crazy. I am too, or I wouldn't—listen, Nicholas, I was drunk. I let him get in there—yes, sure, into the laboratory. Last night. I was drunk. I must've told him. And now——"

"Be quiet. Come in the back room."

"Never mind *me,* damn the thing. You've got to find Walker——"

Nicholas raised his puffy hand again. Hodding cringed. "Back room. You need a drink. Quit worrying. I'll take care of everything."

"But Walker——"

"I can find Walker." While Abraham and I stood bewildered and silly, they were gone. The door closed without a slam.

"Abraham, what was that all about?—if you know."

He said shortly: "I don't."

"They worked on virus mutations at the Wales Foundation. Before Dr. Hodding left the place. . . . Got a laboratory of his own now?"

"How would I—hell, yes, you heard him speak of it."

"Money and incentive supplied by the Organic Unity Party?"

"Ben, I don't have anything to *do* with all that, with—with the Party. And why should you?"

"I shan't, from now on. It was just a device for getting in touch with Keller, in the hope of finding you."

"Well," he said emptily, "you found me. But why question me about the Party?" He was frightened. In some limited, unwilling way, he was lying to me. "I'm not even a member, and nobody's urged me to join. I just live here."

There was an answer to that, but he knew it as well as I. "Abraham, come and have lunch with me. We need to talk about a lot of things."

He moved away. "I ought to be practicing. . . ."

"I saw Sharon Wednesday evening, after the recital. I think I'll see her again this evening. Will you come along?"

He was far away across the room, pressing his forehead against the coolness of window glass. Presently he said: "No. . . . She wouldn't remember me. That was childhood. Can't you understand?"

"She does remember you of course. We talked of you."

"Then let her remember the kid she used to play with, and leave me out of it. Ben, please understand. All right—I've got a brain. I was a damned prodigy, and ran away from it. Because I couldn't stand what my brain showed me. So I'm a coward. Born one."

"You use an imaginary cowardice as a shield."

He winced at that, but went on as if I had not spoken: "And the only way I can keep from going nuts is *not to think at all.* You mean well. But you're trying to stir me up into being something important. I don't think I could. I don't think I want to be anything."

"Except maybe a musician?"

"Different sort of thinking. You never meet anything mean or cruel in music. I'd like to be able to play Bach before they blow up the world. I'd like to be at the keyboard when they do it."

"Quite sure they're going to?"

"Aren't they?"

"I wouldn't even dare predict whether the baby will have a harelip. Will you come and have lunch with me?"

"I'm sorry."

"Tomorrow? Meet me tomorrow noon, Blue River Café?"

"I'm—going away for the week end."

I wrote my address on a notebook leaf and tore it out. "Keep this somewhere, Abraham." He reached for it, red-faced, miserable at his refusal but not changing it. The voices of Namir and Hodding were blurred noise beyond the door. I think Abraham watched me as I went out. I don't know. . . .

New York
Friday midnight, March 10

4 I wrote that last entry here in my apartment only a few hours ago. I feel so changed tonight that the day seems a long time past. When I finished writing this afternoon I telephoned Sharon Brand. I told her nothing of Abraham: she didn't ask, unless some of her silences were questions. I invited myself to call on her and Sophia Wilks in the evening. They live in Brooklyn. Yes, I

147

remember you did too for a few months, Drozma; 30,883, wasn't it
—the year the bridge was opened to traffic? It's still in use, parts
of it a hundred years old. (Don't know yet how the Dodgers are
shaping up this spring.) I needed Sharon, if only to remind me that
I don't always blunder. . . . Now it is midnight, and I imagine
new sounds out there, underneath the city's murmurous quiet. They
are not there: my mind is creating them because I am frightened.

Drozma, you must have often reviewed the logic of our Observers' laws. By what right do we intrude on Abraham's or any other
life?

No right at all, I should say, since "right" in this case would
imply the existence of a superworldly authority dispensing privi-
leges and prohibitions. We Salvayans are agnostics born. Having
neither belief nor dogmatic disbelief in any such authority, we interfere in human affairs simply because we can; because, conceitedly
or humbly, we hope to promote human good and diminish human
evil, so far as we ourselves can know good and evil. How far is that?

After three and a half centuries I have found, for an empirical
ethics, no better starting axiom than this: cruelty and evil are vir-
tually synonyms. Human ethical teachers have insisted over the
ages that a cruel act is an evil act, and men on the whole endorse
the doctrine no matter how repeatedly they violate it. There is
inevitable revulsion against any blatant attempt to make cruelty
a law of behavior. Unrecognized cruelties, cruelties generated by
primitive fears or sanctified by institutional habit—these may continue for centuries; but when human nature sees Caligula in his
plainest shapes it will vomit him up and sicken at the memory.
Conversely, I recognize nothing as evil unless cruelty is its dominant element. Here, manifestly, human nature isn't quite so willing
to follow the logic through. To satisfy semantic order, one must
distinguish between mindless cruelty and the malevolent sort. It's
a humanly evil thing if a tiger chews a man, but the tiger is impersonal as lightning or avalanche, merely getting his dinner with
no malevolence involved. A butcher killing a lamb is similarly
impersonal, and I think he drives a rather decent bargain, though

148

an articulate lamb might bleat reproach at me for saying so: the lamb's juicy little carcass in return for a sheltered, well-fed life and a death more merciful than nature is at all likely to provide. If the term "cruelty" is allowed to include the non-malevolent causes of suffering I think the axiom will stand. I notice that a massive amount of human cruelty is non-malevolent, a result of ignorance or inertia or simple bad judgment and misinterpretation of fact.

It doesn't follow that any such mild and limited conception as kindness is synonymous with good. Men trick themselves with the illusion that good and evil are neat opposites: one of the mental short cuts that turn out to be dead-end traps. Good is a far wider and more inclusive aspect of life. I see its relation to evil as little more than the relation of coexistence. But evil nags us, obsesses us like a headache, while we take good for granted as we take health for granted until it is lost. Yet good is the drink, evil only a poison that is sometimes in the dregs: in the course of living we are likely to shake the glass—no fault of the wine. It is good to sit quiet in the sun: there is no nicely balanced opposing evil to that. Where is there any matching evil to a hearing of the G Minor Fugue? As absurd as asking, What is the opposite of a tree? Recognizing many partial ambivalences between birth and death, we overlook their partial quality and are fooled into supposing that ambivalence is exact and omnipresent. It seems to me that men and Martians will never be very wise until they carry their thinking much further beyond the sign language of deceptive and tempting pictures. I would defy anyone to measure, as in a scale, even the homely equipoise of night and day.

If I must justify my actions on the impersonal level (and I think I should), I concern myself with the life of Abraham Brown because I believe him to have potentially great insight. If I am right, he is bound to train that insight (he cannot help himself) on the more dangerous and urgent of human troubles. If he can reach maturity without disaster, with that growing insight fully grown, I don't know why he shouldn't aid others of his breed to hold the glass steady and throw away the dregs. His means might be any of

149

several—artistic creation, ethical teaching, even political action; that question is secondary, I think. It is certainly not his intelligence alone that made me search nine years for him. Intelligence alone is nothing, or worse: Joseph Max is damned intelligent. Nor is it his heart, which is wounded and confused, nor is it his present self. His present self can be foolish, timid, and disagreeable, as I found out this afternoon. No: in Angelo (and in Abraham) there was and there remains a blend of intelligence, curiosity, courage, and good will. The intelligence is perplexed and tormented by the enormous complexity of life outside him and within. His curiosity and courage, reinforced by blind chance and the inevitable loneliness of the intelligent, have brought him face to face at twenty-one with more ugliness than his heart is ready to endure— he will see greater ugliness in the future, if he lives, and find that his heart is stronger than he thought. His good will is a river blocked with rubbish, but it cannot remain so: it will flow.

I suppose that, like anyone else, Abraham Brown would like to be happy now and then before he dies. I have had much happiness, and expect more. I never won it by seeking it. Long ago, when I loved and married Maja, I thought (just like a human being!) that I was engaged in the pursuit of happiness. Neither she nor I ever found it until we stopped searching; until we learned that love is no more to be possessed than sunshine and that the sun shines when it will. When she survived the difficult birth of Elmaja, we were richly happy, I remember. If one must hunt a reason for happiness, I say it was because we were living to the full extent of our natures: we had our work, our child, our companionship; the sun was high. After I lost her at the birth of our son, my next happiness came a year later, when I was playing the "Emperor" Concerto with the Old City orchestra, and found that for the first time I knew what to do with that incredible octave passage—you remember it: the rolling storm diminishes and dies away without a climax, where anyone but Beethoven would have written *crescendo*. I understood then (I think I understood) why he did not. My hands conveyed my understanding, and I was happy, no longer

150

enslaved by a backward-looking grief but living as best I could—not a bad best. And so I think that if his maturing mind can guide him through the complex into the simple, if his curiosity and courage can show him the relative smallness of a reform school in Kansas City, if the river of his good will can find its channel, Abraham Brown will be happy enough, more than most. And I think, with all respect to one of the most vital of human documents, that the pursuit of happiness is an occupation of fools.

Drozma, if you're as clever as I know you are, you may deduce from the tone of these reflections that I have already seen Abraham again. That is true. He is in the next room, a room of his own if he cares to use it so. I don't think Max's people have followed him here, but I don't intend to sleep anyway, and I dare say I could handle any of them. There may be a worse thing abroad in the city, or perhaps beyond the city by now, a thing before which the human or Martian mind winces and draws back, refusing belief. Abraham thinks it's there. I am still able to doubt, to cherish a hope that he could be wrong. Being helpless in any case to act against it tonight, I stay awake in partial contemplation, and have written these subjective matters for you, Drozma, with a sense that there may be no opportunity for such things in the days and nights coming toward us. Abraham is sleeping off a pill I prescribed. It should hold him in peace until morning. He snores occasionally, rather like a puppy who's run himself ragged during the day. Now about Sharon:

It's still tough to find your way around Brooklyn: good thing for humanity, to hang onto a few problems it just never can solve. Nowadays you can go over in a new tunnel equipped with an electronic road—Robbie-roads they call 'em—which is actually a continuation of Second Avenue Lower Level. Sharon had claimed that if I took the Greene Avenue turnoff I couldn't miss it—sure, she's human. Maybe I couldn't, but my taxi could. We got lightly involved in something that was called Greenpoint, it didn't say why, and then we tried a handsome avenue which gradually became more or less Flatbush. In the course of time we located Sharon's

151

quiet street, away the other side of Prospect Park. She was right about the turnoff, I'm sure, only we were supposed to turn right after leaving it and then do some other rights and lefts and then— the hell with it. Next time I'll use the subway.

The apartment house is a sort of colony of musicians, refugees from exasperated neighbors. A feminine living room, but Sharon's studio is severe as a laboratory—nothing but the piano, a bookcase, a few chairs. No decoration at all, not even the conventional bust of Chopin or Beethoven. When she took me in there I said: "Not even one flower vase?" And she said: "Nup."

But that was later. When I arrived she was maturely concerned with getting a drink in my hand and surrounding me with cushions. Almost a snowstorm of cushions. I could have done without them, but it made Sharon happy to work away at it, inserting a cushion here and a damn cushion there, wherever I had or might have a bone. Some of them spilled when I stood up to shake hands with Mrs. Wilks, but Sharon got them back. Laughing at herself, but quite determined. Inexorable. And pretty enough to make you want to cry out loud.

To Mrs. Wilks I was an ancient ex-teacher and musicologist, old enough to remember hearing Rachmaninoff in Boston almost fifty years ago. I had taught "out West" until my health began to fail. I was fascinated by Sharon's talent, and had introduced myself when I "happened to recognize" her at the Blue River Café. The lies come so easily, Drozma! I didn't mind that one too much. Sharon was quite willing to collaborate on it. It would have been impractically difficult to explain a resurrected Ben Miles to Sophia Wilks, for she has aged greatly in the human way. In every part of life except music and Sharon's welfare, Sophia has grown dim and forgetful. Faraway memories have taken on a present life, confusing her. She met me graciously, but did not even ask to "see" my face with her fingers. She settled in what was evidently her accustomed corner of the living room with some complex knitting, aware of us but not quite with us, tranquil among images not ours. When she joined the conversation, as she did only two or three

152

times, her remarks were not completely apropos, and once she spoke in Polish, which Sharon has never learned. However, by unspoken consent, Sharon and I did not talk then about Angelo. . . .

I had bought a late-edition newspaper on my way over, and stuffed it in my overcoat without a glance. Coming back from the kitchen with a second martini for me, Sharon pulled out the paper for a look at the headlines and said: "Huh!" I got up, spilling cushions but holding fast to the drink, and looked over her shoulder. Because it was an ugly and tragic thing which might have disturbed Sophia to no purpose, Sharon made no more comment except for a silent finger on the black front-page type:

UNITY PARTY WORKER PLUNGES TO DEATH
Leaps Thirty Stories from Max's Penthouse

"Let me show you the studio," said Sharon. She hovered briefly by Sophia's chair. "Comfortable, darling?"

"Yes, Sharon." Sharon inserted a cushion or two to be on the safe side. She hooked a finger in my shirt so that I could walk, drink, and read the paper at the same time.

March 10. Daniel Walker, 34, a worker at the offices of the Organic Unity Party, jumped to his death late this afternoon from the thirtieth-story penthouse of party leader Joseph Max. Mr. Max told police that Walker had apparently suffered a nervous breakdown from overwork. Walker had called at the penthouse earlier in the day, in what Mr. Max described as a "distressed and incoherent" state. He was alone in a room of the penthouse while Mr. Max spoke on the roof garden with other visitors, among whom were Senator Galt of Alaska and video actor Peter Fry. Walker ran outside and climbed the parapet before the others sensed his intention. He stood there some moments; witnesses agree that his speech was incoherent. Then he either lost his balance or jumped, falling thirty stories to the Esplanade.

Mr. Walker was unmarried, a native of Ohio. He is survived by his mother, Mrs. Eldon Snow, and a brother, Stephen Walker, both of Cincinnati.

153

That was when I looked around the good sober studio and made my maundering contribution about a flower vase. "Nup," said Sharon. "Ben, you're acting different, as if something had happened. Come clean."

"I found him."

"Ah?" She whispered it, and caught hold of my coat lapels and stared up a long time, trying, I think, to learn without words what finding him had done to me. "He—is he mixed up the way you thought he might be, with those"—she nodded in distaste at the paper—"those people?"

"Yes, indirectly." I told her everything—everything in the way of fact, that is. In trying to describe what Abraham Brown was like in this year 1972, I probably made a mess of it. "He heard your debut. He thinks you wouldn't remember him. . . ."

"Reform school—poor kid!" But I hadn't made him real to her as a person: words can't do that. She was still concerned with what might be happening to me, and though it was sweet and flattering, I wished she would abandon that preoccupation.

"I met Walker yesterday. A sort of greeter for high-class suckers, and rather good at it. He pulled a very small boner on Party slanguage, and I believe Billy Kell alias William Keller reamed him out for it."

"So for that he jumps off the roof?"

"I had a glimpse of him when I was leaving the office. Keller'd had him on the phone. Walker looked as if he'd had it—between the eyes."

"And this—Hodding?"

"I don't know, sugar. And I'm sure Abraham didn't. It's like seeing only the tail of a beast vanishing behind a tree."

She shivered, thrust her hands into her hair, looked for comfort to her other friend in the room, the piano. "Not that I know beans about politics, seems like a terrible lot of noise for small returns, but I did join the Federalist Party a while back. Infant school branch, seeing the lady's under twenty-one. Card and everything,

154

heck. Was that sense, Ben—I do mean Will, Will—or was I swope off my feet by good dialectic?"

"I like their views."

"You're going to try to get Angelo away from those neo-nazis?"

"He must get away under his own power."

"And if he doesn't?" She studied me with worried tenderness. "What if he's sold on their stuff and spits in your eye?" Somehow I must make her stop thinking about me.

"He isn't and wouldn't. He hasn't changed that much, not down inside. He's tied by gratitude to Keller for practical kindnesses— as I don't doubt Keller meant he should be. Trapped into loyalty toward something that's foreign to him, a loyalty with roots dangerously deep in childhood. He's still the boy who admired Billy Kell. Funny: I just remembered watching you and Angelo bury that little pup of his in the back yard. You probably didn't know I was in my window. You were wrassling a chunk of paving stone— I remember the way your skinny little behind stuck up in the air——"

"Mister! My present dignity!"

"Well, previously you'd been sitting on something dusty, you and your white drawers. Yes, the old things come back."

"Ah, they come back!" she said. "Or they've never gone away."

"The cloud-capped towers—look at them again, Sharon."

"Why, we had a country, Ben, one of our own. A year or so before you came to Latimer. It began at a special crack on the sidewalk of Calumet Street, a twisty crack that looked like S and A together. . . ."

"Go on, Sharon."

"We'd known for a long time that the country was there. And speculated about it. The population was primitive, or say quasi-medieval—mighty high percentage of kings and villainous viziers, afreets all the time monkeying around, heck, you couldn't hold 'em. . . . Angelo drew a gorgeous map of the place, so I had to draw one too, only his was better. I had a river going right over

155

a mountain range, he wouldn't stand for that. It was *my* river, and I got mad, so"—she pressed light finger tips over her eyelids—"so he said, 'Well, then it's a river that goes underground, under the mountains.' And redrew his own map to accommodate it, worked swell—caverns and subterranean lakes and stuff. . . ."

"There might have been a blue-white light that came from nowhere, and your voices came back to you from the wet rocks."

"Oh—*you'd* know! Well, one day we decreed that we'd step over that crack at last in a certain way, and remain in—the name of the country was Goyalantis—remain there as long as we chose. Of course to others it looked as if we were still in this world. A necessary convention. We felt quietly sorry for the poor souls because they'd look at us (and oh! even make us wash and comb our hair and eat oatmeal and not say damn) and they'd think we were with them when heaven knows we weren't at all. We stayed— in fact I don't remember any ceremony of coming back. I think we never did bother to come back." She opened her eyes, and they were swimming. "Your hands haven't changed. Play for me."

Small stuff. One of Field's sentimental nocturnes I happened to remember, because there was a warming night of March beyond the windows. And then the First Prelude of Chopin, as Sharon had taught me it might be played. She was looking down at me, but seeing Goyalantis too, never having left it, and though there were colored mists in Goyalantis, its air could be crystal, a crystal lens for observation of this other world which is not alone in possession of a special seeing we like to call truth. She said: "I wasn't mistaken."

"About what, dear?"

"About you. You see, I never believed you were dead. I remember flatly denying it when I was told. I think I went on denying it, though I learned I couldn't talk about you even to Mother Sophia. I knew all along that the 'Waldstein,' at the recital—that it was for you. You know, they didn't want me to program it—even Mother Sophia didn't like having it follow the Carr suite. But it had to be there. As I knew three years ago when I started serious toiling over it. . . ." She added, so softly that I barely heard it above an idle chord I had touched: "You want me to see him?"

"Only if *you* want to."

"I'm afraid to, Ben."

"Then let it wait. But he hasn't left Goyalantis."

"Do you *know* that?"

"Almost."

"But maybe he ought to leave it. It's good country for me. I live with dream stuff, and now they're beginning to pay me for it, bless 'em. But for Angelo? You said he was trying for music."

"Miserably. Fighting it. Like this." I spoiled a few measures of the Two-Part Invention as Abraham had done. Sharon winced. "Then goes back and plays it again—same way, *du lieber Gott!*"

"That won't help," said Sharon Brand. "Think he's reaching for what he can't ever have?"

"Kid with both hands full of cake reaches for a plum and drops the cake. But you could judge of that better than I."

She laughed, not happily. "You get sort of wicked now and then. Oh, you know I'll see him—sometime soon. Feminine curiosity."

"I'll settle for feminine curiosity."

I left early, for I learned that Sharon had been working hard that day. An appearance with the Philharmonic, in response to popular demand, had been arranged for April, a first fruit of her triumph. Time to prepare for it was short. She was to give the Franck Symphonic Variations, and told me she still had the thing only three-quarters memorized. Wasn't worried about it either —brr!

The door of my apartment was locked. But I had left it off the latch, on the chance that Abraham might come while I was away— sneering at myself for such a hope but compelled to act on it. Now I had trouble with the key.

The light was off when I opened the door and glimpsed the coal of his cigarette. He knocked a lamp over by groping, laughed helplessly as I found the wall switch. "Graceful," he said, and lost his cigarette trying to retrieve the lamp. We got straightened

157

around. He was glad to see me, ashamed, scared. He said: "The c-cat came back. Kind of singed."

"Did you think I was sore?"

"You had a right to be."

"Nah. Hold everything." I mixed him my Double Grenade: three fingers brandy to one of applejack. Nobody can like it, but if you already feel ghastly, it likes you. Abraham gasped and commented: "Why'd they bother to split the atom?"

"Go another?"

"Soon as I get the burnt meat out of my throat, not right away. . . ."

"I read about Walker in the paper."

He shuddered, not at the drink. "What're they saying?"

"They quote Max: nervous breakdown from overwork."

"And that's all?"

"His speech was incoherent, it says here."

"It wasn't, Ben. I was there."

"Will—Will Meisel. Get used to it. Could be important."

"I'm sorry. I'll try. I've thought of you the other way."

I built a milder drink. "Take this one slow. It's supposed to glaze over the charred spots." He was looking at horror, and words wouldn't come. But his young face was not, as it had been this morning, a battleground. It was the face of a sleeper beginning to wake—to a most ugly day, but at least waking. "Abe, suppose I run through what I know or guess. You catch me up if I have any facts wrong." He nodded gratefully. "Daniel Walker is—was—a man for big emotional conversions. He couldn't just step out of the Organic Unity Party. If he fell out of love with it he'd have to hate it, probably with a phase of hating the whole world and everyone in it. Call him manic-depressive, for a label. No middle ground: all black and white for Daniel Walker. I was at the Party office twice yesterday. Walker slipped up, told me something that was out of favor, already obsolete when I went back in the afternoon. Keller jumped on him for it. Walker's mind flopped over on its other side. Much faithful service and then a kick in the teeth——"

158

"Bill? Bill jumped on him?"

"Yes. Had him on the phone, and I happened to see Walker afterward on my way out. Looked sandbagged. So—Walker, in his tailspin, and Dr. Hodding, pie-eyed drunk, conferred last night. I saw 'em at Max's, among the pretty toy soldiers. Then Walker got into Hodding's laboratory and took—something." Abraham whitened under his tan; I was afraid the glass would jump from his hand. "Just guessing: a new virus?"

He managed to set his glass on the floor. "New. Can be airborne. Indefinitely viable, and no defenses in the human—no, no!—*mammalian* organism, that's what Dr. Hodding was mumbling when —well, Mr. Nicholas gave him sleeping powders, after you left, but, poor devil, he wasn't quite out, he started mumbling and tossing on the bed after Mr. Nicholas went upstairs and left me with him. Mammalian—it isn't just us, Ben—Will—it's everything. Medium of distribution too—some stuff like pollen—green——"

"Slow down, boy. Walker did get it, then?"

"Yes."

"Contagious-plus, of course."

"Respiratory system. He kept muttering about his monkeys and hamsters. Kept saying: 'Macacus rhesus eighty-five per cent.' I don't know if that meant mortality. I think it did. Neurotoxin. Reaches the nervous system through the respiratory. Spinal paralysis. . . ."

"And Walker?"

"Had it with him this afternoon. I stayed with Hodding—hours, I guess—chewing my damn nails, not knowing anything to do. Bill came home early, at three. Hodding was sound asleep then. Bill went up to Max's. I tagged along, don't think he wanted me to. They were out on the roof garden: Senator Galt sounding off about nothing much, Max pretending to listen. Miriam was there. That drip Peter Fry. Mr. Nicholas"—Abraham was shaking all over, reaching toward the drink but not taking it up—"Nicholas, taking it easy in a lounge chair built to hold him. God, what a beautiful afternoon! Warm. . . . I don't think Galt and Fry knew

159

Walker was there in the penthouse. I saw Miriam was worried about something, got her alone a second and asked. She started to tell me something about Walker in there building up a jag, but right then he came tearing out, ran to the parapet. Nobody could've stopped him, but nobody tried. He was balancing there with that—that damned peewee test tube, looked like green powder. Waved it at us. He was yelling: 'Airborne! Airborne!' He wasn't incoherent. Laughing like crazy, but wasn't incoherent. He flung it out over the Esplanade—must've shattered into dust, you wouldn't even find the cork. Then he went after it. Not like jumping. Like floating out, as if he thought he could fly. . . . Max—Max had some kind of fit. Heart maybe. Turned white and started to fold. I think Miriam took care of him. Mr. Nicholas said: 'Get the kid out of here!' And Bill hustled me downstairs. I didn't see the police. The others must have agreed to say nothing about me, I don't know why they bothered. Police didn't hear about Bill's being there either, I think. He stayed with me, couple of hours, I guess, until somebody phoned down from Max's and he went back up there. Then I—then I——"

"Then you came to me. Do they know you're here?"

"I don't think so. Just walked out, didn't meet anybody." He could finish the drink now, the glass rattling against his teeth.

"Are you through with them, Abraham?"

He cried out: "Christ, I had every chance to ask myself, 'What's a political party doing, paying a man to invent—to discover'—I knew! I must have known, and wouldn't look. Just some important abstract research, Bill said—yes, that's something Bill said to me, when I was curious——"

"Quiet down, friend. Probably what Hodding thought himself, at least when it started. He used to be a good scientist. Emotional flaw somewhere, maybe just an overdeveloped ability to kid himself about anything not related to his field——"

"But why didn't I—why didn't I——"

"Why don't you get some sleep?"

He raved then about how he'd only bring trouble to me too.

160

I won't record that. There were questions I could have asked. Nicholas, "taking it easy in a lounge chair," must certainly have known what Walker had with him. Max perhaps didn't know until too late. Max and Nicholas together could surely have overpowered Walker and taken the thing away. I asked none of those questions. I fetched a sleeping pill and made the boy swallow it.

So it's out there, Drozma—probably. I cling to frail scraps of possibility. Walker stole the wrong test tube—no, because Hodding discovered the loss in a horribly sober morning and knew what it meant.

Maybe it's not as "successful" as Hodding thought. He couldn't be positive that the human organism has no defenses. Maybe wind will sweep it away, and factors not discoverable in the laboratory will make it not so viable. Maybe the tube fell unbroken in the river. Oh sure, Drozma, maybe there are "canals" on Mars.

New York
Saturday night, March 11

5   Sunrise was gradual and deep this morning. I sat by one of my living-room windows and saw the grayness above the East River take on a slow flush and then a hint of gold. Spires and rooftops on the Brooklyn side were catching hold of light like cobwebs on the grass after a rain. I watched a tug slip across the river on some errand clothed in magic by the latter end of night. It drew a soft line of smoke on the water, for there was a small breeze out of the east. The line broadened to a pathway, white and gold at my end, total mystery beyond.

Abraham stirred and sighed. Without turning my head, I knew it when he crept into the room with his shoes in his hand. I said: "Don't go."

He set the shoes on the floor and limped toward me in stockinged

161

feet. In that dimness I could see that his face was calm, without anger and perhaps without fear. An empty calm, spent, like despair. "Lordy, didn't you even go to bed?"

"I never need much sleep. You don't need to go, Abraham."

"But I do."

"Well, where?"

"I don't know—haven't thought."

"Not back to Keller and Nicholas."

"No. . . . I can't bring on you the trouble I bring to everyone who knows me."

"That's nothing but vanity upside down. Something made you come here, so why go away?"

"I had to talk to someone who could listen. Selfish need. So I—did talk. But——"

"You never brought any trouble on Keller and Nicholas. They brought it on you. You could see that if you'd look at it straight."

"I don't know. . . ." He knelt at the window sill, staring out with his chin on his arms. "Good, isn't it? And doesn't need the human to be good. Except for eyes to see it. Ears for the boat whistles— that won't be there if—oh well, who's to say a chipmunk couldn't enjoy a sunrise? But then, maybe there won't even be——" He was silent a long time. "Have you thought about it that way? Will? What if all those buildings over there were empty? Heaps of steel and stone. How long would they stand, with nobody to care about 'em? Maybe not even any rats to gnaw away at the wooden parts. Birds might use the roofs, don't you think? Gulls—where do seagulls build?"

"Dead trees."

"Other birds might use 'em, though. They ought to make good small mountains, cliffs. A world of birds and bugs and reptiles. Orioles, ephemerids, little snakes with nobody to tread and kill 'em. Trees everywhere, or grass. First just a funny little green finger between two paving stones, and then before too long—you know, I read somewhere that the water level is rising much faster than in the last century. Maybe that'll take care of everything. The big

162

waves would make short work of the best of towers, I'm sure of that. Nice old Hudson an inland sea. And the Mohawk Valley. New England would be a big island, New York State a bunch of little mountainous islands, and just nobody to bother the garter snakes."

"Kind of rough on Gimbel's Basement. Abe, the Black Death of the fourteenth century probably knocked over only about half of Europe, and that was in a time when everybody and his brother had fleas, to make things easy for *Bacillus pestis*. The flu of 1918 killed more than the First World War, but statistically it hardly made a dent in the human race."

He rolled his forehead on his arms. "Yes, they might find it necessary to use a few hydrogen bombs to help things along. That'll do it, that and a rising water level."

"Abe, I really do believe there's time for coffee before the end of the world."

He sighed sharply and stood up, smiling faintly, perhaps making up his mind, or yielding to my insistence only because he no longer cared much about anything. "All right. Let me get it. I won't run away."

"You mean you won't ever run away from anything again?"

He glanced back at me from the doorway, stooping to push his shoes on. "Why, I wouldn't even predict, and I quote, whether the baby will have a harelip. You like it strong and black?"

"Strong enough to grow *short* hair on a billiard ball."

We were still lingering over breakfast in the kitchen—a good breakfast at that, and Abraham didn't refuse to enjoy it—when Sharon came.

I write that baldly, because I don't know any words that tell what it is that happens when someone enters a room. The air changes. The whole orientation is something that never happened before. If the person is Sharon, the changed air has spice and sparkle, the orientation is toward warmth, toward what we call hope: merely another name for a desire to go on living. A lot of talk, maybe, for the process of hearing the doorbell, telling Abraham to sit still,

163

walking through to the door, seeing a bright bit of human stuff in a wrapping of bunny fur—and of course, being Sharon, no hat.

"I'm coming in anyway, so may I? How can anyone *be* so early? How do I know it's early? Because you've still got egg on your chin." She kicked the door shut behind her. "Nup, on this side." She rubbed the place with a peewee handkerchief and pulled me down to kiss it. "Just to make it well, poor egg." She flung the coat somewhere or other. She was wearing leaf-brown trousers— they don't call 'em slacks any more—and a crisp yellow blouse that made music with ocean-blue eyes. It's always trousers nowadays except for evening dress-up, unfortunate for fat girls but fine for Sharon. "Smoke me a light, Will—I mean light me—I mean I couldn't stay away. You won."

"Things happened when you couldn't sleep?"

She watched me with a rather helpless smile above the match flame. "Do you telepath or something? Not that I'd mind awfully.... Oh, I began remembering more and more, couldn't stop— please, Will, without prejudice to my right of being nine years older, huh? But—take me to him."

"Sure?"

"Why, you sevenfold so-and-so, I can't rest till I see him. Once anyway. And you knew I couldn't. Green Tower, you said—I sort of wouldn't care to go alone. Well, look——" She unfastened a button of my shirt, puffed a lungful of smoke through the opening, and stood back to study the effect. "Like that, you—you character. Make people start smoldering with silly ideas, you've got to take the consequences."

I slipped an arm around her and walked her into the kitchen. I felt the shock in her like an electric charge, and took my arm away.

Abraham was standing on the other side of the cluttered table. I saw his small brown hands spread out, finger tips supporting him, and heard him say raggedly: "Don't look now, Will, but you're still smoking."

I ignored that, as Sharon did. I don't know how long they stood quietly, staring at each other. Long enough for a universe to spin a while. I remember picking up a spoon and setting it down with great care lest I hurt the silence. Neither had spoken when Sharon walked around the table. She raised her hands to his forehead and moved them down slowly, over his eyes and cheeks and mouth, until they were resting on his shoulders. He said nothing, but she spoke as if answering something, with gravity and a little surprise: "Why, did you think you could love any woman but me?"

I said: "For your information, Abraham, the world won't blow up." He might have heard it; I don't know. I stepped into the living room and shrugged on my overcoat. At the door I glanced down and muttered: "Nah, Elmis, not slippers." My shoes were by the armchair where I had kicked them off, so I studiously shoved my old four-toed feet into them. I didn't hear any conversation from the kitchen. I went out to the elevator and rode down and walked a mile or so into the city's morning. The wind was chilly but very fresh and sweet.

After a time I was aware that someone was following me. I put on an act of window-shopping in one or two places, but couldn't get a fair look at him. A small man in nondescript gray-brown, busily peering into windows himself, his face averted. I tried a few aimless turnings, enough to make certain that I was his quarry: there was no doubt of it; he clung. I climbed to Second Avenue Upper Level, and walked a few blocks before pausing at a bus stop to look back. He was no longer with me. That I found strange— if a bus came now he'd lose me—unless he had turned over the task to some other shadow. I strolled away from the bus stop and entered a drugstore on the Upper Level, finding a seat at the soda counter from which I could study the sidewalk over my coffee. No one else came in while I lounged there. No one even looked in, except a harmless-seeming woman who halted to glance at the menu in the window and moved on.

I couldn't detect anyone tailing me as I gradually retraced my course to the apartment house. I had used up about an hour and a half. It was past ten o'clock and the sky had grown dingy, preparing a spring storm.

Someone with a familiar back was hurrying for the self-service elevator when I came into the lobby. Bright platinum hair, a fine hip-swing. Not good. I grabbed the elevator door as she was about to close it. "Oh, hel*lo*, Will! But how lucky! I was on my way to see you."

"Fine." I searched a bumbling and semiparalyzed brain for something that might work. "Things are kind of upset—can't I take you out somewhere? Had breakfast? Coffee anyhow——"

"Oh my, no!" She batted cute eyelashes at me. "Too much trouble, and anyway I had breakfast." She poked the button and the cage started up. I could have asked how she happened to know my floor. I didn't. "I don't mind a bit, Will—I've seen how you helpless men keep house, everything just everywhere——"

"But——"

"Now, that's all right, don't give it a *thought!*" She captured my arm and hugged it to her side. "Simply had to talk to you about something, awfully important, that is to me——" Miriam Dane chattered on, managing to say actually nothing at all, until we were in front of my door.

I tried again. "Got a friend staying with me, he's been ill and—well, sleeping late. Small apartment. Really be better if we——"

"Now you stop fretting. I'll be *so* quiet, and it's only for a minute." She wasn't exactly the woman I had met at Max's. In some subtle fashion she looked older. I had not sensed any steel of determination in her then. She had it now, and there was coldness in the steel. She quit smiling and chattering, because I had quit being Santa Claus. She watched me as if she intended to hypnotize the key ring out of my pocket. It wouldn't do. I stared back at her, not wanting to get rough or disagreeable, not reaching for my keys either. The smile was all gone. A tiny shoe with a rhinestone buckle began to tap on the floor. She said without any pretense, evenly and clearly: "It's necessary that I see Abe Brown."

So they had followed him last night. Followed, but hadn't done anything. Until now. Too busy maybe: Max and his boys might not be having an easy time over the death of Daniel Walker, with a New York police force which they say has been incredibly honest for the last thirteen or fourteen years. "Why, Miriam?"

"Why!" Her neat shoulders rose and fell. "After all! We're engaged. As you know. I could ask, why's it any of your business?"

"He came to me. That made it my business."

"Really! He's of age. And this happens to be Party business." It was already open war. I said: "I still want to know why."

"You're not a member. What right've you got to know?"

"He's not a member either." I was making my voice reasonably strong, hoping it might carry through the thick door.

"Needn't shout." She was showing the whites of her eyes. "That's got nothing to do with it, Mr. Meisel. Don't be so difficult."

"All right. Come in. But do you mind if I look in your handbag?"

"My—handbag?" I saw then that she used a trace of rouge: her cheeks displayed unhealthy little roses as the blood drained out of them. Her right hand darted to the blue bag, and my hand closed over hers before she could open the catch. It could be tough for me, if she screamed. I didn't think she would, and I was right. She let the bag go, stood away with fingers pressed to her bright mouth.

It was there, in the bag. A .22, like a toy but big enough. I hate the things anyway. I made sure of the safety, dropped the gun in my hip pocket, and returned the bag. "I carry it for protection," she said, pathetic now. "Have to go around—queer places sometimes." The pathos became precariously held dignity. "I've got a license for it. I can show you. It's here—somewhere." As she groped in the bag a tear spilled and rolled to her mouth corner. Uncalculated. So was the sniff, the flirt of her little tongue to her mouth corner while her hands were flutteringly busy. "You don't have to be so damn *mean*——"

"Keep the license," I said, "and I'll give you back the ordnance, when you leave." I punched the bell a couple of times and thrust my key noisily in the lock. "Coming in?" Impolitely I marched in ahead of her.

167

Sharon was in the armchair by the window with her feet tucked under her. Abraham at least had not noticed our voices out there. He sat on the floor beside her, full of quiet, drowsily conscious of her hand in his hair, not of much else maybe. Sharon smiled and murmured: "Knew it was you so I didn't get up. We've talked ourselves into a coma, and——"

Then Miriam stepped in behind me and said: "Oh."

I waved my hand, a foggy human gesture that tried to say this wasn't my doing. At the sound of Miriam's exclamation Abraham looked around but didn't rise at once, only stared in shock. When he did stand up Sharon laced her fingers in his, and I could see he wanted that. Sharon was intent, outwardly cool. So is a good artilleryman getting ready for a big one.

Miriam had probably never looked prettier herself. She had won her small brush with tears: they only swam in her eyes without falling. Trim and exquisite in her blue trousers, white fur jacket, a little sparkling something-or-other of a hat on the white shining of her hair, she was a gentle pin-up deeply wronged. Sharon said neutrally: "Miss Dane, I think?"

Miriam tried to dismiss her with one contemptuous flickering glance. "Abe, don't on any account let me *disturb* anything, but Bill Keller wants to see you, I do mean right away."

"I'm sorry." Abraham spoke evenly; painfully conscious of his own words, but there was quiet in him; I knew it. "I don't want to see him."

"What!"

"I'm sorry, Miriam. That's how it is." I leaned back feebly against the wall, an old man obscurely minding his own business. That would do, what Abraham had said. The next few minutes were not going to be nice, but the boy needed no help. "If you see Bill, you might as well tell him that. I'm not going back there, Miriam, not seeing any of them again."

I don't believe Miriam had been braced for anything like that. She had come looking for a confused, easily managed boy. She stared into her hands, flushed and paled, unable to conceal her

168

growing sense of defeat and a growing panic which, I sensed, had little to do with her relation to Abraham. After a few false starts she said softly: "Abe, there's such a thing as loyalty. Or wouldn't you know?"

Abraham nodded. "They'll have to think of me as a heel, Bill and Mr. Nicholas and the rest. That's all right. I do myself, but for a different reason: I gave my loyalty where I should've known it couldn't remain. I'm not going back, Miriam."

Sharon said: "There are other loyalties, Miss Dane. Your leader Joseph Max is what I'd have to call disloyal to his fellow men."

I didn't think Miriam's policy of ignoring Sharon would work much longer. But she went on trying it. Staring at Abraham and then at the ring on her left hand, she whispered: "None even to me, apparently. . . ."

Sharon said: "People change."

Even that did not make Miriam look at her. It was like another answer to the same thing when Abraham said: "Dr. Hodding was already broken when the Party bought him—wasn't he, Miriam? Sick, turning to alcohol dreams for escape because even the good work he did at the Wales Foundation had alarmed him, alarmed part of him anyway. Miriam, tell me this: why did a thing supposed to be an openly registered political party want to subsidize a man to invent a new disease——"

"That's a lie! It wasn't *like* that, Abe!"

"It's what happened." Abraham shook his head. I could see pain growing in the deep shadow of his eyes, pain and perhaps a hint of uncertainty. "You were there on the roof garden, Miriam. Once you told me yourself that nothing happens in the Party without your knowing all about it."

"But you don't understand. We didn't know what Hodding was——"

"Didn't *know!*"

"No, we did not. He—I could tell you—all right, I will tell you, though I wasn't supposed to. . . ."

Sharon noticed her free hand had become a fist. She relaxed it

169

carefully. She said: "Yes, do." And still Miriam managed to ignore her.

"Abe, Max has only just found out what Hodding really was, only just this morning. That's why you've got to come back. Nicholas says you were alone with Hodding, heard some of his talk. Max has got to see you, hear about it directly from you—you owe us that much, seems to me. And Bill, Bill Keller is *sick*, Abe. He broke down. We didn't have any sleep, any of us, and Bill is sick, can't get hold of himself, keeps asking for you. . . ."

She could see as well as I did that it made him waver. Perhaps she didn't see Sharon's hand, which was saying more than I could have said with any verbal interference. "Why, Bill's never sick——"

"But he is! I just came from him. Oh, Abe, he's done so much for you—and nobody's asking you to do any Party work, just to come and see him, talk to him. Did he ever ask you for any help before——"

"Miriam, if he's sick it's not going to help him to see me, when I've rejected the things he believes in. And you haven't told me what you started to. . . . What is Dr. Hodding, as of this morning?"

"That's a nasty thing to say." Miriam had dignity when she wanted to use it. "I don't think your present company's improved you, Abe, do you mind my mentioning it? Hodding's what he always was, only we didn't know it. All right—and you'd better listen. You won't like it, maybe you'll refuse to believe what we finally got out of that poor crazy old man——"

Sharon said to no one in particular: "Methods?"

Miriam swung toward her at last. "I *beg* your pardon?"

"Interested in the methods used, for getting information from a poor crazy old man."

It was war of course, and Sharon had chosen a moment when a little goading might sweep Miriam toward revealing hysteria. It didn't quite work. Miriam stared, and sputtered, and turned back to Abraham. "Abe, if you can get your mind off your imaginative friends long enough to listen: we haven't done a single thing that wasn't justified by the emergency. A man like Hodding can't be

170

handled with gloves. I'm trying to tell you what he is. We found out." Her voice was rising. "Never mind how—you've got that weak, soft streak—it doesn't matter anyway. Abe, Hodding has been in the pay of China for the last three years." I believe I laughed; Abraham didn't. "He's been using our American facilities to work up something to use in Asia. And fooling us with talk of abstract research, research that might have a humanitarian purpose—Max went for that, naturally—Max thought Hodding was working on a—a——"

Abraham had gone very white. He understood her hesitation too, I think. He said: "Is that going to be given to the press? Like that?"

"Certainly!" Miriam cried, and the high edge of hysteria was there. "Certainly, when we're ready."

Sharon cocked her head at her little stockinged feet and dropped them softly. She started to speak, but Abraham checked her. He said: "All you need now is a written confession from Hodding? Something like that?"

"We have it already," she snapped.

"Then you don't need me. Miriam, it stinks."

She pressed her hand to her forehead with the pathos of weariness. "So you can't see. Like a spoiled child. With a new toy too." She studied Sharon with the same show of weariness, dazed indifference: "Just who are you, or aren't I supposed to ask?"

"A junior member of the Federalist Party."

"Oh. One of those. I might've known. And this cheap clumsy spy"—she looked me up and down; I let it ride—"what do you pay him, may one ask? Not that it matters. Well, Miss—Miss——"

"Brand. Sharon Brand."

"Oh yes. Thought I'd seen your picture somewhere. You write children's books or something, don't you?"

Sharon chuckled. "Uh-huh. Nice big ones."

"Well, you might tell your nigger boss in the Federalist Party that, as a spy, friend Meisel is a flop——"

"Oh, that tail you had on me this morning," I said. "Wondered

171

why he quit so easy. It was to phone you, wasn't it? Let you know I was away from the apartment house or something?"

But she was ignoring me now. "Your own methods seem to have worked better, Miss—Brant? Must be hard on the heels, starting so young. My fault really, only I never would have thought Abe had a yen for children. Oh, here, you might want this when you're of age." She twisted off the ring and flung it clumsily. Except to twitch her feet aside so that the ring rolled under the armchair, Sharon didn't look at it or move.

Even after yielding to that need for a gesture, Miriam must have held some frail hope of success, slow in dying. She approached Abraham with outstretched appealing hands. Though I had almost no doubt of the outcome, I found I was holding my breath. Miriam had talent.

It was not his distant quiet that broke her control. Something else; something I saw in him, and though I know he tried to hide it, Miriam must have seen it too. Pity. I heard her gasp, saw her make a savage unthinking motion toward her handbag. I saw Sharon jump up; if Miriam had completed the motion, I believe Sharon would have thrown herself in front of Abraham before he could stop her. But Miriam's mind remembered where the gun was, more quickly than her hand. She choked and turned away, harmless and pitiful. "I'll take—what you said, to Joe Max." It was interesting to me that she said "Joe Max" just then. "Abe, you're making a terrible mistake."

I was glad that Abraham answered nothing. She went by me slowly, not looking at me, perhaps not even thinking about the gun, which I would not have returned to her. She didn't slam the door.

Sharon's arms were around Abraham, tight and close. "Will," she said over her shoulder, "Will, is the sun by any chance over the yardarm, and I don't mean on my account?"

6 Sharon went into the country with us today. A holiday, a half-impromptu picnic. Not an escape, unless Sharon may have thought of it that way, a little. Spring has come earlier than ever this year. There was some small rain last night, and today the earth was washed and sweet and ready; we found bright winter aconite in the woods, and the first of the tiny white violets that hide in corners of the rocks.

We rented a car, Abe and I, and rather than oblige us to grope through Brooklyn, Sharon met us at a subway exit uptown. We didn't venture on a Robbie-road, but went over the old bridge and followed one of the fine North Jersey highways until we came on a modest road that promised to lead into the Ramapos. Just the three of us, and by unspoken consent we said not a word during the drive about what had happened or might have happened at the Green Tower Colony Friday afternoon.

It seems that in order to contemplate a major calamity to the human species you need distance. More than the Martian distance. When the black wings swoop too close your eyes blur; Martian or human, you must look away, not so much for the sake of hoping or pretending, but because your heart says: "I am not ready." Or it says, perhaps: "There was no need of this. There could have been another way. . . ." The pilot over Hiroshima—could he look down?

Certainly there was nothing in the spring woods to remind us of grief.

There had been no more approaches from Max's people since Miriam's visit. Abraham and I were not followed when we hunted up that rental garage. Nothing was prowling behind us when we

173

took that little road off the highway. Sharon had brought a basket with lunch, and we had wine—good Catawba wine from somewhere in the smiling lake country.

I could turn my face away from the homely ugliness of our rented car; I could forget our stuffy American clothes and imagine that we were—no matter where. Perhaps a mountainous island in that country where once upon a time human life was a pleasant thing to explore—or so said Theocritus, Anacreon, other voices. Pan never died. He watches and breathes across the pipes, wherever earth and forest, field and sky can come together and make their harmony for the Arcadian son of Hermes.

Often enough, Drozma, I think of your great-grandfather, how he labored to collect and recopy the writings of his own great-grandfather, who knew Hellas as it truly was, when the sun was high. Those writings could be published, if Union is ever possible. I tried to imagine Union, this afternoon. The dream was blotted away by another image—the image of a neat little tube full of green powder.

I saw Abraham stretch comfortably with his head in Sharon's lap. He said: "Will, I begin to tell myself it couldn't happen. Anyway there's a good chance. Isn't there?"

"A chance."

"What Hodding developed wasn't as powerful as he thought. Or maybe not as easy to spread, not as viable outside the laboratory. Or the tube fell into the river and was carried unbroken out to sea."

"In Hodding's ramblings, did he say anything about the incubation period?" I asked that, not wanting to know.

"Not that I heard. . . . Out to sea—but the cork would come loose sometime, and Lord, what then? The sea's mammalian life—transmission sooner or later back to——"

"Don't," said Sharon, and slid her hand over his eyes.

"Well, it didn't happen," said Abraham, for her sake. "So far as today is concerned, it didn't happen." She bent down until her tumbling hair hid his face, to whisper something that they thought was none of my business; no doubt something to do with the hour when they left me in a contemplation that looked like human sleepiness, and strolled away into the woods. They are very sweet and natural children, when civilization relaxes its grip on them. Capable of unspoken understanding, too—that should help, if it turns out that they have years together and not just a few bright moments snatched before the climax of a world disaster. It seemed to me that he was following a train of thought parallel to mine, for presently he said: "Will, assuming nothing happened when Walker threw that thing—assuming any of us can have such a thing as another slice of, say, forty or fifty years—what about my forty or fifty? I'm thinking about work. This blue-eyed lady's got no such problem: she already knows what she can do. And it looks to me as if most people had no such problem: a few have a very plain call to one kind of achievement or another, and the big majority just think of work as an unavoidable unpleasantness, something to be got out of the way so that they can play at nothing in particular, if they can't find some means of dodging it altogether—which is no good for me, but if I have a call to anything, damn it, it usually sounds like a hundred voices calling all at once. Locomotive with no rails. . . . You told me a while ago that you'd bummed around a lot, tried several different things. Ever hit on the one kind of work you really wanted to do? Something that made all the rest a prologue?"

Yes, but I couldn't say so. Forcing myself back into the human frame of reference, and hastily, I said: "Nothing to offer but a moth-eaten bromide: find out what you can do best and stay with it. Finding out might take awhile. I'm merely passing it back to you."

He smiled. "Yes, but that might be one of the hard bromides the moths can't chew. And one finds out by trial and error? Mostly error?"

"Maybe. At twelve you were rather preoccupied by the plague-take-it mysteries we like to wrap up in a bundle named ethics."

"Yes." He watched me a long while, his dark eyes hazy. "Yes, I was, Will. . . ."

"And?"

"Yes, I still am. Learning more and knowing less all the time."

"Oh, after a while you work out a synthesis that holds up to your satisfaction. In your thirties perhaps, if you're lucky."

"And to translate preoccupation with ethics into terms of life work?"

"Teach. Write. Preach. Act, though action is always dangerous."

"Always?" said Sharon.

"Always, unless you can trace out the possible consequences to a pretty large distance. Sometimes you can, with a moderate degree of certainty, enough for practical purposes. If you can't, then the time-tested actions are—well, safer anyway, as the man in the street has always recognized: not necessarily better of course."

"I wonder," said Abraham, "if I'd ever think I knew enough to act."

"If you don't, then study all your life and talk a little when you believe you have something to say."

He chuckled and threw a handful of pine needles at me. Sharon framed his head in her hands and moved it from side to side, not very playfully. "I'd like to take you home with me this evening. You haven't met Mother Sophia yet." I could see her face as he did not. She was thinking not only of Mother Sophia but of the piano. "How long, Abe, since you've done any painting?"

He hesitated; there was a frown that she rubbed away with a finger. "Quite a while, Sharon."

"Maybe," I suggested, "it doesn't hitch up closely enough to a preoccupation with ethics?"

"Maybe." He was startled and interested. "You can preach in oils, but——"

"Not really," said Sharon. "Propaganda is bad art."

"Aren't you thinking in terms of music, though?"

"No. In music the problem just doesn't exist. You don't even start looking for propaganda in music unless your head's already addled."

"Yes. But in art—well, Daumier, Goya, Hogarth——"

"They live," said Sharon, "because they were good artists. If

176

their social ideas had been the kind we don't happen to like in the twentieth century, their work would last just the same. Cellini was a louse. The piety of Blake and El Greco almost doesn't exist nowadays. Their work does."

"I think you're right," said Abraham after a while. "I think Will is right too. Painting isn't enough for a frustrated moralist late of reform school."

Sharon winced and tightened her fingers, but Abraham was still smiling. I thought I had heard something she missed. I said: "Abe, that's the first time I've heard you speak of the past without bitterness."

He twisted his head to look up at his sweetheart almost with merriment, reminding her, I think, to share the memory of some words they must have spoken earlier. "I don't think I have any, Will. Not any more."

"Not even for Dr. Hodding and the men who bought him?"

Abraham murmured: "Bound on the wheel." He sat up then and pulled Sharon into the hollow of his arm, kissing her hair, sensing that for the moment she wanted to be the sheltered one.

"So now the boy is a Buddhist," said Sharon.

"Of course. Buddhist, Taoist, Confucian, Mohammedan——"

"One moment. One wife will be quite enough——"

"Hoy! Mohammedan, Christian, Socratic, Hindu——"

"Okay, only kind of hard for a girl to keep up with on a Sunday afternoon, and I still say——"

"You get used to it," said Abraham. "We dispense with the veil. It merely means you have to take your shoes off when you go through the house in order to reach the bo tree in the back yard."

I said: "You forgot Mithra."

"Tradesmen's entrance," said Abraham. "Plenty room. Not forgetting the Greek Pantheon, which can use the front door any time." He stuck out his tongue at me, not much more than twelve years old. "Syncretism in North Jersey yet! Will, this bottle still has life in it."

We killed it without help from Sharon, who didn't want to move.

177

But it seemed to make Abraham more sober, not less. He watched me over her drowsy head, and at length he asked: "Do you still have that mirror?"

Dubiously I said: "I've always carried it with me, Abraham."

"So . . . ?"

"And never exactly forgiven myself for letting you see it when you were twelve." Sharon looked up at him, with questions unspoken. "Since then I've looked in it many times."

"And found . . . ?"

"Oh, if you can stand it, if you turn it often enough this way and that, you can usually find something like the truth you look for. Most people would say it's only a distortion in the bronze, imagination supplying the rest. I wouldn't say yes or no to that."

"Mirror?" said Sharon sleepily.

"Just something I carry around with me. Call it a talisman. It was given me years ago by an archaeologist. A little Cretan hand mirror, Sharon, said to be about seven thousand years old."

"You see, honey? Just modern stuff after all."

"Uh-huh," I said. "Yes, if you're interested in ethics, you could do worse than think in terms of geological time. Well, Sharon, you can't find any wave or imperfection in the reflecting surface, but there must be one, for the plague-take-it thing never looks the same twice. I wouldn't care to have you peep into it unprepared. Usually it doesn't show your face as other people see it. It might show you very old, or very young. Different. Things you might never have guessed yourself—and who's to claim there's any truth in it? A trick. A toy . . ."

When I said nothing more and made no move to take out the mirror, Sharon spoke with her head drowsy again on Abraham's shoulder: "Will, don't be so damn gentle."

"Really I'm not. But I learned some years back that human nature is volatile stuff in a world full of lighted matches."

Meeting my eyes tranquilly, Abraham said: "We wouldn't be scared to look, Will."

I unfastened the mirror from the strap hidden under my shirt, the same strap that holds my old grenade and the new one Supply sent me, and put it in Abraham's hand. They gazed into it, two young and uncorrupted faces side by side. Not so very young. Twenty-one and nineteen. But out of certain black places even I could never explore, Twenty-one had groped his way, undefiled; and Nineteen was a grown-up, proud, and humble priestess in what may be the greatest of the arts.

Drozma, I felt the beginning of that peace which we Observers know when the end of a mission is not far away. What Abraham had predicted was not quite true: they were frightened. That was almost unimportant. What mattered was that nothing they felt—fright, shock, amazement, disappointment—made them turn away from what they saw. I can't know what that was. They are both articulate with words. They also knew as I did that this was beyond the narrow territory of words. I could guess, from the passage of emotional lights and shadows in their faces—puzzled, rapt, startled, hurt, sometimes amused and often tender. I could guess as much as I had any right to know. I asked nothing when Abraham handed the mirror back to me. Showing that sleepy smile which I remembered from long ago, from a summer afternoon in the cemetery at Byfield, from a few other nearly silent summer afternoons in the pine woods, Abraham said: "Well, it would seem we're human. I did have a suspicion of it all along."

"Yes. You, and the maker of the mirror, and Mordecai Paxton."

He grinned and remarked softly: "Hi-ho, Mordecai! Wha' d'ya know—is she asleep?"

"Not entirely," said Sharon. I think that's what she murmured. I had glanced into the mirror before putting it away, and I saw nothing of myself.

I saw nothing of myself, Drozma.

Did you know, my second father, that there might be a time when I would look there and see only the motion behind me of friendly trees and open sky? A bush of viburnum, a rank of heavy undergrowth dividing the clearing from the forest and full of the innocent secret hurry of birds. This and the maples with leaf buds newly

179

stirring, and the pines, and far and high the passage of a white cloud. . . . Did you also foresee that there might be no pain in that moment at all—or at least only such daylong, nightlong pain as we and humanity must live with because of our mortality, finding it a sort of background music not very different from the love song of tree frogs at night or the imagined music of May-flies in the late sun? Did you know that I might be able to smile, and put the mirror carelessly away, stretch like a human being, and remind Sharon that we ought to be starting home?

"He's right," she said. "I don't want Mother Sophia trying to get supper for herself. . . ."

This time we ventured with the car into the maze of Brooklyn, Sharon acting as guide and pretending there was nothing to it. I observed a different Abraham there at Sharon's apartment, one I had known about but never truly seen. It was manifest in his behavior toward Sophia Wilks, a tenderness and consideration without any of the condescension of extreme youth. He liked her, and found easy ways of making it plain. She looked at his face with her fingers, prolonging that inquiry probably because of the singing note in Sharon's voice, and she smiled at whatever she found there—she who seldom smiled even when she was amused. After supper, when Sharon and Abraham went into the studio, I sat and talked with Sophia about Abraham. Most of her questions had unspoken ones behind them: she was more interested in his temperament than in any practical circumstances, and I told her only those things Sharon might have told me of the boy who used to live in Latimer. In Latimer Sophia had never known him, except after his disappearance, and then only through the halting and grief-confused words of a ten-year-old girl. I was careful with my voice, but there was scant danger that Sophia could ever connect Meisel with the funny old quasi-Polish gentleman who had wanted a monument: her mind was elsewhere, and her own quiet memory of Benedict Miles another monument. "Should an artist marry, Mr. Meisel? I did, but only after I had learned that the heights were not for me—in any case my husband was also a teacher. Sharon is all fire and devotion.

180

Do you know that for seven years now she has never practiced less than six hours a day, often ten or twelve?"

I said something comfortably useless, about how it had to be a separate problem for every artist, one that only the artist could answer. Unfortunately that was true as well as useless, but Sophia already knew it as well as I. "We never drove her, my sister and I. There was a year, Mr. Meisel, when she was fifteen, after she had come to live with us—she would get up from the piano not knowing where she was. Once my sister saw her blunder into the doorframe on the way to her bedroom because, you understand, she was not in the room at all, she was in some place—I think you understand —some place where nobody else could be with her. We were so frightened that year, my sister and I. It was too much, we thought— we never drove her, and sometimes tried to hold her back, but that we couldn't do either. The fears were foolish, you see. Such a flame does not ever burn out. It is only the little flames that—ah there!" The piano in the studio had spoken. "No—no, that isn't Sharon. Why, does he——"

I said quickly: "He's a beginner. Something pulled him toward music, I don't know what. He'll probably find out his talent is elsewhere, before too long."

"I see." I am not sure she did, and she was not pleased. Abraham was playing the somber Fourth Prelude of Chopin almost correctly, with a fair touch and some insight. I muttered to Sophia that I would be back in a moment, and I strolled into the studio as Abraham was finishing it. I saw his upward glance of inquiry—why, there was amusement in it too, how genuine I don't know, defensive perhaps. I also saw Sharon shake her head a little, involuntarily, I believe.

She softened it at once by saying: "Not yet." And stepped behind the piano chair to put her arms around him, bring her mouth close to his ear. "Do you really *want* it, Abe?"

"I don't quite know."

"It's rougher'n hell—well, you know that. Point is I don't think you'd want it just for your own pleasure—if you did it would be

181

good, but if I know you, Abe, you'd want to give, with it. That takes eight hours a day, for years, and it might not be there." She glanced up at me over his head, and she was very frightened. "And it might take away from—oh, other things, things worth more, things you could do better." Yes, she was horribly frightened, and I couldn't help.

But Abraham said: "I think it was a fever, Sharon. I think I notice some nice cool sweat on the brow." His mouth was unsteady, but he was smiling with it. "Do something for me?"

"Anything," she said, nearly crying. "Anything, now or any time."

"Just play it the way it ought to be."

"Well, there's no one way it ought to be," said Sharon Brand. "But I'll play it as well as I can." She did of course. It would have been a cruelty to play at anything less than her best, since he would have known it; but I wonder how many others would have sensed that at such a moment? I've known a lot of pianists, human and Martian. They fall readily into two classes: Sharon and then all the rest of 'em. I never could quite bear that prelude anyhow. She blinked at me rather desperately, and followed the prelude immediately with the tiny, half-humorous one in A Major, the Seventh, simply because something had to follow it, it couldn't hang in the air.

"I have a special corner in the temple," said Abraham, and put a cigarette between her lips and lit it for her and kissed her forehead. "The corner where you can hear best. Remind me to tell you sometime that you're slightly snub-nosed."

"Are you p-partial to pug noses?"

I went back to Sophia. . . .

Abraham needed to talk to me, a little, as we started home. Fortunately the automobile is one human gimmick that doesn't overawe me. I feel almost at home with it so long as it stays on the ground. Don't think I'll ever try the plane-car they're experimenting with nowadays. The damn thing has wings folded over its back like a beetle's; it's supposed to snap them out at a comfortable

182

seventy miles per hour and take off. Retractile propeller. Slow stuff, not intended to do anything over three hundred when it's airborne, but all the same I think they can keep that one. Nice, of course, for kids anxious to find some new way of breaking their necks. Poking through those quiet and sober streets that had grown empty toward midnight, I was able to listen to Abraham without thinking much about my driving. He wanted to talk about the reform school. Not, I think, on his own account, but to satisfy possible questions that I had not spoken.

He had grown a shell in that environment, except for a few friendships. And those, he said, were all shadowed by the sense that nothing could ever last very long. I said something commonplace to suggest that human growth had much in common with the growth of insects: old chrysalids tossed on the rubbish heap and new ones grown. "Still," he said, "as a larger bug I probably have a better memory of earlier states of bugginess than, say, a weevil." He went on to make a rather horrible and intricate pun deriving *pupil* from *pupa* which, out of respect for our Martian community, I decline to record. He told me more about how the lost boys came and went. It had been a large school with, I guess, a fairly sensitive conscience somewhere at the top. The boys were of all sorts—the sickly, the morons, the majority called normal, the few bright ones; making a fenced-in, neurotic community, it seemed to Abraham that they had had little in common except bewilderment. Even bitterness was curiously absent in some of them. They were abused more by each other than by authority. Such violence as he saw was mostly furtive. Discipline was rigid enough, and the school had made a serious effort to weed out bullies or clip their claws. "I carried a knife," Abraham told me. "Never could have used it, but it was the thing to do. Like a fraternity pin, I guess. A new boy would get beat up a few times, then someone would befriend him, see that he learned to carry a knife, talk the accepted language, and he'd be let alone. I was able to get some books. Last two years I had a sort of trusty job, in the so-called library. Except for the physical thrills, even beating up a new candidate was a sort of—oh, dutiful routine. . . .

Well, they did have one thing in common besides bewilderment. The nobody-loves-me feeling. Those who had parents coming to see them had it worst. But we all felt or imagined or tried to imagine that no one had ever cared much about us. I knew better, Will, so did a lot of the others, but you couldn't say so. Saying so would have been admitting that you might be partly to blame yourself, but it was more than that. You *had* to believe you were unwanted, or you'd be a social outcast. The school of paradox. Maybe not such a bad preparation for what's outside. You know, Will—the old school tie. Alumnus Brown recalls the golden age." But there was no overtone of bitterness. "Will, I wonder—can anything turn around and kick itself in the teeth like the human mind?"

"I dunno. Did you ever help beat up a new one?"

He said with remarkable gentleness: "You could almost guess the answer to that one."

"Uh-huh—you never did."

"Almost right. I never helped beat up anyone, but to offset that, I never had the guts to try to stop it either. Except once."

"And that time?"

He rolled up his left sleeve and showed me his arm in the dashboard light. The scar was nearly white, running from elbow to wrist. "I'm proud of that hash mark," he said. "It tells that on one occasion I did have a little guts, and it taught me something." Still I heard nothing in his voice except a reflective serenity neither sad nor happy. "It taught me: unless you're a gorilla, don't interfere with the pleasures of chimps." And somewhat later he said: "Punishment—that's the idea that taints the whole system, reform schools, prisons, four fifths of the criminal law. Cure the curable, keep the incurable where they can't hurt others—anything else is just humanity picking at a sore and half enjoying the pain." He was talking to himself as much as to me. "From all I've read, Will, it seems that enlightened people with experience have been hammering that idea for at least a hundred years. Reckon the law will catch up with them in another hundred?"

"First you need a science of human nature, that doesn't exist. I

184

don't blame the law for being not much impressed by the battle of terms we call psychology. The various Freudianities can't stop to hear the various behaviorisms, and vice versa. We have the beginnings of a knowledge of human nature, but it's a study that has to creep slowly because it scares people to death. It was all right for the Greek to say, 'Know thyself'—but how many would dare to do it even if they had the means?"

I spoke mainly because I hoped he would go on talking to me, in any way he chose. He would have, I think, but the world stood still.

Is it my biased sense of history, Drozma, that makes me use those curious eroded human phrases for such a thing as this?

I saw the man step off the sidewalk half a block away. It was a well-lit street near the bridge approach, and quiet. There were no headlights behind me, only one red taillight a block or two away. Endless time. No urgency. My foot found the brake, without panic, for we were not moving fast, and there was no possible danger of hitting the man, who had dropped to his knees in front of us, under my lights, under the orange glow of a sodium street lamp. All in control. I came to an easy, soundless stop five or six feet away from him. He was in profile to us but never turned his head, only knelt there, first with his hands raised toward his chin in the ancient attitude of prayer. The arms dropped, limp; I saw the fingers of the left hand go into a lively dance as if he were scratching the air at his thigh. His mouth hung open and he began to sway from the knees as I forced myself to clamber out of the car and go to him.

He was toppling over when I reached him. I was able to ease him down on his back and keep his head from striking the asphalt. A small, elderly man, well dressed, clean. He made me think of a sparrow, with his little jutting nose and brilliant eyes that would not shut. His cheek was flame-hot. I never felt such fever but once before, long ago, in a human friend who died of blackwater malaria. I think this man was trying to say something; nothing came out but "Uh—ah——" sounds without control of throat or tongue. There was no choking. For several moments the glitter of

185

his eyes was firmly, intelligently focused on me. I am sure he would have liked to speak.

I stared across him at Abraham, who had also touched his burning flesh. There was no speech for us either, then.

7

Only today comes the first newspaper announcement of the disaster. Last night at ten o'clock—Wednesday night, just one little week after I heard Sharon's miracle—there was confusing mention of trouble on the radio. We heard it, Abraham and I, heard the repressed hysteria in the broadcaster's voice as if someone were plucking a taut deep wire behind his rapid gabble. He said only that there were "several" cases of what might be a new disease in Cleveland, Washington, New York, and the West Coast. Medical circles were interested, although there was "obviously" no occasion for alarm. "West Coast?" said Abraham. The broadcaster lurched on hastily to the most recent vital information on a divorce case involving a video star and a wrestler.

"Plane travel," I said. "Paris and London are only a few hours away. . . ." Abraham brought me a drink. We couldn't talk much, or read. He sat near me most of the evening in my dull little living room, which seemed to me more than ever like a well-upholstered cave in a jungle of the unknown; both of us haunted, understanding the panic in each other's minds. Now and then we tried the radio again, but there was nothing except the usual loud confusion of trivialities. Toward bedtime Abraham telephoned Sharon. It was just a lovers' conversation—"What've you been up to all evening?" —and since he didn't mention the broadcast to her I assumed she hadn't heard it. After hanging up he simply said: "I couldn't. . . ."

The three days since Sunday had allowed us to crawl back on a

186

flimsy raft of hope. That man we found in the street—oh, it could have been pneumonia, a dozen other things. So we told each other then and for three days. Abraham had called an ambulance, which came quickly and whisked the fallen man away, after a few inquiries from an intern who seemed to have a worry in the back of his mind that wouldn't come into words. Other similar cases? I almost asked the young doctor that, but held my tongue. As we drove home Abraham and I began passing each other counterfeit words. We knew they were counterfeit, but they bought us a little phony peace.

This morning the *Times* as usual had the best soberly factual account, offering statistics with a rather terrible restraint. There have been 50 hospitalized cases in the New York metropolitan area, and 16 deaths. In Chicago, 21 reported cases, 6 deaths. New Orleans, 13 and 3. Los Angeles, 10 and 3. This is the fourth day since Sunday, the sixth since Friday. The first reported case, according to the *Times,* was a Bronx housewife—Sunday morning. She died Monday afternoon.

The *Times* prints a statement from the A.M.A.: the disease "resembles an unusually virulent type of flu, with several atypical features. Nationwide medical resources are being mobilized to meet the unlikely event of an emergency, and there is no cause for alarm." Close quote.

The *Times* goes on to describe the thing without quotation marks and apparently without pulling any punches. The first symptoms are merely those of the common cold—sniffles, moderate fever, general malaise. After a few hours of this, fever rises abruptly, there is deafness with violent head noises, perversion of the senses of smell and taste. Numbness of hands and feet, legs and forearms, followed quickly by more general motor paralysis, which in all cases so far has included paralysis of throat and tongue; patients cannot speak or swallow. Fever remains at a very high point for several hours—twelve in one case; it follows no pattern of fluctuation. Evidence of delirium in most cases, and the behavior of the speechless patients suggests vivid visual hallucinations before un-

187

consciousness intervenes—as it does at the third or fourth hour after onset of major symptoms. Death, when it has occurred, has come during deep coma, after a gradual subsidence of fever, and may be due to paralysis of cardiac muscle. Cheyne-Stokes breathing very marked in all fatal cases so far. In "some" other patients the temperature, instead of dropping to deep subnormal, has leveled off at about 101°, the patients remaining unconscious but with some improvement of involuntary reflexes: prognosis obviously unknown. Except for the quote from the A.M.A. the *Times* isn't telling us there's nothing to worry about. Nor do they speculate about origin and cause. Nor do they say directly that the arsenal of drugs and antibiotics has proved ineffective, but there is one small sentence difficult to forget: "Patients have responded to supportive treatment in some cases." So it's that bad. I suppose a newspaper reader would have to be somewhat familiar with medical argot, to grasp the implications. You couldn't expect the *Times* to say: "They try to keep them comfortable, knowing nothing else to do."

I have seen no follow-up account on the death of Daniel Walker. No mention anywhere, these three days, of Max or the Organic Unity Party. I commented on that this morning, wondering out loud if Max had gotten away with it. Abraham said: "No. He won't."

It is terrifying to see controlled and quiet anger in a face designed for gentleness. It was all the worse because of his physical slightness and soft voice. I waited for the look to go away. It did not. He had spread the paper on the table and stood looking down at it, but as if the black and white square were a window, as if there were unmeasurable distances beyond. "What's going on in your mind, Abraham?"

He only said: "They won't get away with it."

"You're thinking of what Miriam said? Hodding in the pay of China and all that?"

"Hell, they won't use that pipe dream, Will. I think that was spur-of-the-moment, and a poor effort. No, I think they'll hope for

188

silence, hope that nobody can make the connection. And nobody could, unless one of us talks—I mean one of those who were up there on the roof garden. I don't think Fry or Senator Galt understood anything of it—they're freaks, nobodies. Nicholas, Max, Miriam—and Bill, and me—those five may be the only ones who know."

"Should you speak, Abraham?"

He was all grownup when he said, with no tension in his voice, without even looking at me: "I haven't quite decided. . . ."

We went for a walk that afternoon. No objective, simply here and there in the streets, a bus uptown, west on 125th, back downtown through the West Side, walking. We saw no one collapsing in the street. Perhaps things were rather too quiet for a weekday afternoon. There wasn't quite the normal amount of talk and laughter in those who passed us. We heard the bell and siren of ambulances five or six times in our aimless journey—but one does anyhow: illness and accident have always claimed their victims through the nights and days of any city. . . .

Hodding is dead. We got that from the evening paper.

His house and laboratory in a Long Island suburb caught fire from "an explosion of unknown origin." His body and those of his wife, daughter-in-law, and grandson, aged nine, have been identified. The four were in the laboratory when the explosion occurred. The laboratory, says the paper, was a private enterprise which Dr. Hodding had carried on after his retirement from the Wales Foundation. Dr. Hodding's son had been away from the house; the paper quotes him as saying that the laboratory was designed for some limited type of biological research, hardly more than a retired man's hobby. Young Hodding is an architect, and claims he knew nothing about his father's line of work; but he is certain that nothing was ever kept in the laboratory that could have caused an explosion. Police, says the paper, are investigating the possibility that a bomb may have been set by a crank. "One," said Abraham. "One who can't talk any more. If Fry and Galt are insured, the companies ought to be worrying a bit." And then, pursuing another

189

line of thought: "Will, such a thing could be no use to anyone as a weapon, unless there were a means of immunizing the users. I keep coming back to that. I think Max wanted to dictate terms to the world, including Asia. I think he hates the Federalists worse than others because he sees himself as—oh, the first President of a world government, something like that. He'd feel it was quite all right to kill off a few million commonplace human animals if that would make him Leader—for the world's good of course, always for the world's good. But first he would have to have a means of immunizing the faithful."

"Perhaps Hodding was working on that, and got only halfway. He developed the disease but not the protection."

"I think so," said Abraham, with the same dangerous quiet that had been in him all day. "So now, in order to hide the truth and escape the consequences, they've killed the one man who knew most about it, who must have already done a lot of work toward finding an immunization or a cure. Killed his family too, but they wouldn't consider that—another product of the doctrine that the end justifies the means. I met the little boy once. He was a bright kid. . . ."

"Promise me something, Abraham?"

"If I can."

"Don't start anything unless I'm with you."

He came and stood over my chair, smiling down with more straightforward unconsidered affection than he had ever shown me. "I can't promise that, Will."

Presently I said: "I know you can't." Nor could I have made the same promise to him, so I had to tell myself that it was fair enough. I have learned a little since that night in the cemetery when Namir escaped me. Namir will not escape again, and I think Keller will have to die with him: Keller is a well-trained son of his father, and I don't think the Old City hospital could do anything with him. The only problem now is to isolate them from human contact long enough to do what I must. And I must do it before this flame in

190

Abraham explodes into some action he may not have the strength to carry through.

That evening paper added nothing to our knowledge of the spread of the disease. More demoralized than the *Times*. No statistics. The radio has been silent about it all evening. Abraham is sleeping, I think. Fortunately I do not need to.

New York
Friday, March 17

From this morning's paper: New York area, 436 reported cases, 170 deaths.

I think they were right to hold the St. Patrick's Day parade. It would have been against the public interest to cancel such an expected and time-honored thing, in spite of the clear danger that large gatherings might help to spread the contagion. We didn't go to see it. Abraham has been in a faraway abstraction all day, his mind talking to his mind, demanding answers. The evening paper says the crowds were small, and there was "some disturbance" when one of the paraders fell from his horse in a "sudden heart attack." A heart attack?

There was also a broadcast statement from the White House at six o'clock, urging the nation to keep calm. Panic, said President Clifford, was more dangerous than epidemic. The country's medical resources are adequate to deal with the—emergency. He had some slight trouble with that word, his voice not quite in control, his deep-lined, still handsome face tightening itself to force out the syllables smoothly. His television make-up wasn't too good. I think they had tried to soften the furrows in his forehead, but they couldn't make him anything except a frightened, essentially brave and decent little man carrying a burden too heavy for anyone. Civil Defense organizations, he said, have been placed under the direction of the Surgeon General of the Army—who followed Clifford on the video with a fair display of jaw and stop-this-nonsense eyebrows. Avoid crowds, said Surgeon General Craig, stay home from everything but essential work, obey all, repeat all, orders of local medical authorities and Civil Defense personnel. All theaters, stadia, bars, other public meeting places will be closed for the duration of the emergency. Use your radio to keep in touch with the efforts of your government. The pandemic—Craig stopped there for a second, shaking his big head as if at a buzzing fly; he had meant to say "epidemic" but the other slipped out. The pandemic, Craig said, is caused by a new virus, possibly a mutation from the virus of poliomyelitis. Promising efforts are under way to isolate it and to develop a serum. This will take time. Repeat, avoid crowds, stay home except——

From a ten o'clock broadcast: the disease is reported from Oslo, Paris, London, Berlin, Rome, Cairo, Buenos Aires, Honolulu, Kyoto.

Friday midnight

I have got up from a sleepless bed to write down something Abraham said before he went to his room. I force myself to admit that the disease could strike him too; that he could die tomorrow; my need to write what he said derives from that admission.

After I turned off the radio we talked a little of what men call the Second World War, meaning that phase of the twentieth-century war which came to a partial end in 30,945, six years before Abraham was born. In giving him some (humanly censored) memories, I referred to the "expendable millions."

Abraham said: "No one is expendable."

8   From the *Times:* in the nation at large, 14,623 reported cases, 3561 deaths, as of Friday, 8 P.M. More than twenty-five per cent mortality: the proportion is rising. Those patients whose fevers level off above normal merely take longer in dying. But several of those stricken earliest are showing "probable" signs of recovery—temperature normal or nearly so, consciousness recovered although usually with sense impairment and varying degrees of localized paralysis apparently due to damaged or destroyed neural tissue. They are calling it paralytic polyneuritis. The headlines have already shortened that to para.

Abraham went over to Brooklyn early this morning to see Sharon. I went to the Green Tower Colony.

Para. . . .

The streets are not as they were Thursday afternoon. Human beings still pass you, in groups of two or three, not more. They glance at you quickly, and away quickly, huddling together, clinging to the selves and the faces they know, afraid of strangers. You hear their voices, not always like individual voices. The city is whispering *para.* Over and over, the one word, a faraway drumbeat, or a giant muttering in tormented sleep. *Para.* One word, which means . . .

A man staggers on the sidewalk, reaches out for the wall of a building to steady himself with one hand; the other hand joins it, as if he wanted to embrace what was never there. Both hands begin to dance at the finger ends. No one hurries to help him as his knees give way and his forehead touches the wall. The couple who had been walking behind him swerve and run scramblingly across the street, the woman pressing a handkerchief over her mouth, the man

193

glaring back as he runs with a meaningless square-mouthed smile. They would like to help, but . . .

Para means a little dog trotting down the center of Third Avenue dragging a leash. Traffic has thinned to nearly nothing. The golden spaniel isn't quite right in the legs: a hind leg gives way now and then, but he hurries on, hunting for something—help, I suppose. The small head jerks repeatedly to the left; he tries to bark, with only a strangled wheeze. Then both hind legs fail him, and he struggles to keep moving, pulling with his forepaws, a dog's patient determination in unaccusing eyes. A car approaches slowly, turns out to avoid him. A woman screams at the driver, pointing: "He's got it! Finish him!" Obediently the car backs and shoots forward, then crazily off uptown as if the mechanism itself had sickened at a thing which at the moment seemed necessary. The woman snatches up a wire waste receptacle and hurls it at the little smear of blood and golden hair. Ordinarily she could hardly have lifted it. She takes out her lipstick, carefully paints a new mouth, fumbles at a place where the wire snagged her dress, but walks away without looking for the compact that fell from her fingers and rolled into the street.

Para means a man throwing open a front door to stare up and down the street. He is crying, and shouts (not to me or anyone else): "Those bastards won't *ever* get here!"

Para means a mob looting a liquor store. I saw that on Third Avenue from the corner of Twenty-third Street. There were a dozen or so, including a few women. The store must have been locked, for there were plate-glass fragments on the pavement. The looters seemed comically serious about it, until a woman broke away from them and plunged toward me, clasping three bottles like a baby to her breasts. She called back: "You can't live forever!" And squalled with laughter when two men started after her. I don't know what happened when they caught her; I turned into Twenty-third Street to get out of the way. By evening they will be shooting down looters, most likely. Vigilantes will organize to do it if the police can't.

194

Para means a man lying in the gutter, his gray hair moving curiously in a brown stream from a leaky hydrant. He has a four-day beard and his clothes are frayed, with buttons sprung open on innocent meaningless nakedness. He is elderly. He isn't drunk. His stiffly upright shoes are cracked, with holes in the bottom, and he isn't drunk: the wagon will come when it can.

Para means a rat running out of an empty restaurant. There weren't supposed to be any rats left in New York. This one stops in front of me, not frightened, not aware of me, just dying. No resistance when my foot pushes him into the street.

The busses weren't running on Lexington Upper Level. As I went back down the stairway I noticed eight or ten crows flying northwest. Odd—you never see crows over the city. Northwest toward Central Park. I think the Robbie-road was functioning, but I didn't see a taxi anywhere. I went on down to the subway level, and there the robot change-maker was in operation. I passed through a turnstile to a deserted platform and waited a dreary while. One other man came through, saw me, and walked to the other end of the platform to wait.

The train came in at low speed. I noticed two men in the motorman's cab, another outside—in case one should collapse? The car I entered had only two other passengers in it, a thin woman whose lips moved silently, a frozen-faced Negro studying his shoe tips. They sat at opposite ends of the car; something in the way they both glanced at me suggested that I ought to sit in the middle or go to the next car. I sat in the middle. . . . Only a few pedestrians were on Lexington Upper Level when I climbed back to it at 125th Street. They hurried as if on desperate secret missions, giving each other wide clearance. I saw no one stirring when I looked through the big windows of the Organic Unity Party office. A policeman stopped me at the entrance. "Staff?"

"No. Place closed?"

He spoke with the harassed patience of a man forced to repeat the same thing to the point of nausea: "No public gatherings allowed. Only the office staff goes in."

"Do you happen to know Mr. Keller by sight?"

He looked me up and down coldly. My Santa Claus appearance may have restrained things he would have liked to say. "I don't know any of 'em, mister. I just work here. On the sidewalk. Only staff goes in."

"Okay, I don't want in. But—uh—it's just the rule about public gatherings, isn't it? What I mean, there isn't anything to the rumor that's going around about these Organic Unity people?"

He was large and quiet and Irish and most unhappy. "Now what rumor would that be?"

Drozma, I shall never know if what I did was right. It was an action deriving more from emotion than from reason. It had the human thread of vengeance in it: I have been away from Northern City too long. I said: "Talk I overheard in the subway. Other places too—everyone's whispering it. I've got nothing to do with this damn Party, but I'm slightly acquainted with Keller, man who works here, thought I'd like to ask him about it, about that rumor."

He was monumentally patient. "What rumor?"

"Hell, you must've heard it." I tried to look more than ever distressed and stupid and ancient. "About that fella Walker who jumped off Max's roof garden, week ago Friday, I think it was." He stiffened with alertness, and some woman, half seen, was passing on the sidewalk as I spoke. I can't be certain that her steps paused for a listening second. I think they did. "The rumor was that Walker had a test tube with some kind of bugs in it, virus or something, and chucked it over before he jumped."

It went home, I know. A moment of dark intentness, perhaps horror, before he rumbled: "I wouldn't be repeating stuff like that."

"Why, I won't. But other people are. On the subway was where I just now heard it, one guy yakking at another." I shrugged and moved away. "Well, hell, Keller wouldn't tell me the truth anyway." I walked on slowly, terrified that he might call me back for questioning. He didn't. My impersonation of a half-witless antique must have been convincing. With the tail of my eye I saw him step inside the building—to a telephone, I imagine. I don't know,

196

Drozma. Maybe it was the old bum in the gutter. Or that little golden spaniel. It was not what an Observer should have done, yet under the same pressures I would very likely do it again.

I walked on, west, on 125th Street.

I cannot see the thing as a whole, Drozma. Not yet and maybe never. I know (with my mind only) that, because of the blind madness of a few and the almost unknowing acquiescence of the many, human beings have once again stumbled into calamity with no assurance of survival. I know (in theory) that a wiser society might be able to detect and isolate such creatures as Joseph Max before they have done their work. Yet who can shape the realities of any such society in his mind, or tell how to arrive at it? With the study of human nature in its half-sickly infancy, we come back (in theory at least) to the unwillingness of men to look at themselves: but that is too simple. Even self-knowledge, if it should ever be achieved by more than a handful in each generation, is simply a means to some end that neither man nor Martian is wise enough to guess. I know these things with some clarity, but at this moment I can truly see only certain disconnected pictures from today's bleak journey.

Para means a little Negro girl, about the age Sharon was when I first knew her, walking directly into me on 125th Street, wide-eyed and tearless. She said mechanically: "I'm sorry, mister. I didn't see you. My pop's dead." I kept her from stumbling; maybe she knew it, but she moved on, stiff-legged, while I fought back the need to follow and tell her—well, what? What? I couldn't make him live.

I climbed from 125th Street to the Esplanade. Not many blocks north of here, a small tube of glass . . .

The express elevators in the Green Tower Colony were not running. There was a bank of self-service elevators, and there has been no power failure—yet. I used one of those, and stood for a time outside Keller's door, not thinking much. It was like waiting for some signal which of course never came. I noticed that the card with Abraham's name was still above the bell; I took it out

197

and dropped it in my pocket, a touch of cold metal reminding me, quite casually, that I was still carrying Miriam's automatic. Then it was also a casual thing to punch the bell. One and perhaps both of my grenades would have to be used. Both, if Keller and Nicholas were both here, or if I should be wounded and unable to escape.

Nicholas opened the door.

I reminded myself further that I had not used scent-destroyer for several days. It hadn't seemed to matter. And although as soon as Abraham decided to go over to Brooklyn I knew where I would go, it still hadn't mattered. Nicholas opened the door. He recognized Will Meisel and stood back with a human stare of resentment, dislike, anger, sternness—all quite irrelevant, as he understood himself when I had shut the door behind me and my Martian scent reached him. He said with sober quiet: "I should have known."

"Is your son here, who goes by the name of William Keller?" I spoke in English; it has become almost more natural than my native tongue.

He waddled away to close the door on the back rooms, and held his voice to a neutral dead level: "My son is in Oregon, or maybe Idaho, with a new face. You'd only waste your time trying to find him—I couldn't myself, probably." It had a flat sound of truth; I think it was truth. If it was, then I must leave Keller to be dealt with by other Observers in the course of the years. Such a being cannot hide himself long, and we have always had patience on our side.

I indicated the closed door. "What's there?"

He leaned against it, perhaps to block me away with his mass. "One of my students, who should have lived to do his work."

"Joseph Max? He took refuge here?"

"Refuge? No one was looking for him. He came to consult me, and he was stricken while he was here. The hospitals are already crowded, and have nothing to offer. It shouldn't matter to you, Elmis. He's dead."

"Para. . . ."

"Yes."

"It's fitting, I think. . . . The Organic Unity Party is dead too, Namir. Or will be soon. There may be some trouble down there at your office. A mob perhaps. At any rate the party will receive due credit for what's happened. Did you think it could be any other way?"

"Why, I hadn't thought." He lifted and dropped his fat hands. I think he laughed a little. "It doesn't matter where the credit goes, if the thing works, does it? The Party doesn't matter—a tool useful once, thrown aside. Like myself—as you see, I have only a year or two to live."

"Well, less than that. A year or so could be too long."

"Vengeful, Elmis?"

"No. A matter of sanitation. I shouldn't have fumbled, nine years ago." He didn't look interested. "If there's anything you want to say to me, I'll hear it. The laws require that much." I showed him the automatic. "Sit down over there."

He obeyed me, smiling dimly. With my left hand behind me I locked the door on the back rooms. He asked: "May I have a cigarette? I've become quite fond of them."

"Of course. Just keep your hands in sight." I tossed him a pack, and matches. "In the future as you saw it, you'd have had to keep a lot of human beings alive—you know, to cultivate food and tobacco, run a few machines, sweep the streets if you intended to have streets."

Namir laughed in the smoke. "I never racked my head over blueprints. I only wanted to help get the creatures out of the way. The building of a sensible culture would have been for others— but as you say, they might have wanted to make human beings good for something."

"I think you came to enjoy destruction as an end in itself, didn't you? Any other ends you might have had at the beginning were swallowed up in the pleasures of smashing windows, tying a can to the tail of the poor human dog, chalking up words on blank

199

walls. Is there any way I could show you that the pursuit of evil is a triviality?"

"You see it that way." He shut his eyes. "I see, as I always have, that it was best to help men destroy themselves, because they aren't fit to live."

"Not fit, by whose decision? Whose scale of values?"

"Mine of course." He was tranquil behind closed eyes. "Mine, because I see them as they are. There's no truth in them. They project the wishes of a little greedy ape against the blank of eternity, and call it truth—there's triviality if you like. They invent a larger ape somewhat beyond the clouds—or somewhat beyond the Galaxy, which is the same thing—and call it God; they use this invention as an authority, to justify every vice of cruelty or greed or vanity or lust that their small minds can imagine. They talk of justice, and say that their laws derive from a sense of justice (which they have never defined); but no human law ever derived from anything except fear—fear of the unknown, the different, the difficult, fear of man's own self. They make war, not for any of the noisy noble reasons they produce, but simply because they hate themselves almost as much as they hate their neighbors. They gibber of love, love, but human love is merely one more projection of the ape-self, superimposed on the invented image of another person. They invent religions of charity such as Christianity—if you want to know how they practice them, look at the prisons, the slums, the armies, the concentration camps and execution chambers; better still, look into the not very well hidden hearts of the respectable, and watch the maggots squirm, the maggots of jealousy and hate and fear and greed. They are stupid, Elmis. They have always done their best to smother and destroy the few abnormal ones who have a little vision, a little ability beyond the ordinary, and they always will. Do you think Christ could live any longer in the twentieth century than he did two thousand years ago? Galileo recants again, Socrates drinks the hemlock again, every day of every year—but now there are three billion units in the swarm, in a smaller world, and they have

200

learned simpler methods of crucifixion, without embarrassing publicity. The three billion crawl about, all over the helpless earth, destroying and defiling, killing the forests, polluting the air with smoke and radioactive dust and the torturing noises of the machine. In place of meadows, filling stations. The lakes are puddles of human filth. Two years ago the whole area of San Francisco Harbor was covered with dead fish: even the ocean is sick from the human taint, and this they call progress. I have done what I can, Elmis, and I hope you will make my death reasonably tidy. The floor of this room is some new kind of glass—the grenade won't affect it. I always hated disorder."

"You make a reasoned indictment," I said. "I notice you put it all on abstract grounds. You must have had a more personal reason, to hate them as you do."

"No." His half-hidden Salvayan eyes watched me curiously, honestly, I think, temporarily interested in what I said. "No, I don't believe so. As an Observer, I suddenly realized the blindness of Salvayan hopes, the futility of any effort depending on human nature. I abdicated because I saw that the only cure for the human situation was annihilation. Of course, once you declare war on the human race"—he shrugged amiably—"it tends to become a personal matter. Possibly my own vanity and ambition entered into it, after a while. Unimportant. Oh, I worked hard over Joe Max." He yawned heavily. "I didn't overlook the pitiful instability of creatures like Walker and Hodding—that was the material I had to work with, the chance I took. . . . As a favor to me, Elmis, would you spare me listening to the counsel for the defense, and use that gun now? I'm tired."

"No defense. I admit almost every charge of the indictment. The only thing wrong with it is that it's too partial, too trivial. You've spent your life hunting for counterfeit money in a pile of treasure. You looked for evil all your life, to prove your case— naturally you found it, and where it was absent you created it. Any fool can do that. I've looked for good in human nature and elsewhere, and found it, heaped up and flowing over. Anyone

201

can do that too, though good may be a little harder to see, because it's all around you, no further away than the nearest leaf, the nearest smile or pleasant word, no further away than every breath of air. You say there's no truth in men. Do you know what truth is, any more than Pilate did? Human beings are in the early stages of trying to accept and understand empirical truth. It's difficult. It's like going into a jungle without weapons or foreknowledge. No other terrestrial animal ever tried it, or even guessed the jungle was there. Well, Namir, our views of man are not altogether different. We both see him as someone stumbling through that jungle. You want to slip a knife in his back because you don't like him. I'd rather take his hand, knowing that he, and I, and you are all in the same jungle, and the jungle is only a small part of the universe. Justice? That's an ideal, a light they see ahead of themselves, and try to reach. Certainly they stumble: because they try. If that weren't so, they couldn't even have invented the word. The same is true of their visions of love and peace. Fear goads them from behind, because they're flesh and blood. If you blame them for being afraid, you're only blaming them for being alive and capable of suffering. The products of fear—war, hate, jealousy, even greed develops from fear—those will diminish as fear diminishes, if they have a few more centuries to learn. Centuries are short for us, rather long for them, Namir. On the whole, I don't think they're much more stupid than Martians. As for the ugly aspects of their twentieth-century progress—another temporary sickness, I think, like the different sickness of, say, the ninth century, probably no more important. The earth will heal—my planet Earth, Namir, that might have been your planet too if you hadn't blinded yourself with the very human sickness of hate—it will heal, when they learn how to live with it. Perhaps another century of learning how to control the machine——"

"Oh yes, yes." He spat out his cigarette on the floor. "They want the stars. Kill me, Elmis. It turns my stomach, to think of men reaching the stars. Regard it as an act of mercy, if it troubles you."

"It is," I said, for I could regard it in no other way. I suppose

202

the little gun finding the center of his forehead—because even now I had to remember the cemetery in Byfield—I suppose that was as merciful as death ever is. I rolled back the rug. The floor was inorganic, as he had said. I spread his pathetic bulk there, and stood well away until the purple flaring and sputtering had ended, and nothing remained but some coins from his pocket and the distorted bullet. The rest was dust; the rug could cover it. A lump of lead, a half dollar, two quarters, a dime, and a handful of dust—Namir is dead.

But not his son.

I went through the back rooms, having a certain need to know with my own senses that Joseph Max was dead.

I found him in a bedroom at the back. He was quite dead, lying in pallid dignity; someone had had the courtesy to close his mouth and eyes—Miriam, I think, for she was not dead, not yet. She sat beside him on the bed, her hand moving aimlessly through his hair and over his cheek. Her nose was reddened, but not from tears: her eyes were dry and somewhat feverish. *The first symptoms are those of the common cold. . . .*

It was of interest (to state it in the coldest way) to note that as a woman she had loved Joseph Max, perhaps a great deal; that her engagement to Abraham had been on her side a matter of politics, a device of Keller and Nicholas to bind Abraham into the Party in the hope of using his abilities. I had guessed that, much earlier; now it was hardly even of academic importance. When history moves swiftly it leaves us all behind, men and Martians. She said something to me, hoarsely and with difficulty. I think it was: "Go away. . . ." I could not speak to her, as one cannot speak to an insect forced to live a while after its body is crushed. In this room, para was and would be merciful.

Abraham had not returned. It was early afternoon when I got back to the apartment. The subway was still functioning and there were more passengers, though nothing like the normal crowds. In the walk from the subway to my apartment I saw nothing more that I want to record. Other Observers, Drozma, will be telling you of these things. I knew, as I came home, that I had seen only the small beginnings of the disaster. Before long—a day, a week—there will be, not one old man dead in the gutter and waiting for a wagon that can't come quickly, but many more. There will not be a wall in the city that doesn't hide a human loss. There will be breakdown of communication, transport—for New York and most other modern cities, that means starvation. There will be riots; some will die even while throwing stones at what they believe to be some enemy. There will be lime pits. If even the rats die of it . . .

Abraham did not come home all afternoon. At three I telephoned Sharon, and she answered quickly, asking at once whether I was well. Abraham had been there in the morning, she said, and had left a little before noon. She took it for granted that he would be going home, though he hadn't said so. She was well, Sharon told me; she and Sophia were well. . . .

Never mind the next six hours. I lived through them. Abraham came home at nine, and limped to the sofa, taking off the prosthetic shoe and nursing his left foot on his knee. "Just standing on the damn thing too much," he said. "I wanted to call you from the hospital, but every line was jammed all day."

"Hospital——"

"Working there. Cornell Center. Impulse—one I should've had sooner, only that brain you say I have wasn't operating. Sure, just walked in, volunteered. Maybe it takes a pestilence to slice the red tape. They'll use anybody who can still crawl, run errands, carry a bedpan. I'm to go back at 3 A.M.—bit of sleep and something to eat." He gulped the drink I brought him, half blind with an exhaustion more than physical. "Will, I didn't know—you couldn't imagine—the babies, the old, the great husky men who look as if nothing could hurt 'em—down like the corn in a hailstorm. There aren't any beds left, you know. We'll use the floor while the extra mattresses last, and then—go on using the floor. We try to be sure they're really dead before we——"

"I'll go along with you at three."

This was not the first time that human nature has put me to shame, but it is the time I shall always remember best.

9   Sophia Wilkanowska died this morning. So did President Clifford, but I think of Sophia, and one other.

Yes, the President of the United States died this morning. According to the newspaper, he went out like a gentleman, after some seventy-two hours without sleep, upholding the massive burden of duties and decisions even after the cold symptoms began and he knew the virus was in him. Disaster, as human beings would say, always does separate the men from the boys. He was still quite young—fifty-nine. Rest in peace. Vice-President Borden is the usual political unknown; time enough to worry about him if he survives the siege. I am thinking of Sophia and one other.

Abraham and I came home at one o'clock Sunday, after ten hours at the hospital. We were to return at eight in the evening. Sharon's telephone did not answer. I think that for Abraham the hours had become a black tunnel with a light at the end, the light of the moment when he could talk to Sharon. Now the telephone did not answer, and I had to watch the light go out. I heard the dead impersonal rings. He broke the connection. "Maybe I dialed wrong." He tried again. He hadn't dialed wrong. "I'll go over," he said. "You'd better get some sleep."

"What about that leg?" His left leg had swollen at the ankle. He had not stumbled at the hospital; now he did, a little, as he crossed the room to retrieve a wet raincoat. There was a sorry drizzle on the streets, and March chill had returned.

"That? Oh, the hell with it, it works. You're going back at eight, Will?"

205

"I think I'd better. But you should stay with Sharon. You'll find she's just stepped out somewhere, but—stay with her anyhow."

"Sophia—almost never goes out, Sharon said: her blindness."

"I know. You stay with them. It's more important."

"Yes—'importance' is a word"—he was reeling with fatigue—"and you taught me not to be used by words."

"Besides, another ten hours on that leg and you couldn't walk, Abraham—better admit it."

He found second wind—or third, or fourth. It was not to steady himself that he turned in the doorway and caught hold of my coat lapel. "Will—thanks for everything."

I tried to look irritated. "Cut that out—this isn't good-by. I'm coming over to Brooklyn myself tomorrow, soon as I'm through at the hospital. You stay with them, and keep off that leg as much as you can."

"All the same, thanks." His dark eyes were upturned, inescapable, blazing with the unsayable. "Sharon told me how it happened that Mrs. Wilks started her school. I was thinking about the woods too—the woods in Latimer." He grinned suddenly, and shook my coat lapel, and limped hurriedly for the elevator, leaving me—not exactly alone.

He called back in the late afternoon, but found it difficult to talk. I asked: "Sharon——"

"She's all right. She's all right, Will, but——"

"Sophia?"

"Has it. . . . Sharon had gone out, when I was trying to call, out to find a doctor. There aren't any available. Not one."

"Yes, it would have come to that by now. Better to keep her there, I think. Better than a hospital."

"Yes, we've seen that." Sophia would die. We both knew it; both remembered a statement in a newspaper we read on the way home from the hospital: *So far, all patients showing signs of recovery are under thirty-five years of age.* "They say, Will, they say two Brooklyn hospitals are turning them away—simply no place to put them."

"I'll come tomorrow, soon as I'm through. You stay there."

"Yes," he said.

"You're certain that Sharon——"

"I'm certain," said Abraham, and his voice cracked all to pieces as if someone had struck him in the chest. "I'm certain." He hung up.

Abraham had not stumbled there at the hospital. I did, a few times, that night, not so much from fatigue as from a sense of helplessness that became physical, as if I were trying to swim in molasses. They came in so fast! There was no such thing as separating the light cases from the severe—there were no light cases, not there at the Center. My duties were to fetch and carry on three wards, lend a hand wherever I was at anything the nurses or doctors thought I could do. I did my best, but it was not like Abraham's best, and now and then I stumbled.

They were strangely silent wards. Full of the sound of tortured breath, the feeble scraping and shuffling of bodies that could move a little, but no groaning, no speech except among us who tried to care for them. When one died there was scant struggle; no convulsions or violent contractions of the muscle: you might not be sure until you stooped to feel the coldness. The smell of the wards was foul of course—two or three worn attendants can't keep paralyzed patients clean, when there are sixty or seventy of them in a room meant to hold not more than twenty. Ten million are said to have died in the flu of 1918; that was nothing, Drozma, compared to this. There has been nothing like this since the fourteenth century. Statistical charts have gone into a fever like that of para. By this time, I suppose, technicians will have fed the nightmare figures into some of the electronic brains that have become so important in the last twenty years; but I don't think the papers will publish what the machines have to say.

As night crawled into morning I found I was leaning more and more on the memory of how Abraham had done this same work with me the day before, and yet his way would be difficult for me to describe to you, Drozma. In actual work, perhaps he did

207

no more than the other devoted attendants, although he seemed to: he was everywhere. There was what I must call some kind of communication between him and the conscious patients, even when the deafness of the disease prevented them from hearing anything he said. Sometimes I saw him shaping words carefully for them; sometimes he would scribble a note, or it might be only a smile or pressure of the hand or an almost telepathic understanding of an unspoken need. They knew it when he was there; those who could moved their heads to watch for him. . . .

Most dreadful of all were those patients in the stage before unconsciousness, when their eyes glared at unknown images and their hands twitched frantically in a struggle to rise and push away some monster of the mind. Three times I saw Abraham achieve communication with such patients, making them aware of him so that his real and human face became a shield between them and the hallucinations. For one of these, a giant Negro who could have strangled a bull a few days earlier, Abraham lifted the straining hand and brought its fingers against his cheek to prove the reality; the wildness passed, and there was a kind of peace, a third victory. That man, and one of the other two, were still living when I went back Sunday night; their fevers were not very high, and the nurse had tagged their mattresses with a blue X, which was emergency shorthand for *Good resistance, possible recovery.* If Abraham lives, I can return soon to Northern City.

Mission accomplished. If Abraham lives . . .

I worked a twelve-hour shift that night, and it was ten o'clock in a rainy morning when I reached Sharon's apartment in Brooklyn. She let me in, and cried in my arms. I could see Abraham sitting across the room frowning at the floor, and through an open door beyond him I saw Sophia's room, and Sophia herself, already composed, her eyes shut, hands quiet. Abraham nodded, though it wasn't necessary to tell me. Two men were coming up the stairs behind me. I had not closed the door because Sharon still clung to me, and one of the men tapped my shoulder gently. "You sent for us, sir?" They had gauze masks over mouth and nose, a singular futility. Sharon smothered a scream.

208

Abraham took charge, motioning Sharon and me to the studio. She was explaining to me: "You see, there can't be any regular funerals——"

"I know, Sharon. Let Abraham——"

"Because the dead outnumber the living, do you see? Why, they always did, didn't they? Oh yes." She coughed and blew her nose and shivered. "And so they just come and take them, do you see?" She pulled the chair away from the piano and sat down facing me, lacing her hands together, wanting to explain. "Ben, she always liked a little ceremony. Oh, she was a very formal lady, I always tried to live up to it. I think she'd've liked me to play a Polonaise—not the *Marche funèbre*—no, *no!* But a Polonaise, only I don't think I could, anyway she's not here, is she? We have to think of it that way, don't we?"

"Of course. Let yourself go, Sharon. You're all wound up——"

"Oh no, because the dead outnumber us, and some of them like a little formality, I'm sure of it. It's a matter of keeping up appearances." I heard the front door softly close. "Would you get me a wrap, Ben? It's miserably chilly in here, isn't it?" It was somewhat chilly, but she was warmly dressed. "The janitor is sick, I heard. I suppose the furnace is out. I think I'd like to sit here awhile. Look at the keyboard, but I don't think I could play anything. Would you like to, Ben?"

"No, I—I'll get you a coat."

Abraham came in then, and I went to look for a coat or blanket. I found her bunny fur in a closet, and as I was taking it down I heard the piano for a moment. Not playing, just an upward ripple of notes. She would be standing by it, moving the back of her finger up the keyboard, a kind of caress to a friend, as if she were saying—— I hurried back with the coat, but Abraham was bringing her out of the studio then, and she smiled brilliantly. "Thanks, Ben. That's what I wanted." Putting out her arms for it, she stumbled. Abraham kept her from falling. I picked her up and carried her to her bedroom—cool it was, orderly and virginal, with white walls, a blue bedspread. Simplicity and innocence. She said carefully: "I've had a bit of a cold all morning, but I don't think it's anything. Feel my hand, Abe. See? I'm not feverish." I had carried her; she was hot as a coal, and the hand that Abraham was not holding was restless at the finger ends.

"Of course you're all right, Sharon," he said. "Shoes off. I want you to get under the covers——"

"What did you say, Abe?"

"Shoes——"

"I can't hear you." She must have known it, must have been living with the thought for hours, but this was the first time that the shield of brave pretense had been torn away from her, and now she cried out: "Abe, I love you so! I wanted to *live*——"

After that she could not speak. . . .

It must be near midnight. Abraham has never left her, of course. I spent some of the morning and afternoon trying to find a doctor who could come. A desperate waste of time: they are all red-eyed wrecks, working twenty-four hours a day at the hospitals and elsewhere. Not only with para: people still run their cars into lampposts, carve each other with knives, die of other diseases. There can be no home visits, and to send a victim to the hospital at this stage is merely to give him a more crowded place to die. I do not feel able to think of Union, Drozma. The end justifies the means, Joseph Max believed, following certain earlier theorists who should have died in infancy. I doubt if I ever knew before what it is to hate. Loving their best and hating their worst as I do, I can never go out again as an Observer. I am disqualified. I shall be old before I can look at this under the aspect of eternity.

I was right that what I saw Saturday was only a beginning. These streets are full of the dead; crews work with panel and half-ton trucks, taking them—I don't know where. Such a crew is usually followed by a protecting patrol car. Other police cars cruise slowly, watching, I think, for any knot of citizens that might become a mob. I bought a paper. It was a *Times,* down to an eight-page skeleton with no advertising. Some foreign news, almost all of the spread of para. Nothing about Asia. The death of President Clif-

210

ford—that, of course, is the long banner headline, and at any other time the front page would have held almost nothing else; but the story of his death reads as though the writer had done it with his left hand, or as though his own head were aching with the symptoms of the common cold. . . . The front page carries public notices, giving the telephone numbers of what they call Civil Defense Relief Crews—those are the men with the panel trucks. Statistics too—I've already forgotten most of them: over a million cases in the New York metropolitan area alone. In boldface type, standing instructions for treating victims who cannot be hospitalized. Supportive measures: keep the patient warm and quiet; don't try to make him swallow, too likely that he will strangle; keep the head level with the body to avoid constriction of the windpipe; the room should be darkened, since the eyes are hypersensitive during the conscious phase. . . .

Sharon passed through the delirium in the middle afternoon. We were both with her. I could only be quiet while Abraham fought with devils, and the gentleness of his hands and face were the only weapons he could use. As I knew from our service in the hospital, there have been many deaths during the delirium, from a spasmodic closing off of breath, perhaps due to pure fright at the nightmare hallucinations. Sharon did not die.

I think she knew even at the height of her distress that Abraham was there, touching her, watching for every shadow that might cross her face, demanding that she stay with him and be afraid of nothing. It was natural to see my friend as the young St. George—it would have been so much easier, so much simpler, if he could have opposed his frail body to a tangible dragon spouting flames! But the real dragons are always quiet, without form, and the profoundest courage a man can have is the kind that will uphold him against the attack of shadows.

We knew it when Sharon passed into unconsciousness, and shut her eyes in the stupor of the high fever. Abraham lost his grip then, briefly; probably because she had gone beyond communication, and there was nothing he could do. He was shaken with a

211

kind of convulsive crying that had no tears in it. I forced him to swallow some black coffee. I found a cot in the spare bedroom, and brought it into Sharon's room, and made Abraham lie down, though I knew he would not sleep. He came out of the collapse quickly, and sat up again to watch her. At the hospital, a few patients have been kept alive with artificial respiration. He could not take his eyes away from her, for fear of missing the moment when she might need it. There had been something on an inner page of the newspaper: no more oxygen cylinders; a transportation break-down was blamed. Since I knew there was no way to get any for Sharon, I couldn't care. . . .

It must be nearly midnight. I am in the living room with this notebook, where I can hear if Abraham calls me. The fever is 105°. But average for this phase of the sickness is nearer 107°, and she is breathing well. She is strong; she wants to live; she is very young.

These hours stretching ahead of us must be moving toward some sunrise. It is quiet here, everywhere. I can hear her breathing, evenly, not too weakly. The city is strangely silent. This journal will be miserably unimportant, if she dies. I'll go in now, see if there is anything I can do.

Tuesday afternoon, March 21

Sharon's fever broke this morning at four o'clock, after four-teen hours of the burning. There was no ominous leveling off at a high point. She is unconscious still, but it could almost be taken for natural sleep. 99.1°—you can't call that a fever. In the early afternoon I went out to buy a paper—the radio broadcasts are maddening gabbles, and two of the best stations have gone silent—and found a newsstand with a few of the four- and eight-page sheets they are putting out. The dealer wore one of the useless gauze masks, and tossed change to me, careful not to touch my fingers. . . .

Monday afternoon, it seems, a mob destroyed the offices of t^{l.}

Organic Unity Party. The policeman guarding the entrance—I shall always wonder if it was the same big decent Irishman—fired into the crowd as a last resort, but they trampled him to death in spite of that. They set fire to the interior, and slaughtered another man who was probably an innocent caretaker. Partly my doing. I can never go out again as an Observer. I threw away the paper, and told Abraham I couldn't find one.

He was at last willing to sleep. I have promised to wake him if there is any change, and I will. Incredible that in spite of all Martian and human science of the last thirty thousand years I can do nothing but sit here, sponge her lips, watch, wait.

Tuesday night, March 21

She is still unconscious, but her temperature is 98.7°; her breathing is excellent, not entirely mouth breathing now; there have been some apparently voluntary swallowing motions. I thought I saw her hand move slightly, but may have imagined it. That was early this evening; Abraham did not see it, and I did not mention it for fear I was wrong. I thought too that there was some dim responding motion when I felt her pulse just a few minutes ago, but again I could have been wrong. Anyway the pulse was good: regular, strong, fairly slow, none of the fluttering, pounding, hesitation that were so marked during the fever.

They recommend stimulants as well as liquid nourishment as soon as the patient can swallow. She must be conscious first. That will come. The wasting, the terrible hollows under her cheekbones that have appeared in the last forty-eight hours—those will pass. We have coffee and warm milk ready. It may be difficult to buy food outside now, but they had a well-stocked freezer, and so far the power has not failed. Canned stuff too, enough for four or five days. In the few exhausted words that Abraham and I have for each other, we take it for granted that very soon she will open her eyes and be able to see us. He speaks to her often; there has

213

been no response to that, but I thought or imagined that the unknowing mask did change faintly once, when he kissed her.

We talked of other matters too, this evening. I wanted to draw Abraham away from the inner violence of his personal ordeal, and I said something vague, to the effect that human society as we knew it could never be quite the same again after the pandemic had run its course.

"It must be known," said Abraham, "that this thing was manmade. They must have that fact driven into them, driven into their guts, driven into the germ plasm. And I think their great-grandchildren had better remember it."

"It is known," I told him. I told him what I had done, and what the mob had done.

"I think you were right——"

"That I'll never know, Abraham. It's done, and I shall be judging myself the rest of my life—likely with a hung verdict."

"For what my opinion's worth, you did right. But it's not enough. After this is all over, Will, I ought to write down everything I know—after all, Hodding and Max are dead: who else is there to talk? Somehow I ought to see to it that there isn't a corner of the planet where that truth hasn't reached."

"Are men going to listen any better when it's over, Abraham? If you approach authority, for instance, and they say, 'Where's your proof?' "

"Why, I'd even lie and say I had a hand in it myself, if that was the only way to get the fact across."

"Wrong, for several reasons——"

"Oh, Will, the individual isn't so much as all that——"

"He is, but that's not the greatest reason. I'll ask you to look at this one in particular: if you did that, you'd be a scapegoat, nothing more, and haven't you stopped to wonder why men want a scapegoat? What is it, what was it ever, but a device to help them avoid looking at themselves? This is the kind of world where it's possible for a Joseph Max to run wild. If there must be blame, then all citizens—you, I, everyone—are responsible for letting it

214

be that kind of world, for not placing ethical development ahead of every other kind. We understand ethical necessities quite well; we've been capable of understanding them for several thousand years; but we haven't been willing to let them rule our actions—it's that simple. Spend yourself in the long labor, Abraham, not in the passionate gesture or the unheeded sacrifice. On the personal level—because I've always seen a special flame in you that burns more dimly in others, and because I've always loved you—I forbid you to give yourself to crucifixion for no purpose."

After a while he said, to me, to himself, to the girl who was so silent but not dying: "Is maturity the acceptance of conflict?"

And I said, silently, to myself only: *Mission accomplished.*

Wednesday, March 22

Early this morning, before dawn, she moved her hands up to her face, and her eyes opened—wide, knowing, full of recognition. "Sharon——"

"I'm all right," she whispered. "I'm all right, Abe."

"Yes, you're out of it. You——"

"Darling, don't whisper. I want to hear everything you say."

"Sharon! Sharon——"

"I can't hear you," said Sharon Brand. "I can't hear you."

Aboard the S.S. *Jensen*
out of Honolulu for Manila
July 24, 30,972

10   The ocean, forever changing and the same, was awake with deep music tonight; I was alone and not alone at all. Not alone, looking down some hours from the moving bow, seeing the flash and lingering subsidence of the noctilucae, those living

215

diamonds of the sea, their light as transient as the sea foam and eternal as life, if life is eternal. Everything goes with me, the cherished faces, the words that endure although no embodied voice is near my body but only the great continuing voice of the sea and of a westerly wind out of the open regions of the world. I am not alone.

As we measure time it is not long, my second father, since I was in Northern City with you: nine years, a moment—it will seem nothing indeed when I am there with you again, in a few weeks or months.

You have my journal. Now that more time has passed, letting some pain recede, some anger die away, I must ask you to destroy that letter which I wrote to accompany the journal. I wrote it only one day after I knew that Sharon was deaf; I should have known better than to write anything at such a time. It was several weeks before I dared entrust the journal to the crippled human transportation system with any hope that it would reach Toronto and be forwarded to you, but in those weeks the anger and despair did not release me, and perhaps I could have written nothing better at the end of them. Now, however, I ask you to destroy that letter. From pride and vanity, and from the thought that my children are almost old enough to study my work, I do not want such a mood to be preserved. Put with the journal this message I am writing you now, and throw away what was written at a time when I was too heartsick to know what I said.

I cannot truly hate human beings for anything they do. If I said I did, that was an aberration of weakness, because I love Sharon more than any Observer should allow himself to love, and because I knew, as well as anyone can, what effort, sacrifice, and devotion it had cost her to make herself so fine an artist, only to have it torn away. "I live with dream stuff," she said. Yes, she did; and to all who could hear she gave those dreams with a most free sharing. And the world responded—with para, with permanent deafness, not curable, not to be remedied with any device, for the beautiful magic nerves themselves are destroyed: she must live

216

all the rest of her life in total silence. And for a while, as I admit now, I was not myself and I could not endure it.

It was Abraham who saved my reason, and probably Sharon's. He upheld all three of us, forcing us to understand what richness of life remained in spite of everything. Well, let me tell in a couple of dozen words what Abraham has done since I wrote that wretched letter. He married her in April, as soon as she could be up and about, and took her to a small village in Vermont. Now he's a clerk there, in a general store: dry goods and fishhooks and a pound of this and a pound of that. Laugh at it, Drozma—he does—and you'll see that it makes sense. I'll come back to that presently.

This freighter is an old tramp in no hurry. The air liners are flying again. There are fast boats. The whole huge complex of human transport and commerce and communication has staggered back to maybe forty per cent of normal; by the end of a year I suppose things will seem very much as they did a year ago. Superficially. I chose this old tub because I wanted a month with the ocean, and near it, where I could feel the voice of it, not slipping across it in a vast fission-driven city or soaring above it more swiftly than sound, but down here in the swells, the salt smell, the long whispering, the blue and green and gray. I wanted to watch the humorous pace-setting of the fulmars, whose flying is a kind of singing; the hasty brilliance of the flying fish; the large unhurried fins of danger that sometimes follow; the distant spouting of leviathan. I wanted to see the Pacific sunshine on the water through the hot days, the uncaring splendor of its setting in the evening—and with the sense that I was in that sunset, not overtaking it, not challenging it with my tiny conceptions of duration and motion. I wonder whether, some day, human beings will settle down, relax a little, discover that eternity is a long time.

I'll talk with you directly from Manila, Drozma, if I can. If there should be difficulty about that, I suppose this may reach you first. I want to arrange matters so that Sharon and Abraham will learn of my "death" in a way that will distress them as little as possible and yet leave no doubt. They know I am going to Manila

217

—"for a sort of vacation and to see some old friends." I told Abraham once, casually, how I had always hoped that when I died it would be in the ocean, a relinquishment, a slipping downward into calm without a grave. That was not true, to be sure— I want to die in Northern City, after many more years of interesting work. But it was a humanlike notion that Abraham would not find strange in me, and I said it to prepare the way. I want about two months in Manila. Then I'll take another slow ship for the States. If one of our little exploration subs could meet the ship, say about thirty miles out of Cavite? I could be a "man overboard" with not too much fuss, and Abraham would think that the old man died the way he wanted to. But if this would be too expensive and troublesome to arrange, Drozma, we can work out some other gentle fraud when I get in touch with you.

The worst was over at the end of April. Gradually, grudgingly, the curve on the graph sagged downward. By the end of May the fire was out: no new cases were reported, and the survivors found that there was still civilization, of a sort. How much it may have set back the "progress" that Namir hated so badly, I don't know; and about ten years from now, I think we might begin to assess what it has done to men's thinking.

It is known everywhere, as Abraham desired, that the tragedy was man-made. Known from a rather unexpected source: Jason Hodding's son, who found a tormented diary the old man had kept during the final weeks of his work, and gave it to the authorities— and then shot himself. He must have felt, as Abraham did, that it was a thing men had to know; he was also the son of a man who was neither good nor bad, but human.

These are some of the figures I remember. The United States, with a population of more than two hundred million, lost forty-two million dead. This was from para alone: it does not include those who died in riots, and in the famines that gripped many communities, causing panic evacuations into a countryside that had no means of caring for the refugees. It does not include the millions who survived with major disablements—usually deafness

218

like Sharon's, but there were some who came out of it with limbs crippled as if by poliomyelitis, and some whose throats never recovered speech; and there were a few—I am speaking in terms of thousands—whose brain tissue was so damaged that they are not actually among the living. The United States of Europe, and South America, suffered in about the same proportion; Africa and India rather more. Interesting to note, however, that the death rate was only slightly higher in those countries where sanitation and public health work had never advanced to anything like the American level. It is supposed to have been somewhat higher in those countries merely because convalescents could not receive the care they did in more prosperous places, and therefore many died from inevitable neglect who might have lived.

The disease certainly reached Asia. That much we know. It must have done its slaughter there, after two years of major war, more horribly than anywhere else. But we also know, from the Satellite Authority, that some kind of war still goes on there, a slow fire of death, perhaps dying down, perhaps not. There is talk of sending in medical rescue expeditions—with armies in front of them for protection. I don't know. It couldn't be done soon; not until the rest of the world has had a little time to recover. It should be easy enough to by-pass Canton, Murmansk, Vladivostok, where they combined demolition with radioactive cobalt, but all effort at communication since the war began has been met with the sullen fury of silence; so far as I know all the land approaches to the sick continent are still viciously guarded in depth; their radar is good, and somehow they still have the means—aircraft, anti-aircraft, guided missiles—to destroy all foreign planes without inquiry, as they have done for the last three years. To break through would require a major military operation. The Western world has no heart for that at present; quite probably the slave populations would consider it an invasion, and hate the foreign devils as thoroughly as their masters do. It may be the logical finish for a national paranoia—all the same, you can't throw away a third of

219

a planet. Sooner or later sanity will have to tear down the barrier, if only for its own sake.

What has been the quality of the years for you, Drozma? In your letters you say little of yourself. I know you stand apart, watching both worlds with a clarity I have never achieved. I hope (though you do not say so) that the administrative burdens have been lightened, to give you better hours of contemplation. In spite of the plague, in spite of the continuing division of the world and the great weariness that will linger everywhere for a long time, I still believe that Union may be possible toward the close of my son's lifetime. We must discuss that when I see you, that and many other slow-maturing fruits of the centuries. I gave the Minoan mirror to Sharon and Abraham, thinking you would approve the gift.

They have the essentials of maturity. Now I wish you could see Abraham waiting on the customers in that little store, or sometimes presiding over the rambling talk of old men and young on the rickety porch! He has even picked up a trace of the accent, though nobody could take him for a Vermonter. The small village was ravaged by para, like all the rest of the world—about a hundred dead from a population of less than four hundred—but it coheres and goes on about its decent business in the stubborn Vermont way. The owner of the store is an old man who lost all his family to para; he is worn down to a gray shred of humanity, but he is not confused. He thinks of Sharon and Abraham as his "new children," and for himself he chiefly wants just to sit in the sun and wait a while.

They live over the store. One room has become a library, and Sharon reads a great deal. . . . "We shan't be here always," Abraham said to me. It is a pleasant and probably necessary temporary retirement from the livelier world. They need some years of quiet and study—Sharon to build a wholly new life on the ruins of what she lost, Abraham to digest and understand the past and the present and go on to new discoveries, new efforts that I would never dare to predict. He learned the deaf-mute sign language before

Sharon did; learning it from him was one of the first steps she took out of her private maze of despair. He has other methods too of bringing the world to her. Sharon had never read a great deal before; the piano took the place of it. Now she is following his mind wherever it goes, and they are never lonely.

There is no undercurrent of guilt in his devotion to her, only love and a receptive interest in the endless mystery of another personality. He has no tendency now to blame himself for the world's troubles. He sees himself very simply, I think—as a human being with possibilities that are not to be thrown away or lost or stultified. He has learned, Drozma, how to look in a mirror.

He is painting, too, for his pleasure, and Sharon's, and for whatever others may choose to see in his work. I have two new canvases he gave me, in a waterproof cylinder, and am bringing them home to you. I wish you could see a certain fantasy of the underground river of Goyalantis—but I couldn't accept that one, because I knew that Sharon wanted it even more. And tentatively, not too humbly, Sharon is approaching that art herself, partly under his guidance, more under the guidance of her own warm imagination—something may come of that; it's too soon to tell. They are never lonely.

All that I have told you has the pathetic incompleteness of words. I remember my report of 30,963, and my journal of this year, and I am constantly amazed to think how intricate was the reality, how partial my story of it, like those telescopic photographs of Mars that tickle and excite the human imagination with a sense of truth just beyond reach. I remember Latimer, New England's queer blend of history and tomorrow: I can smell it, and hear again the street sounds, yet my words were feebler than a photograph, and a photograph would have told you very little.

I remember my first meeting with Angelo Pontevecchio. How can I describe the certainty of recognition in myself when he limped into the house, set down the *Crito,* studied me with twelve-year-old curiosity behind his mother's friendliness—the certainty that I was in the presence of what I must always love without ever understanding it?

Did I make you see Feuermann? Or any of those other bewildering complexes of contradiction we call human? Mac—I'll never know if I wounded him by shoving that damn toothbrush out of alignment. Mrs. Keith and her amethyst brooch . . .

I shall always remember Rosa, the pretty eyebrows in her round face always slightly lifted in wonder at her son and at the world beyond him.

I remember Amagoya.

I remember too the first time I saw the Satellite. In the Americas they call it the Midnight Star, and I saw it rising from the north and passing, not swift like a meteor but far more hurried to the eye than any star. The most dramatic achievement of human science, I think, and something more than science too—a bright finger groping at the heavens. It moves in daytime, invisible, over the Pacific, but I shall see it again when I am coming home.

I remember the sea, from centuries past and from tonight, the sea that changes forever only to be the same.

Never, beautiful Earth, never even at the height of the human storms have I forgotten you, my planet Earth, your forests and your fields, your oceans, the serenity of your mountains; the meadows, the continuing rivers, the incorruptible promise of returning spring.

afterword

This is not likely to come out particularly unbiased or dispassion-
ate, not that such an afterword would be worth—as John Nance
Garner said about the vice-presidency—a pitcher of warm spit to
anybody. I have loved Edgar Pangborn since I was fourteen years old,
back in that unimaginable time when questions were legally required
to have answers, and people expected things to get better. I remember
that I sent a dollar away to the Science Fiction Book Club, and they
sent me, as their introductory offer, Kurt Vonnegut, Jr.,'s first novel,
Player Piano, and Edgar's second, the book you have just finished. I
liked Vonnegut well enough, but I was *aware* of Edgar Pangborn in
a different way, and (as I had done with William Saroyan, Jane Austen
and P. G. Wodehouse) I promptly set out to read everything the man
had ever written.

That wasn't easily done in those days. It isn't easily done now: when
Edgar died in 1976, only one of his books was still in print; and since
then the rest have blinked on and off in various momentary edi-
tions—gone today, here tomorrow, and gone again by Thursday. Over
the next ten years, the only other work of Edgar's I could locate
anywhere was "Angel's Egg," that astonishing story with which he
announced himself in *Galaxy* out of next to nowhere in 1951. Finally,
in the mid-sixties, St. Martin's Press published *Davy,* which is still
probably his best-known and largest-selling book. For most of his
career, it was the only one you could find.

In 1968 my own novel, *The Last Unicorn,* was published, and
Edgar wrote me a letter. It was a note, really, brief and shy and

223

wonderfully courteous, and it ended with the words "Don't ever be discouraged." He was not the first person to say that to me, or the first who said it as one artist speaking to another; but he was the one who bore the truest witness to it with his own life. He still does, inside me. *"Don't ever be discouraged."* I always find myself trying to talk about Edgar to writing classes: trying to bring that line of his to life for a roomful of people who sit there believing that there is a trick to it all, and that learning the trick—from me or from someone else— and getting a book published will somehow validate them as writers, and bless them further with some kind of permanent definition as human beings that they have never known. And I always wind up telling them about Edgar Pangborn, and they hardly ever understand.

Edgar and I had been corresponding for a good while before I learned about his other four novels. Today you can find *West of the Sun* (his first book, and possibly his only real attempt at the classic science-fiction story) and *The Judgment of Eve* without devoting your life to the search; but it was many years until I saw any other copies than the ones Edgar sent me. You can prowl the used-book stores forever without turning up *The Trial of Callista Blake,* that nagging, disquieting, uncomfortable novel that was so far ahead of its time— and so far from anything Edgar had written before—and that would do so well today if someone had the wit to reprint it and promote it properly. And as for *A Wilderness of Spring,* Edgar never once mentioned it to me. I had to discover that one on my own.

A Wilderness of Spring is, for me, Edgar's best book. It is a dizzying treasure house of a historical novel, set in early eighteenth-century New England, and breathing with such richness of language and character and such intellectual bite that I reread it every few years with the same new amazement and roaring envy. I remember writing to Edgar on the day I finished it—for once in my life too astonished to be anything but candid—"I've known since my childhood that you were a good writer. I never knew you were this good."

Edgar wrote back to tell me that *A Wilderness of Spring* had been published in 1958 "and was out of print—oh, say, within ten minutes, maybe fifteen." The reviews were apparently devastating, and the book seemed to go directly from such stores as ever ordered it to the remainder tables. It has never been reprinted in paperback, and the only copy I have ever seen is still in the Santa Cruz Public Library until I can find a way to steal it. I would start a publishing house of my own just to bring back *A Wilderness of Spring.*

It seems to me that Edgar's greatest strengths as an artist—his curiosity, his originality, his unfailing willingness to risk (as Jessamyn West says of all real writers) not only looking like a fool but discovering that he might actually *be* a fool—all worked against him in the commercial publishing system. If it's a truism that most popular fiction writers merely tell the same story over and over, it is also true that most readers would just as soon know exactly what they're getting when they drop a book into their shopping carts. The magic word in the modern conglomerate-run book business—as where not?—is *packaging;* and Edgar, by nature and choice, made a lousy package. The elbows always stuck out, or the feet, or that damn tender, implacable intelligence.

From what I know of his life, I doubt that Edgar ever really fit in anywhere for long. The fact is, however, that what I truly know—even now—of the events of Edgar's life can still be fairly summed up in the brief sketch that he wrote for an old Penguin Books reprint of *A Mirror for Observers:*

Edgar Pangborn was born in New York City in 1909, and was educated at Brooklyn Friends School. He attended Harvard from 1924 to 1926, but did not graduate. He engaged in literary hackwork under pen names, and in other random activities, including a few years of backwoods farming in Maine. After his army service, 1942–5, he began publishing science fiction and other work. . . .

Whatever remained of the fifteen-year-old music major Edgar once referred to as "that lonesome little wise guy," besides a deep happiness in playing the piano, or of the scuffling dirt farmer, besides a slight Maine accent and an abiding landscape, the man I knew might have come into existence at the age of forty-two with the publication of

225

"Angel's Egg." Edgar seemed to prefer it that way. He spoke often of his Army years as a watershed time, during which he finally began to learn how to write; his feeling about the work and the life before then is clear enough in the passage above. I remember him telling me once, "I didn't finish things. The writing was slapdash because *I* was slapdash. I had a very prolonged adolescence, even for an American, and it still makes me squirm sometimes."

The Edgar I knew lived with his sister Mary—herself a first-rate scholar and fiction writer—in a lovely old fish-scaled house on the Bearsville Road, just beyond Woodstock, New York. (Directions never help: it has no number, and I know beyond contradiction that it doesn't stay in the same place all the time. I find it to this day, as I always did, by getting lost and stopping when I come to a house that looks like the sort of house in which Edgar and Mary would live.) He gardened passionately, and he painted and played music; and when he wore his grizzled brown hair in braids, he might have been a cross between a Native American and a rather small Ent. Neither he nor Mary ever married, but children always seemed to find their way to that house, to be adopted and talked to and worried about. I have no anecdotes about him—just some fifty or sixty wise, candid, angry, wonderfully silly letters that still retain my friend's twangy cadences and zigzag humor. He talked like this, in a letter dated June 8, 1973, discussing the foundation of a greenhouse he was building:

Paraphrasing Mehitabel, there's a dance in the old boy yet. I got the back-hoe work done on May 17, and it rained, and it rained, so I spent three weeks or so scooping the glops of clay mud out of the bottom of the trench. Thought I had a helper lined up from a local, rather soulful, help-the-dropouts outfit. Muscular character going on thirty, took one look at the shovel and the trench, and retired down the driveway gracefully and *so* fast, speaking about other jobs he had lined up, suddenly they couldn't wait. . . . So I dug it out myself. Got it ready for the ready-mix concrete truck this week, and after it was poured and the cheerful operative was packing up, I stepped across the trench to get on the other side, (a good reason, I thought) and fell in it. Up to here. If you want to know how much a pair of pants can weigh and still remain attached to the corpus, fall in concrete. But unless you're in need of that information, avoid it, me bhoy, avoid it. There's really nothing in it. True, there's a knack to it—you're supposed to get the hell out before it starts to set, and this, after some thought, and with the kindly help of the Operative after he quit laughing, I did. It has set without me. Only afterward did I understand the Inner Motives that Papa Freud would instantly have recognized—I was trying to punish my parents by making myself a monument more enduring than brass. Clever of me. Today, anyhow, I got my materials for revenge—200 concrete blocks, mortar and sand. Tomorrow, weather permitting, I shall begin Putting the Blocks to It. . . .

Rereading *A Mirror for Observers* for the first time in some years, I am reminded that Edgar's work is occasionally accused (by Edgar, among others) of a besetting sentimentality; and in some respects it's easier now for me to see why. It isn't that his intelligence or his vision was inherently bathetic—his humor alone would have preserved him from that—but rather that Edgar had a strong tendency to fall in love with his heroes and heroines, especially if they were young, beautiful, and in some way innocent. Sharon Brand suffers most from this trait in *Mirror*: Edgar adores her from the moment she hits the page as a ten-year-old introducing the Martian narrator Elmis to her own inner planet of Amagoya; he revels in her gifts, suffers all her sorrows, and allows her none of the interesting petty faults and inconsistencies that might have made her truly human. She is a dear fantasy, but almost never anything more.

Edgar was far too clear-headed about his writing not to see this himself. In another letter he spoke of

. . . the efforts of a good many "great" male novelists trying to create women—one thinks for instance of the ghastly female constructions of Henry James, or even of Mark Twain, whose women are never there at all unless they can be quaint and elderly Aunt Pollys. On Olympus, the Hall of Literature is a large building, but the rotunda (where you check out the rotund books) is dominated by a statue of Hermaphroditus, and the little fella may be Parian marble and all that, but he watches every move you make. I have been guilty of a number of sins in trying to write about women myself, and

I know. Nickie in DAVY was an idealized flop, and Eve not much better. About Sharon Brand and Callista, I don't know. . . .

Angelo Pontevecchio fights off Edgar's love more successfully, to the great benefit of the book. Not only does he resist being a genius, but he struggles throughout the entire novel for the human right to make whopping mistakes, to make a complete fool of himself, and generally to commit those sins of willful stupidity for which those who love us may forgive us, but from which even they can never really liberate our cringing, pitiless memories. At the end, it is possible to believe that Angelo has grown, changed, been scarred, learned something—no small achievement for a character so burdened by an author's cherishing. Yet, saying this, I realize how greatly I prefer Edgar's weakness to its sullen counterpart: the book that clearly hates all its characters, from protagonist to the least spear-carrier, and exists only in anticipation of killing them all off in a dully gleeful grand finale. Edgar never went down that dead-end street, in his work or in his life.

What continues to make *A Mirror for Observers* rewarding and resonant for me is the running war—physical and philosophical—between the two Martians, Elmis and the renegade Namir. On one level, of course, it's the God and Satan of the Book of Job all over again, contending mightily for a single human soul; on another it is the plot-spring that puts all humanity at risk and kept a Bronx fourteen-year-old reading to find out what happened. But it is the third level—the endless internal battle that everyone fights who cannot quite abandon hope of one day waking from the nightmare of our species' history—that holds me still after thirty years. Speaking for myself, it is not only Namir who cries out contemptuously in his final confrontation with Elmis:

"They aren't fit to live. . . . There's no truth in them. They project the wishes of a little greedy ape against the blank of eternity, and call it truth . . . They invent a larger ape somewhere beyond the clouds . . . [and] they use this invention as an authority, to justify every vice of cruelty or greed or vanity or lust that their small minds can imagine. They talk of justice, and say that their laws derive from a sense of justice . . . but no human law ever derived from anything except fear—fear of the unknown, the different, the difficult, fear of man's own self. They make war, not for any of the noisy noble reasons they produce, but simply because they hate themselves almost as much as they hate their neighbors. They gibber of love, love, but human love is merely one more projection of the ape-self, superimposed on the invented image of another person. They invent religions of charity such as Christianity—if you want to know how they practice them, look at the prisons, the slums, the armies, the concentration camps and execution chambers . . . They are stupid, Elmis. . . . It turns my stomach, to think of men reaching the stars."

Elmis, forever "racked by an old malady, a love for the human race," replies, as I believe Edgar did inside himself, and as I would like to, as I try to, sometimes:

"No defense. I admit almost every charge of the indictment. The only thing wrong with it is that it's too partial, too trivial. You've spent your life hunting for counterfeit money in a pile of treasure. . . . [O]ur views of man are not altogether different. We both see him as someone stumbling through [a] jungle. You want to slip a knife in his back because you don't like him. I'd rather take his hand, knowing that he, and I, and you are all in the same jungle, and the jungle is only a small part of the universe. . . ."

In the last pages of the book, having struggled and suffered and loved "more than any Observer should allow himself to love," Elmis the Martian is still able to say with passionate credibility, "I cannot truly hate human beings for anything they do. If I said I did, that was an aberration of weakness. . . ." Whether or not I can ever say that with him, what I hear in those words is Edgar's voice, and I miss my friend and am grateful still to have this book.

Peter S. Beagle
Kona-Kailua, Hawaii
September 1983